Best
Miki Bennett

Forever in the Keys

A Florida Keys Novel

MIKI BENNETT

First Edition

ISBN-10: 0-9988481-1-5
ISBN-13: 978-0-9988481-1-2
Library of Congress Control Number: 2017902588
WannaDo Concepts Publishing, Charleston, South Carolina

Dedicated to my most wonderful husband, Jeff. I'm one lucky girl.

* * *

She had just fallen asleep when the phone rang. She could barely make out the caller at the other end of the line, but finally realized it was Lance. As he spoke the words, Abbey felt a complete numbness envelop her body. This had to be a dream — this couldn't be real.

"Abbey, are you there?" she heard Lance say.

"Yes."

"Meet us at the hospital. He's going to be fine. Are you OK to drive?"

"Yes. Yes, I'm OK. How did this happen, Lance? When?" Abbey heard herself talking, but she still felt like her whole world had just turned upside down. Everything seemed surreal.

"Let's talk when you get to the hospital. I'll let you know what the police have shared with me," Lance said quietly. "See if Josie can come with you."

"All right. I'll be there in a few minutes," Abbey said emotionlessly, and she clicked the disconnect button on the phone. Even though she still felt paralyzed with fear in her gut, she quickly got up, dressing in the first pair of jeans, T-shirt, and flip-flops she could find. She grabbed her purse and keys, then headed out the door.

"Goodness, what has you here so late?" Josie said as she opened her door. Then she saw Abbey's face, tears streaming down her cheeks. "What's happened?"

"It's Zach, Josie. There has been an accident."

* * *

1

Abbey couldn't believe she was finally here! With a smile on her face, she read the sign on the side of the road: "Welcome to Key West." She bounced up and down in the seat of her Jeep while pumping her hand in the air, shouting "Woo Hoo" as loud as she could while she sat at the light. She was getting ready to turn right, using her GPS to guide her to her brand-new apartment. She was really here! And her own little place awaited her. "Margaritaville" played on the radio as she maneuvered her Jeep and a small U-Haul through the streets to her new home. Even though it was late in the day, she wanted to move as many things as possible into her apartment before sunset. Hopefully, the keys to her little piece of Key West would be in the small compartment in the flowerpot where her landlord had said he would place them. Abbey also had to remember to call her parents as soon as she was in the front door to tell them she had made it safely. She was home!

The decision to move here had been radical and rather quick. It had come on the heels of attending a wedding on the Florida Key of Islamorada. Just a few months before, her best friend from college, Hope, had invited Abbey to her mother's wedding on Anne's Beach. It was the first time she had been to the Keys, and Abbey immediately fell in love with the little islands. She loved Hope's mom, Maddy, and had been in awe of how her month-long getaway to the island had led to her meeting the man of her dreams. Abbey was a hopeless romantic and loved every bit of Maddy's story when Hope told her all the details, and she was especially glad when she got the invitation to the wedding. And it was beautiful. Both bride and groom stood in the clear waters of the beach, saying their vows, becoming husband and wife in one of the prettiest places she had seen. Afterward, Abbey, Hope, and Shawn, Hope's husband, had made a quick trip to Key West for a few days of fun, and she instantly felt at home in the little city.

It was an island full of creativity, relaxation, and friendly people. The best part for her was the many types of art she found in galleries, shops, and booths of street artisans that had nightly shows at Mallory Square, the place where everyone gathered to watch the famous Key West Sunset Celebration each evening. Everywhere they went, everything they did, Abbey instantly felt a kindred spirit in the old city. They were only in Key West for a few days, but that was enough to let Abbey know this was the place she fit in.

The night they went to Mallory Square and she caught sight of the artisans setting up with their own tables to sell their artwork, she was immediately intrigued. Abbey wondered if she could do the same thing with her miniature sculptures and paintings. She had sold some in Asheville at a local gallery, but it was just a hobby.

Abbey had majored in art and design at Princeton after receiving a full scholarship. Hope also had a full scholarship, but otherwise they were completely opposite. While Abbey was the artsy, creative person, Hope was all logic and science. But they were assigned the same dorm room their freshman year and became the best of friends. Abbey couldn't understand the first thing about Hope's classes, and Hope was constantly asking Abbey to clean up her paper, pens, and art messes that usually scattered their floor. None of that mattered to the two girls, who basically did everything together during their four years at college and had been great friends ever since. They even saw each other at least every other month, because Hope lived in Charleston, South Carolina, and Abbey in Asheville, North Carolina, only four hours apart.

The decision to leave the mountains of North Carolina for the sunny island of Key West had been both easy and difficult. Abbey had a wonderful job at the top advertising agency in Asheville where she was the head illustrator and graphic-design artist. She honestly loved her career but longed to see if she could become an independent artist. Could she actually move to Key West and make her artwork her profession, something she had always wanted to do since leaving college? She contemplated the idea all the way home from the wedding, even writing the pros and cons in her notebook on the plane ride back to North Carolina. As soon as she got home, she researched everything about Key West, including jobs, places to live, weather, safety, and more. Within three weeks, she had made the final decision to move.

Her family couldn't believe Abbey would leave the security of the life she had. At twenty-eight years old, she had her own home and a high-paying job located in the beautiful Smoky Mountains. Her boyfriend, Max, was a handsome, successful real-estate agent. According to the outside world, Abbey Wallace had it made. But she didn't see it that way. Yes, she had a good life, but it felt as though a piece was missing. Abbey wanted more simplicity and creativity. She wanted what she had witnessed during the wedding she attended in the Keys. That "head over heels in love" relationship, the kind that made your toes tingle. This was something that Abbey didn't have with Max. Though she cared deeply for him, it wasn't true love. So within a span of three weeks, Abbey had found a job and an apartment in Key West. She put her house on the market, and even though Max had told her not to expect a quick sale, she had a contract in the first week. This was a sign, Abbey thought, which meant she was on the right path.

When she told Max of her plans to move, it was her way of breaking off the relationship. At first he was upset and hurt, but after a long, honest talk, they both knew that it was only a matter of time before they went their separate ways. They cared for each other and would always be friends, but that deep soul mate love Abbey longed for wasn't there, and they both knew it. Max told her he was sad to see her leave and that he would miss her, but he was happy that Abbey was finally going to pursue her art dreams—and what better place than a tropical island paradise.

Her hardest good-byes were to her parents. Abbey came from a close-knit family, but she was the last one to leave not only home but also the city where she had lived her entire life. Her two brothers had moved shortly after they finished college. Her older brother, Mark, went to Houston to work for a large church as the director of their worship team after earning a degree in music therapy. Her baby brother, Drew, was off to New York City to pursue his desire to be a journalist. Abbey had stayed in her hometown, having weekly dinners with her parents and spending time with them whenever she could. Telling them of her plans to make the move to the Keys was one of the most difficult things she did before she left. Her parents were her rock. Not being with them and seeing them almost every day would be hard. And even though they were sad to see their little girl leave, they were also happy for her, telling her to make room for them soon, because they would be frequent visitors. Abbey even kidded with them that they might come south and decide to leave their mountain home, but she seriously doubted it. Their roots were in the mountains and always would be.

As Abbey wound her way through the streets to her new home, she marveled at everything around her. Though she had been here only a few months ago for the wedding, and then a quick interview shortly after that, it seemed like years to her. Driving her Jeep through the city towing the small trailer was a bit unnerving, but Abbey had made it this far, and it wasn't long before she was parked in front of her new address. There wasn't much room to maneuver along the street, but she parked the trailer as close as she could to the curb, taking only two parking spaces hoping it wouldn't be a problem since it was only for the night. Abbey was sure she could unload first thing in the morning what she wasn't able to get to tonight. Then as soon as she was done, she would return the U-Haul. She hadn't brought much with her—only what she had to have. The apartment was furnished, but Abbey had already decided to buy a few new things once she got here. A bed was at the top of the list, because it was the one thing her new residence did not provide.

Abbey stepped out of her vehicle and stood looking, marveling at her new neighborhood. The trees were beautiful. The colorful flowers dotting the street were lovely, lending to that feeling of landing in the tropics. The breeze flowing across the island from the Atlantic to the Gulf of Mexico felt good on her skin. Her little apartment was three streets from Duval Street, the hub of excitement in this island town. Her new job was for a small graphic-design agency that primarily built websites for big-name companies across the world but also made digital graphics for logos and more. Abbey would start in a few short weeks, and it was only four blocks from her house. Hopefully, she would be able to walk, or better yet, buy a bike and ride, since she had noticed on her first trip that it seemed to be a very popular form of transportation here.

She remembered when she had discovered the job opening on the Internet. Within a few days after Abbey sent her application, the owner, Lance Peterson, called her. He was very impressed with her résumé, and after two interviews, the job was hers. She was amazed at the agency's client list and, considering the office was small and located in Key West, not a major metropolitan city like New York. That was what Abbey would have expected after seeing the names of the people and companies they worked with.

During the second interview with Mr. Peterson, she learned that he had originally been based out of Chicago for the first twenty years of his business. The agency began doing more online design and website work as the Internet grew, and before long, ninety percent of his business was done primarily online or through phone calls and teleconferences. That was when he and his wife, Donna, had made the decision to move from the big-city life and chosen Key West, a little over ten years earlier. Their two children were already grown by then, so it was just the two of them. It was also a perfect move for his wife, since she was a wonderful and well-known artist. The downstairs was her own art gallery, and the upstairs was his agency. He told Abbey that it was the best decision they had ever made. Plus, now both their children, married with families of their own, had moved to the Keys and were just an hour away, so they were able to visit their grandchildren as often as they liked. Abbey liked Lance, as she was told to call him, from the first time they talked on the phone. In person, he was even sweeter. She couldn't have picked a better person to work for, and this made her even more excited to start her new job.

It was during her second trip for the follow-up interview with Lance that she found her new apartment. She had flown in to talk to him in person, and after confirming she had the job, she stayed a few days longer, looking for the perfect place. On her second day of hunting, she found the two-story light-teal-painted building that looked more like a beautiful house than a place that held four nice-sized apartments for rent. It reminded her of a bed-and-breakfast from the outside with the white fence and gate that opened to the sidewalk. The wraparound porch on both the first and second floors was beautiful, and Abbey instantly saw herself sitting out there, in a rocking chair, sketching her newest piece of work or reading the latest juicy novel.

Upon opening the white gate, it was only a few steps to the staircase that led to the second floor, where her new apartment was. There was a set of two steps that led to the first-floor porch, and she could see the two separate doors indicating the bottom apartments. When she reached the top of the steps, she was directly in front of the place she had come to look at. The other door around the corner led to the room that over-looked the street.

As soon as she opened the door, Abbey immediately felt at home. It was much smaller than her house back in the moun-tains, but as she looked around, Abbey could see a place for everything she would need. The kitchen was small but nicely organized, with enough room for cooking and some of her small appliances. The one bedroom was large enough for her, and she could already envision it completely decorated. The bathroom was smaller than what she was used to but perfect just for her. The rest of the space was one large room with two French doors that led to the outside porch balcony. Abbey would have to decide how to divide it into a living room and art studio, but that would come later. It only took one visit, and she knew this was the place for her.

2

Josie couldn't believe someone was already moving in up-stairs. She had hoped that it would take a while to rent the place above, but the landlord didn't waste any time accepting whoever came along. There had been so many people, from good to bad, over the years, but no one ever stayed for long. Not like her. Josie had been in her little apartment for over twenty years now, the longest tenant ever, according to her landlord. She probably could have bought her own house by now, but this place and this street had become her haven, and the thought of leaving actually brought her anxiety. Josie had made one big leap a long time ago, and she didn't feel like she could change at her age. She was content with her job and her little place with her tiny mixed-breed dog, Jewel. Josie was only fifty-five years old but sometimes felt like she was eighty.

She had moved to Key West on a whim after being jilted at the altar twenty-seven years before by the love of her life,

Michael. She was completely devastated, and after the shock wore off, depression consumed her. Eventually, Josie accepted her situation only through the love of her parents and friends. It was then that she decided a change of scenery would be the solution to her circumstances. Josie knew she was running away, but in her mind, a change was needed. Living in Montana was beautiful, and she loved the mountains, but Josie decided to move somewhere far away. Key West was the first city that came to mind. It was the farthest south you could go in the United States, and that would put plenty of distance between her and Michael.

She had found out that Michael had finally surfaced after disappearing on their wedding day but didn't come to see or talk to her. Josie was angry because in her mind, rightfully so, he should have at least apologized and explained to her what happened. But he never came to her door. Josie knew there was more to his story but chose not to search out the reason. She packed what she could in two suitcases, took all her money out of her accounts, and bought a bus ticket to Florida.

As Josie traveled the three days to reach Key West, she had so much time to think about how her life had changed in an instant. One minute she was working as a certified public accountant at a small-town firm, living on a farm that she and Michael had bought before the wedding. He was going to raise cattle, and his herd was already growing. Michael loved the land, and she had pictured herself working right alongside him, growing the ranch and watching their children playing in the barns. All it took was that awful day when he didn't show up at the church, humiliating Josie in front of almost the entire small town. She couldn't face everyone anymore. When she reached the Keys, she called to tell her parents where she was but swore them to secrecy, which they kept until they both passed away only one year apart. Even her brother didn't know where she was, since he had left home right out of high school, moving to Hawaii and never to return.

While Josie watched out the side window as the new girl began unloading the boxes from the trailer behind her car, she hoped this one wouldn't be rowdy or, should she say, sleazy, like some of the others who had lived in this building. She had seen all types of people live here, and she loved to keep the place respectable even though she wasn't the landlord. Josie had lived here so long that she felt like she was the keeper of the apartments, and in a way she was. Whenever Karen and Daniel Nunomi, the owners, decided to take a vacation or go away for the weekend, they always asked her to take care of the place. Since she had been such a good tenant over the years, they had become close, and they treated Josie like part of their family. They barely raised her rent each time they made changes, and they even invited her over for dinners and included her in their holiday festivities. But Josie didn't like that they were quick to take the next person who wanted to rent an empty room without knowing many details about the person, except for a little information on a sheet of paper and a signed rental agreement. She could understand not wanting to lose any money each month, and that was why some questionable people had graced the house at one time or another. Josie only hoped that the cheerful girl taking boxes up the steps would turn out to be a good neighbor, quiet and keeping to herself.

3

So, taking boxes upstairs hadn't been the brightest idea she'd had today. Abbey was tired from her drive, and with each load of boxes or bags she lugged up the steps, more energy drained from her body. She should have waited for tomorrow, but her excitement got the best of her as soon as she saw her new apartment. Now that she was halfway through the trailer, Abbey really wanted to see it empty. It would mean less to do tomorrow.

"Looks like you could use a bit of help," she heard some-one say behind her. Abbey turned just before taking the first step up the staircase to see a very handsome man open the gate to the fence that surrounded the beautiful yard. He had a bag of groceries in one hand and keys in the other. *He must live here*, she thought, making him her neighbor. The closer he came toward Abbey, the more nervous she felt. Even though he looked a little disheveled, Abbey could feel the catch in her breath. From his mesmerizing eyes, the chestnut-brown hair that looked windswept, and the dark stubble across his chin, Abbey was speechless. He took the big box out of her arms just as she was trying to get it situated for the trip up the steps.

"Hi, I'm Garrett, and you must be my new next-door neighbor. I live in the other apartment on the second floor." Abbey stared, still silent as she watched the tall, handsome man. He looked to be in his late thirties and very fit, as he was holding with ease the box that she'd just had so much difficulty with. Suddenly she realized that she hadn't even introduced herself.

But before Abbey could say anything, Garrett added, "If you want, I could help you get the rest of your stuff inside. Probably wouldn't take more than thirty minutes."

"I can't let you do that, but thanks anyway." Abbey wanted so much to accept the help, but she didn't even know this person.

"I'm volunteering!" he said cheerfully.

Abbey hesitated for a moment but the thought of all her things being in her apartment made her give in to his generous offer. "If you're sure, that would be great. I really want to turn in the U-Haul tomorrow, but I didn't realize just how much stuff I had in there till I started going up and down the steps. A little more than I bargained for. By the way, I'm Abbey Wallace. It is very nice to meet you, and yes, it looks like I am your new neighbor."

"Glad to meet you, and once you get used to the steps, they aren't so bad. But then, I'm not here that much either. This is sort of a temporary home base for me. I'm mostly out on the water on a boat. I'm a marine biologist doing a study on a coral reef off of Key West. So I'm the best neighbor in the world—I'm hardly ever home," he said with a smile as they headed down the stairs for another load of bags and boxes.

"Your work sounds exciting! How long have you been here?" Abbey asked, trying to get more information on this friendly, sexy man who had come to her rescue. As ridiculous as it sounded, Abbey could already see herself and Garrett having dinner by candlelight. She laughed inwardly at the ridiculous picture in her head, realizing it had to be fatigue for her to be thinking about a romantic liaison on her first day in the Keys.

"It's been almost a year. I have about six more months of work, then I'll be off to Key Largo to study the reef there. Parts of the reef system are dying, so it's my job to see what's happening, to make a long explanation very short. I live in wet suits and scuba gear, but I love it. So, what brought you down to the lovely Conch Republic?" he asked as he sat the next load of boxes inside her doorway.

"I decided on a change of scenery. I visited a couple of months ago and just fell in love with the city. I went back, sold my house, quit my job, and moved. That's my story in a nutshell." When Abbey described it like that, it did indeed sound a bit crazy.

"Aren't you the impulsive one! But you're not the first person I've talked to that has done the same thing. There is something about these islands that is irresistible, except for the heat. Thank God for air conditioners in the middle of summer, except I'm usually out on the boat. And it has an air conditioner in the cabin for those days when the ocean breeze just isn't cutting it." Garrett continued to get more things out of the trailer, with Abbey following closely on his heels, even though she couldn't carry the amount of boxes he did. But within thirty minutes, the trailer was empty, just as Garrett predicted.

As she sat the last bag on the counter in her new little kitchen, Abbey was astonished at all the stuff scattered everywhere in her living room. The Jeep still needed to be unloaded, but for tonight she was done, except for her travel bag and purse, which were in the front seat. Her vehicle would be locked tight, and its contents would have to wait for tomorrow.

"Wow, this is amazing! The trailer is empty. If it hadn't been for you, I would have called it a day and just had a very long one tomorrow, for sure. Thanks so much." Abbey smiled at Garrett as he stood in her doorway.

"No problem at all. Are you sure you don't want to go ahead and get everything out of the Jeep too? It would only be a few minutes more."

"You've done so much already. I can do the rest tomorrow. Please let me pay you for the help. It feels incredible to have that trailer empty," she said hesitantly.

"I leave tomorrow morning for three weeks, so when I get back, I'll let you fix me dinner if you cook. I rarely get home-cooked meals," Garrett said with a smile.

"It's a date!" Abbey said quickly. Then she realized her words, cringing inside. "I know some good Southern recipes my momma taught me."

"I'm already looking forward to it. Welcome to the neighborhood, Abbey. I hope it's everything you dreamed. See you later." And he walked out of her apartment to his own place next door. *Did Garrett just agree to a date? Or was he just being friendly?* A nice and good-looking man living next door to her. She had been in Key West less than four hours, and she already had plans for dinner with her sexy neighbor. *What a way to start your new adventure, Abbey,* she thought with a smile on her face.

4

The rays of sun shining through the blinds were Abbey's wake-up call the next morning. She originally was going to set the alarm on her phone to wake her early, but she was so tired after the previous day's late-evening move-in that she decided to wake on her own. Garrett's help unloading the trailer the night before left her with only the items in the Jeep. Though it was full, it wouldn't take her long before everything would be in her new place. Abbey had been able to dig out her sheets and blankets to put on the couch for sleeping instead of just the flimsy throw she had stashed in her overnight tote. She sat up and looked around at the boxes and bags spread around her. Even though it looked quite the mess, Abbey smiled so wide her cheeks hurt. Yes, at a glance it seemed to be piles of clutter, but this was only temporary. Before long, she would have her quaint little place on the island looking cheerful and welcoming.

As Abbey had promised, she had called her mom and dad the night before after Garrett had gone. As soon as she heard their voices, she was a bit homesick. They were glad to hear that she had made it safe and sound. She had promised to call them the next day using FaceTime so that she could show them where she would be living. Though she was tired during their entire phone call, Abbey chatted nonstop, telling them about her trip and the Keys. Though Abbey couldn't see their faces, hearing their voices sounded so good to her when she realized that she was truly on her own for the first time in her life.

Abbey grabbed her tote bag that had some leftover snacks from her trip. She brought out some crackers and natural peanut butter, which would serve as her breakfast this morning. Though she had a long day ahead, she would have to make time for grocery shopping to stock her cabinets and refrigerator. She had eaten enough junk food on her travel down here. Now it was back to eating a bit more healthily, as she had since she was a teenager, driving her family crazy at times with her "health food." But at the same time, Abbey couldn't wait to explore the local restaurants she had heard so much about.

Finding her suitcase full of clothing was easy. She grabbed a pair of shorts and a tank top, knowing the day was going to be a warm one. Slipping into her shoes, she grabbed her keys and headed to the Jeep to start unloading the last of her things. Abbey stepped outside and was instantly greeted with a warm breeze and bright sunshine. It was beautiful and welcoming. The clear, blue sky above with slightly swaying palm trees surrounded her. Abbey still couldn't wipe away the silly grin that she knew was plastered on her face, because she was really here, in Key West. In her own apartment! It almost felt like a dream.

Just as she reached the bottom of the steps, an older woman walked out the door to the first apartment on the ground floor. *Perfect timing! Meeting another new neighbor,* Abbey thought enthusiastically.

"Good morning," Abbey said as she walked toward the woman and extended her hand. "I'm Abbey Wallace. Just moved in last night in the apartment upstairs." She was met with a blank face. The woman's stony stare was anything but friendly, and Abbey was not quite sure what to do, so she shyly and slowly withdrew her hand.

"Hello. Have a good day." The woman started walking down the stone walkway to the sidewalk, acting as though Abbey was just an annoying person she would rather not talk to. This was her first contact with the woman, so she knew that she couldn't have done anything to upset her. Or had she? Were she and Garrett too loud yesterday while unloading the trailer? It had been a bit late, and she had talked the entire time, with Garrett giving her some great information about the city and things to do. Whatever the case, Abbey had been given the cold shoulder, something she definitely didn't expect from anyone living in this paradise.

As she stood watching the woman walk away down the street, she heard footsteps behind her and turned to see Garrett coming down the steps with a backpack and two huge tote bags.

"Good morning! Off to sea I go—again. Did you sleep OK in your new place?" he said as he reached the bottom of the stairs. But then he saw the look on Abbey's face. "What's wrong? You look perplexed."

"Oh, I'm sorry. Good morning! You certainly look like you are ready for a big trip." Her thoughts were still puzzled by the odd woman's behavior. "Garrett, do you know who lives in the first apartment here?" She pointed to the door.

He gave a small laugh and shook his head. "Now I know why you have that look on your face. I see you have met Josie," Garrett said as he smiled at her. "Just a cranky old woman who couldn't be nice to a puppy if she had to."

"That's a bit mean to say, don't you think?"

"You just wait," Garrett said as he loaded his car. "You haven't been here long enough to know her, but you will. And I wish you luck with that. She is basically a recluse, hardly talks to anyone except our landlords, and when she does say anything, it has never been really nice. Then again, I'm not here every day. You will have to ask Ella, who lives next to her. She will give you an earful about her dear, wonderful neighbor."

As he finished loading his bags and got in his vehicle, he yelled back to her, "Remember, you owe me a dinner." And with that, Garrett drove down the street.

Abbey's thoughts suddenly switched from the woman to the dinner date she had in a few weeks. Garrett was a handsome man and extremely nice. They had gotten along splendidly yesterday, talking and chatting, Garret full of information. There was even a wink here and there, which Abbey interpreted as flirting. She had told herself, on her trip south, that dating and romance were on hold for a while as she settled into her new city and a new routine. But Garrett's charm and friendliness were making it next to impossible not to at least consider a date here and there.

Abbey waved to him as he left and started the task of unloading her Jeep. It only took about four trips, and finally all her things were in the apartment. There was hardly a place to walk except for the little paths she created when bringing her boxes in, but she didn't care. As she looked around at what she had brought with her, she couldn't believe that she had whittled her possessions down to what she saw before her.

In Asheville she had a furnished, nice, three-bedroom, two-bath home. After Abbey decided to move, she had put her more precious items in storage and had a huge garage sale with the things she determined she could part with or that couldn't make the trip south with her. The goal was to use the money from the sale, and a few larger items she had sold on Craigslist, to furnish her place here. Now it was just a matter of deciding what she needed as she unpacked. She would make a list, but after sleeping just one night on the couch, her main focus was to buy a bed. Though the sofa was comfy, she needed—no, wanted—a real bed. But today she would return the U-Haul, get groceries, and unpack. And if she got everything done, Abbey promised to reward herself with a trip to Mallory Square to watch her first Key West Celebration Sunset as an official island resident.

As Abbey she shut the door to the Jeep after taking one peek inside to make sure she had everything, she saw an exceptionally beautiful, dark-haired woman walking hurriedly from the house. This had to be Ella, the other tenant in the building. Abbey couldn't help but stare as the woman walked toward the gate, because Ella was gorgeous—tanned, thin but well toned, with dark-brown, almost black hair that hung in a beautiful ponytail down her back. She was dressed in shorts and a T-shirt with a company logo that Abbey couldn't quite make out.

"Hi there," the woman said with a slight accent as she walked toward Abbey. "My name is Ella. I heard that there was a new girl coming to town. Welcome!"

"Thanks! I would shake your hand, but…" Abbey held up her arms, which were full of the few last things she had to take to her apartment.

"No worries. We will have to talk later, as I'm off to work. The boat leaves in thirty minutes, and I'm already late. Have a great day," Ella said as she practically ran to her bike and rode down the street. *A bike*, Abbey thought. That would have to go on her shopping list. It would be much easier to ride a bike than drive everywhere. Plus, she would be able to cross exercise off her list each day.

Returning the U-Haul was an easy task since the drop-off center happened to be just a few blocks from her home. Next, she went on to the grocery store, where she felt like she was on a food-shopping spree. Abbey was stocking up for the first time, and her cart was overflowing. As she put the bags into her car, she began to think about the trips up the stairs to the take her food in. At this rate she wouldn't need to do any biking or walking to keep in shape. The stairs were her new exercise machine! Her legs and arms were aching as though she had worked out with ten times the weights she used at the gym back home. This was just from yesterday's stair workout while moving in, but she knew it wouldn't always be this way. Hopefully this would be the last time having to move so many things upstairs at once.

Abbey suddenly realized that she was alone in the building today. Everyone had headed off to work, except she wasn't sure about Josie, since she didn't have much to say. Abbey would have to spend a bit of time with Ella to find out about their elusive neighbor. She certainly wanted to start off her new life here on the right foot with everyone around her, including this woman who seemed to be very different from everyone else Abbey had met so far.

5

Getting her groceries up the stairs was a feat, but when Abbey at last closed the door and let the cool air of the apartment envelop her, she felt like she had completed a huge task. As she put up her groceries for the first time, she found that she was actually having fun with something she never thought was very appealing before—but this was her first grocery run. She knew eventually the newness would wear off, but until then, she would revel in all the excitement of living in her new city. One thing that she was sure would never wear off was the relaxed island ambience that surrounded her everywhere she went. At least, Abbey hoped in her heart it wouldn't, because she could already feel the stress level was lower here. People seemed so different—or was she the offbeat one by making this impulsive decision to almost completely change her life so quickly?

It didn't take Abbey long to have all the food in place in the little kitchen. Next she tackled as many boxes and bags as she could, moving quickly. Since she had marked each one as to which room it belonged, she started by putting them in the proper place. That didn't take long, because there were only four spaces: kitchen, bathroom, bedroom, and large living-room area. She ate a quick lunch and then started taking one box at a time, putting things up. Abbey became so engrossed in her work that at first she didn't hear her cell phone ringing. When she finally realized it was buzzing, she couldn't remember where it was but suddenly saw it on the kitchen counter. She grabbed it just in time before the caller hung up.

"Hello," she said tentatively, since she didn't look at the caller ID.

"Are you there? In Key West?" It was Hope, her best friend and the person who was, in a way, responsible for setting Abbey on her new adventure.

"I'm here! I'm really here! I can't believe that I really did it. It still hasn't sunk in that I'm actually living on the island."

"I can't believe you did it either. I have to admit, I loved it down there too, but just for a really nice vacation. Visiting a couple of times a year sounds like a plan to me. I hope you are up for house guests," Hope said excitedly.

"Of course, as long as you don't mind sleeping on an airbed on the floor," Abbey laughed.

"No, you and I will splurge on a hotel down on Duval Street near Mallory Square. We will let Shawn stay at your place and make it just a girls' night."

"That sounds fabulous. I should have this place presentable by the time you guys come for a visit. I'm trying to finish most of my unpacking today and treat myself to a sunset on the square tonight. It's not far from here. I have most of my stuff out, but things still need to be organized. I did my best not to bring much with me, only what I needed, and I'm still amazed by what I was able to leave up north. I can see now how I had accumulated too many things that I really didn't need. I do have to shop for a bed tomorrow and now a desk. I'm actually making my list of things I need to buy...I'm so sorry! I'm just rattling on and on from excitement, still running on adrenaline. How are you guys doing?" Abbey asked.

"Well, I have some news. You are going to be an aunt!" Hope shouted into the phone.

"Are you serious? Oh my gosh, I can't believe it!" Abbey said as she jumped up and down with excitement. It wasn't long before she heard three loud knocks, but they weren't coming from the door. The sound was coming from beneath her feet. *What in the world?* she thought.

"Abbey, are you there?"

"I'm sorry. Something weird just happened. I just heard knocking, but it was coming from my floor, not my door."

"Aren't you on the second floor of the building? Maybe it was a neighbor trying to get your attention for some reason?" Hope asked curiously.

"I didn't do anything. There is a lady that lives on the first floor who isn't very friendly. Tried to talk to her, and she gave me a definite brush-off. But this morning I watched everyone here leave. I'll check it out later. So, give me info." As Abbey and Hope continued to talk about her pregnancy, thoughts about the knocks coming from her floor were in the back of her mind. It didn't make sense.

Hope filled her in on how everyone was excited about the baby, especially her mom and Jason. They were going to be grandparents, and it seemed like that was all her mom was focused on. They lived on Folly Beach, close to Hope's home on James Island near Charleston, South Carolina. Abbey had always loved that beach and went there each time she visited. She and Hope practically lived on the sand every time Abbey came to stay during the summer months. Now, Hope would be taking her little one to enjoy their favorite beach.

"I'm considered a high-risk pregnancy because I have Diabetes, so they are keeping a very close watch on me. Plus, I've had to take a leave of absence from the office, but I'm doing some work via the laptop from home. And Shawn is taking exceptional care of me. Figured I might as well rest now, because when the baby gets here, I have a feeling I'm going to be very busy!"

Abbey could hear the happiness in Hope's voice through the phone, and she was so excited for her. "You will have to definitely come visit, maybe before the baby is born. Anytime, you just let me know. You can travel, right?" Abbey asked enthusiastically.

"Probably, but will have to get the doctor's OK. But let's talk about you. Abbey, I'm so happy and proud of you. When you said that day that you were going to move there, I thought you were joking. Instead, you made a decision, and you did it. Not a lot of people follow through. I can't wait to hear about your job, and let me know if you are able to get a license to sell your art at the square. I would love to be there on your opening day!"

Though they could have stayed on the phone for hours, Abbey knew she needed to get back to work. As they said their good-byes, Abbey was feeling so excited for her best friend. But right now she needed to investigate what was going on downstairs and who was tapping so hard on her floor.

Abbey tucked her phone in the front pocket of her shorts and set off downstairs. She knocked at Ella's door first, knowing that her apartment was directly above hers, but no one answered. Next was Josie's door, but as Abbey raised her hand to knock, her nerves set in, remembering how the woman had treated her in the short amount of time she had been here. And she really didn't want to confront her now, if she was even home. *Here goes nothing*, she thought as she knocked on the door.

The older woman answered the door, staring at Abbey without saying a word. At first Abbey was tongue-tied, but finally she found her voice.

"Hi again," Abbey began. "Uh, just a few minutes ago, I heard some sort of tapping or knocking coming from my floor. Have you ever heard of that before or maybe know what it was?"

"It was me and my mop handle. I don't know what you were doing up there, but I could hear a very loud banging noise on the ceiling. So loud that it startled me." The woman just stared at her, and her voice was monotone, not angry but not friendly either. Abbey knew there was no way her excited jumping could have made that much noise, but she didn't argue. She truly wanted to start her new life here on a positive note with all her neighbors, including this lady who seemed determined not to be nice.

"Sorry about that. I'm not usually a noisy person, but I just got some good news from home and was doing a little happy dance." She was trying her best to be as cheerful as possible, but the stone face that looked back at her was hard to please.

"Just keep it down. We like it quiet around here. Even though your place isn't above mine, very loud sounds travel." She went to shut the door, and Abbey got up the nerve to stop her by putting her hand on the woman's door. The woman stared back at her incredulously. Abbey herself couldn't believe that she had just done that!

"I would like to introduce myself before I go. My name is Abbey Wallace. I'm from North Carolina, and even though I wish it were under better circumstances, I'm really glad to meet you." She hoped that this would help break the ice wall surrounding this woman.

The woman sighed and continued to stare. "Well, Abbey from North Carolina, I'm Josie from Key West. Keep the noise down, and we will get along just fine." And with that, the woman shut the door.

6

Abbey stood there for a moment and then turned on her heel, going back up the stairs. What nerve! She was just trying to be polite, and this woman—Josie—was being so hateful. Abbey knew she hadn't done anything wrong. She had just met the woman, so what could be the problem?

Abbey was still thinking about her encounter with Josie as she continued to put things away, fixing up her little apartment to make it feel like home. Talking to the unpleasant woman had left her feeling unsettled, but as she continued to put things in their proper places, Abbey got lost in a feeling of happiness once again as she watched the rooms around her transform. Though when she hung a few pictures, each time she used the hammer, she almost expected to hear knocking coming from the floor beneath her feet again. Abbey wished she knew more about the woman living downstairs and made a decision as she continued working. One way or another, Abbey was going to show Josie that she was friendly. Even if Josie had no interest in getting to know Abbey, she was going to be nice to her anyway. Hopefully she would bring Josie around to her side, maybe dare to become her friend, because it seemed like Josie could use one. Why this was important to Abbey, she didn't know, but she felt compelled to break through her new neighbor's icy facade. Since following her instincts had gotten her this far, Abbey was certainly going to follow her gut, even though the situation right now looked and felt very bleak.

Around five o'clock, Abbey finally sat down and looked around. Except for a stack of broken-down boxes in the corner, her little place in Key West had come together. She had infused some brightness throughout the rooms with paintings, plants, and special items she had brought from her mountain home. In her kitchen, she had placed her appliances strategically on the counter, leaving her room for prepping meals. She hung brightly colored hand towels by the sink, and a few magnets that she had collected over the years graced the front of her refrigerator, reminding her of home in North Carolina. The pretty aqua rug on the floor was almost large enough to go from one counter to the other and brightened up the light-beige-colored tile floor. She decorated her bathroom with a coral, purple, and off-white shower curtain that was dotted with all types of seashells. Coral-colored rugs on the floor gave more color to the tiny space. Bright, tropical-colored towels adorned the rack, bringing the little room to life.

Abbey's bedroom was still bare because of the room left for a bed, which she was hoping to get by the end of the week. But she had hung pictures, mostly of family, and a painting of a beach scene she had created while in college. It had actually won a contest that had put a few bucks in her pocket at the time. Now it seemed fitting since she was living in a tropical locale. The small dresser and chest of drawers were cleaned and now filled with her clothing. The side tables would be for her journals, books, and such once her bed arrived. All the furniture was made from a beautiful bamboo, lending again to the island atmosphere of her new place. And even though the bed wasn't in the room just yet, Abbey put down the pale-turquoise rugs on the floor to give her an idea of what it would look like once all the furniture was in place. It made her smile.

In the large living room, Abbey moved furniture around till she was satisfied with the arrangement so that it would give her the space she needed to both relax and create. She grouped the couch, love seat, and chair around a glass coffee table. She moved the sofa table in front of the furniture and placed her flat-screen TV on top. In the corner, she arranged the perfect place for a desk and storage. This would be her personal "art studio," a place for her to design and make her paintings, sculptures, and figurines she so loved. Abbey placed the boxes there that held her supplies and now added "desk and storage drawers" to her ever-growing shopping list to complete her little workstation. Even though it was only her second day here, it was truly starting to feel a bit like home.

Abbey realized as she looked around that most things were complete. That meant, even though she was tired, she was going to see her first Key West Sunset at Mallory Square as a resident this time, not a tourist. A quick look at her phone let her know that she had just enough time to take a quick shower, get dressed, and make it to the square, though she would have to drive her Jeep. But as Abbey was getting ready, she thought about Ella and her bike. *It would be nice to ride a bicycle to the square*, she thought, and was glad that she had added "bicycle" to her shopping list. It seemed like everyone who lived in this little town had one.

Just as Abbey got to the bottom of the stairs, Ella came through the gate. "Hi, Ella!"

"Hello, um—" Ella stumbled. Abbey knew she didn't remember her name and came to her rescue: "Abbey."

"Yes, Abbey. So sorry! I'm not the best with names, even though you would think so, since I deal with people all day." Ella looked embarrassed.

"That's OK. I know you just got home from work, but do you have a second for a real quick chat?"

"Sure, as long as you don't mind if I change clothes for work while we talk," Ella said as she quickly walked to her apartment door.

"Didn't you just get home?" Abbey asked, perplexed.

"I work two jobs," Ella explained as Abbey followed her to her place. "I work with the boat tours during the day, and I'm a waitress at night. Trying to save up enough money for my own place instead of renting. I'm even thinking about not staying here in Key West but moving up to one of the other Keys, like Marathon or Islamorada."

"So you don't like it here?" Abbey said as she walked into Ella's place, which was a mess, to say the least. Abbey never wanted to criticize other people's living styles, but there was no way she could live with the clutter she saw as she stood just inside the doorway of Ella's little place.

"I love Key West, but sometimes I just want things to be a bit simpler and have more room. Maybe even have my own garden. It's just something I'm working toward. Oh, sorry for the mess. I've been so busy that cleaning has been the last thing on my mind, though it probably should be a priority," Ella said as she looked for a piece of clothing in the pile of laundry by her couch. "Promise you that it doesn't always look like my apartment has been burglarized. What did you want to talk about?" she asked as she started quickly getting undressed in front of Abbey with no reservations at all. Though it made Abbey slightly uncomfortable, since she didn't really know Ella, she decided to act as though everything were fine. Abbey really wanted to know more about Josie.

"I was wondering if you could tell me a bit about your neighbor, well, our neighbor, Josie. As Garrett was leaving this morning, he said to ask you when I got a chance."

"Did Garrett leave again? I was hoping to finally get him to agree to have dinner with me," she said, pouting just a little. As soon as she said the words, Abbey felt a little awkward, since she did have a dinner date with Garrett in an odd sort of way. Knowing that Garrett hadn't made the commitment to go out with Ella boosted her confidence a bit, because this woman was stunning and seemed to be nice. But Abbey decided to keep this tidbit of information to herself.

"Been trying to get him to go out for two months now, ever since I got here, but it's always something. And he is gone a lot! But Garrett is a really sweet guy and even nicer to look at!" Ella said with a wink, continuing to change into her evening work clothes as fast as she could. "But you were asking about Josie.

"Josie is crabby and old. Sorry, just calling it like I see it. I've tried to be nice, but no luck. She doesn't even acknowledge me when I see her. I asked the landlords about her, and they would only say that she has been here for a while in the same apartment, and she had things to deal with. Something is going on with her, but I have given up trying to be a friendly neighbor. I would hate to be that miserable all the time. When did you run into her?" Ella was finally dressed, putting her long hair back into a ponytail and freshening her makeup. She was so fast that Abbey was a having hard time keeping up with her.

"This morning while I was unloading the rest of my stuff out of the Jeep. I introduced myself, but she basically ignored me."

"Well, get used to it, because we all have. Only time I see her talk to anyone is when the landlords stop by. They are so nice, but I'm surprised that she is friendly to them! Just let her be, and she will leave you alone."

"That's just it. This afternoon I got a phone call from a friend telling me she was pregnant. I jumped up and down in my apartment. Suddenly I hear knocking on my floor! I came down here to make sure I hadn't disturbed you, but since you weren't home, I went to talk to Josie. I tried to introduce myself, *again,* and I was basically told to keep the noise down, and she shut the door. She had used a mop handle to knock loudly on my floor! Really weird when my place isn't even over hers, except for a very small portion. I wasn't bouncing up and down like I was on a trampoline." Abbey was getting a bit exasperated as she told the story but was determined not to let it get the best of her.

"You don't have to worry about me and noise," Ella said as she finished by neatly pinning a name tag on her shirt. "I usually don't get home till around midnight, and then I'm out like a light. Noise doesn't bother me unless it's extremely loud, and you, my dear, don't look like the type." She smiled at Abbey as she gathered her things to head out the door.

As they walked outside, Ella continued, "Don't let it get you down. You can't please everyone, and I'm glad you are here. You seem really nice, and hopefully we can have some girl time soon. I'm sorry but I have to go or I'll be late again. My boss is pretty cool, but he is a stickler about being on time, especially right now when things are so busy. Have a nice evening!" Before Abbey knew it, Ella was back on her bike and riding down the street once again.

Even though Ella had advised her to stay away, Abbey couldn't get Josie out of her mind. After the conversation she had just had, Abbey was even more determined to get to know the elusive woman in the downstairs apartment. But for now, Abbey was going to have to hurry to Mallory Square if she wanted to see her first Key West sunset.

7

By the time Abbey got to the square, it was filling up fast. She was able to secure one of the last parking spaces and made her way through the large crowd to find a great place to sit. Her little spot was at the end of the pier, and she made herself comfortable as she waited for nature's picture show to begin. The sunset was beautiful, with gorgeous colors of yellow, orange, purple, and red displaying like a fan as the sun seemed to sink into the ocean. Abbey captured several pictures on her phone so they could go into her new scrapbook. And even though she was surrounded by a throng of people, she felt content and alone with her thoughts. This was only day two of living in her new hometown, and Abbey already felt like she belonged to this little island that called itself the Conch Republic.

After the sun had settled over the horizon, Abbey headed to the tables of the various artists selling their handmade wares. She was mesmerized by all the talent she saw before her and wondered if her art was up to the standards of these talented people. She promised herself that she wouldn't compare her work to theirs, because it seemed everyone had different ideas and styles, but sometimes it was hard not to. As soon as she was settled in her new job, Abbey was going to become one of these artists here, selling her paintings and figurines. Not just for the money, which would be nice, but more for the love of creating and making things. Then, to be able to watch others get excited when they fell in love with a picture, a painting, or a craft item made Abbey smile inside. Even though she was good at her job and loved designing on the computer, it was creating with her hands that sung to her heart.

By the time she got back into her little home, Abbey was beyond tired but so satisfied. She ate a quick sandwich, took the fastest shower ever, and curled up on the couch. It had been a long but satisfying day. As soon as her head landed on the pillow, she was fast asleep.

Abbey woke again to a room filled with sunlight. *Add "room-darkening shades" to the list*, she told herself as she stretched. Not that the current blinds were bad, but when she slept, she liked her room to be nice and dark. During the day it was just the opposite. Everything had to be bright and sunny. Thinking about the list reminded Abbey that this was her shopping day, and what had begun as just a quest for a bed was now turning out to be a full-on shopping experience around the city. She only hoped she would be able to find everything. Key West didn't have the usual Target or Walmart, so if she couldn't find what she needed, it would have to be ordered or shipped in, unless she wanted to make the three-plus-hour trip back to Florida City. And since she was going to be out today, Abbey decided to go by her new workplace and introduce herself.

When Abbey had come to the Keys for her second interview, she had only met with Mr. Peterson, or Lance, as she was told to call him. It had been a late-afternoon interview, and everyone else had left for the day. Even though there were only three other employees, she thought it would be nice to meet them now instead of waiting for the awkwardness that usually accompanies the first day of a new job. Abbey also wanted to let Lance know that instead of starting in two weeks, she would be ready next week if it was OK with him. If not, she would use the time to explore the city, but she was eager to get started.

Since Abbey was going to meet her fellow employees, she decided to dress up a little more than just shorts, T-shirt, and flip-flops, her usual apparel for a day like today. She picked out a white skirt that fell a few inches above the knee. She paired it with a white tank top, which she covered with a multicolored, see-through peasant top that cinched at the waist. Her shoes of choice were a pair of silver, braided flat sandals. She was dressed nicely but not too dressy. She still wasn't sure of the dress code given that most of the work was done virtually, so today would be a good way to find out.

Just as she reached the bottom of the stairs, Josie emerged from her apartment. Though she made no eye contact with her, Abbey had already made a commitment to herself that she would always make a point to speak and be nice no matter what.

"Good morning, Josie. How are you today?"

This time Josie just looked at her, walked out the front gate, and then continued down the sidewalk. Abbey sighed as she watched Josie walk away. If there was to be a relationship, Abbey knew it would take a long time to nurture. She saw no sign of Ella this morning, and she looked over to see that her bicycle was already gone. And now, even though she was nervous, it was time to go and meet her new coworkers, hoping they were more welcoming than her downstairs neighbor.

8

Josie walked down the street, already dreading her coming workday. It was her yearly evaluation today, and even though she had received exemplary reports for the last fifteen years she had worked at the resort, Josie always felt like she was under the microscope at these meetings. Working in the accounting department of one of the largest private Key West resorts was so different from the small-town CPA firm she had left so long ago, but the benefits and pay were better. The fact that she was as far away from Montana as she could get without leaving the United States was an added bonus. She had done some type of accounting since arriving here twenty-seven years before. She had used that time wisely, building a huge savings account and plenty of investments so that she could easily retire soon. But she continued to work to be around the people she felt most comfortable and safe with. Though Josie wasn't very close to those she worked with, she felt more at home with them than the people in her building and the other neighbors around her little apartment.

There was a feeling of mistrust with everyone that continued to haunt Josie since she had been jilted at the altar. She was scared to form any kind of relationship, not wanting to experience that hurt all over again. Though she knew in her heart it was a terrible phobia, Josie had convinced herself that she was content with her life, even though sometimes she secretly wished she had someone to talk to.

Josie usually shared her stories and sought advice from her landlords, the only people she really trusted, and it had taken so long for her to feel comfortable with them. The thing that hurt the most was that she could still remember what her life was like before Michael had dropped that bomb on their supposed wedding day. There had been happiness, love, and peacefulness. Every day Josie lived with the desire to have those feelings again but convinced herself that it was never going to happen. So she pushed it all down inside and did her best to appreciate the life she had made here for herself in this beautiful tropical city.

"Hi, Josie," Eddie said as she walked in the front lobby doors. "Have a good weekend?"

"Same as always. How about you?"

"Same as always, but I bet mine was better than yours. Big party at the marina. You should have been there. One of these days, I'm going to persuade you to come."

"Maybe next time," Josie chuckled and went toward her office. Eddie was definitely the friendliest guy around and the biggest party person ever. He was always nice to her, no matter what kind of mood Josie arrived in at the resort each day. They had worked together for over five years now. Maybe one day she would go to one of his parties, but Josie knew she would most likely be the oldest person there. On second thought, she would stick to her little place and her loyal dog. Anyway, it would probably interrupt one of her TV shows, she thought as she settled in her office for the day. Even though she loved what she did, working with paper and numbers all day, Josie found comfort in her personal routine each morning and evening. Right now her thoughts were focused on the evaluation. Though she was nervous, she felt confident that her review would be a positive one. Josie just wanted it to be over so she could move on with her day.

At ten o'clock, Mr. Sherwood, Josie's boss, finally summoned her to his office. As she got up and followed him down the hall, her gut instinct suddenly felt panicky. Something just didn't feel quite right. Mr. Sherwood's spacious office looked out over the water, and she could see Wisteria Island in the distance as she took the seat in front of his desk. A few tourists also passed by the window to his office, but since it was darkened, no one could see in. Josie's office was just the opposite. She was stuck in a small room with a tiny window covered by the trunk of a palm tree.

"As you know, this is your yearly evaluation. As always, Josie, your work is outstanding. Your numbers are correct; your work is neat and always on time. I feel like I just repeat the same thing to you each time we have this chat. You are very valuable here, and you have worked here at the resort the longest, except for me," Mr. Sherwood sighed as he looked down at the papers lying on his desk, acting hesitant about continuing.

"With that being said, I wanted to let you know that I've sold the hotel to a large resort group. They have promised to keep all staff, but I know how things work in the larger corporate world, so I wanted to make sure you were the first to know about the sale. The change in management won't take place for three months, and I plan to talk to the employees at a meeting this Friday. If we could keep this right now between the two of us, I would appreciate it. I feel the new owners will keep you on staff because your work speaks for itself, but if for some reason they don't, I will be more than happy to give you a glowing recommendation to any potential employers."

Josie sat still, stunned at the news. She had read enough about corporate takeovers of private businesses to know how ruthless the incoming owners could be. She instantly felt anxiety completely take over as her mind began to race. Those feelings of being left behind were surfacing, something she had thought was long gone.

"I am going to increase your bonus this time because out of everyone here, you are the most hardworking and dedicated. Plus, you'll receive your annual raise. Josie, try not to worry about your position here. Once the new owners see the quality of your work and loyalty to the resort, I don't think you'll have a thing to worry about."

"Thanks, Mr. Sherwood" was all Josie could say as calmly as possible. She stood up and slowly walked back down the hall to her little office. As she sat at her desk and stared at the list of today's work to be done, she couldn't concentrate. Everything around Josie seemed surreal and she felt more alone than ever, with no one to turn to. She knew in her heart that part of it was her fault by purposely keeping her distance from others, not making friends, but now she needed some advice. Josie wanted someone to talk to. She decided she would wait till Karen and Daniel got back from their trip. They would be her sounding board because Josie felt that more than likely, she would be out of a job in three short months.

9

As soon as Abbey found a place to park her Jeep, she got out and looked into her little side-view mirror as best she could to make sure she was presentable. She was suddenly nervous to go into the little gallery with the graphic-design shop on the second floor. It was right on Duval Street, and she watched as tourists bustled from one shop or restaurant to another. Before parking, she had driven past the small building a few times to make sure she had the right place, her stomach churning with a mixture of anxiety and excitement each time she looked at the storefront. This was not like Abbey, so she took a deep breath and calmed herself down. As she walked toward the office, her nervousness deepened but suddenly she was standing in front of the door. She took one last calming breath and went inside.

The gallery looked like it had the day Abbey had come for her second interview. The first floor was used as a showcase for Mrs. Peterson's oil paintings of the Keys, which were very popular with locals and tourists alike. Abbey would be working on the second floor above the small studio/gallery. As she walked around admiring the paintings that graced the walls, Abbey immediately felt at home and loved Mrs. Peterson's painting style right away. The work was exquisite, and Abbey thought, as she continued to look at the pieces of artwork, that she would have to ask for some painting tips.

"Hello, may I help you?" a small voice came from the person standing beside her. She turned to see a woman just about her height, of slight build, with ash-blond hair in a pixie cut. She wore a colorful maxi dress with sandals and appeared to be in her late fifties.

"Hello. Are you Mrs. Peterson?"

"Yes, I am. Do I know you?"

"Sorry. I'm Abbey Wallace, the new employee for your husband's graphic-design business. When I came for my interview, Lance, I mean, Mr. Peterson, told me that you were out of town on a girls' trip to the Bahamas. It is so nice to finally meet you." She shook the woman's hand.

"I heard about you. My husband was extremely impressed with your credentials. And please call me Donna."

"Thanks, Donna. I know I'm two weeks away from my official start date, but I wanted to come by and see the office, hopefully meet everyone. I'm so excited to be here." Abbey instantly liked the woman in front of her, whose warm smile was friendly and inviting.

"Your paintings are incredible," Abbey said as she glanced at the gallery. "I studied art at Princeton, and I paint with mixed media and do sculptures. One of the things that made Key West so appealing to me was all the creativity in the city." Abbey continued to look at the colorful paintings that lined the wall and sat on easels throughout the open space.

"Yes, Key West has a lot of artists and all types of creative people. We love it here, and I know you will too. Can't wait to see your artwork." Just then a few patrons entered the front door. "Follow the hall to the back, and the staircase will be on the right," Donna said as she went to greet her customers. Abbey mouthed the words "thank you" and headed toward the back of the building.

As she made her way up the steps, Abbey could hear voices in the middle of a lively discussion. Lance had told her the names of those she would be working with, but her mind was drawing a complete blank as she reached the top of the steps. She stood there looking into a large room that had four desks, several large drafting tables, and all types of drawing tools, calendars, pictures, and more that lined the walls. Everyone seemed to be huddled around a computer, giving out ideas and passionately discussing whatever was appearing on the screen in front of them.

"Please let's change the font! It will look so much more professional," said a girl who looked younger than Abbey but was tall, with her long hair pulled back in a high ponytail. She wore shorts, a tank top, and sneakers, letting Abbey instantly know this would be a relaxed working atmosphere.

"Bill said he loved this font, so that's a no go." This time is was the older man who sat directly in front of the screen who voiced his opinion.

"I have to agree with Everly on this one, Randy," said the third guy, who looked to be her age. She sized him up and figured he was about six feet tall or more, was extremely well built, and had a bit of a tan, as she could tell by the shorts and T-shirt he wore. His medium-blond hair almost looked sun kissed, with blonder streaks running through it. Finally, Abbey recognized a voice she knew—Lance. He was sitting in a chair next to the desk, staring at the screen like the other three.

"I agree. Randy, talk to Bill. Sell him on the font change, because we all know that it will help the look of the site, and it is easier to read. Let him know that this small change could increase the popularity of the site, thus increasing his sales. That should be enough motivation to sell him on a simple font change."

The man directly in front of the computer screen seemed frustrated that he had been outvoted and turned around, shaking his head. To his surprise, he saw Abbey standing quietly near the top of the steps.

"Can I help you?" he said in a brusque voice.

At that, the entire group turned toward Abbey, and she immediately felt as though she were on display like one of the paintings on the first floor of the building.

"Abbey, you're here already," Lance said as he jumped out of the chair, walking toward her. "I didn't know you were in town, since you don't start for a few more weeks. When did you get here?"

"About two days ago. Already moved in and unpacked. Didn't bring much, so that made it a lot easier. I hope it's OK that I came by to see the office and meet everyone." Even though Abbey tried to sound calm, she was a bit shaky inside as she and Lance walked toward the three people still standing around the desk.

"Let me introduce you to everyone and then maybe ask your opinion on our current project we are discussing. This is Randy, our technical guy when it comes to these websites. He does coding and all that jazz—I don't even understand it, but he is one of the best." Randy stood up and shook Abbey's hand. He was a tall, slightly balding man, maybe in his mid-forties, with a sweet smile. "Nice to meet you. Lance has told us so much about your work and experience. Glad to have you on board."

"Thanks!" Abbey said, her body starting to relax slightly.

"And this is Everly, our computer whiz. Between her and Randy, they can make a website work no matter what."

Everly smiled and shook Abbey's extended hand. "So glad to have more estrogen around here. Maybe we will get some real work done now," she laughed as she glanced around at the men in the room.

Abbey shook the young woman's hand. She was very pretty, with light-brown hair and a tan that let Abbey know she must love the outdoors even though she was described as a "computer whiz."

Before Lance could introduce the last of the trio, the very attractive man quickly stepped up to her. "Zach Isler," he said, extending his hand to her. "Glad to have someone else here who appreciates design." He looked over his shoulder at his other two coworkers. "Nice to meet you," he said with a bright smile. He was so friendly and very cute, Abbey thought, making her heart flutter just a bit as he continued to shake her hand slightly.

"Zach is our graphic designer and the person you will be working with primarily." Lance smiled.

"I'm really excited about working here. Mr. Peterson told me so much about all of you. Seems like you have a great team, and your client list is amazing. I'm just glad that I can be a part of it."

"Remember to call me Lance. As you can see, we are pretty casual around here. Makes the job more fun." Lance was still smiling, and Abbey's nervousness was melting away.

"I'm very glad you are here," Everly said quickly. "Zach here thinks his designs are perfection even though we try to tell him otherwise. It will be nice for him to have some competition!" She smiled as she looked over at Zach, who had his eyes still focused on Abbey.

"Since I'm moved in, I do have a few things I have to settle this week, but I could start next Monday instead of waiting, if that's OK with you," Abbey said as she looked at Lance.

"That would be great. We just received a new client that wants us to take their current website and do a complete redesign. And they would like it to be completed within six weeks."

"Which is almost impossible," Zach piped in.

"But we will make it work, right?" Lance said as he looked at the group, which returned his gaze by giving him fake smiles and nodding before laughing. Watching the group before her, Abbey could feel that this was going to be a fun and relaxed environment to work in compared to her old job back home.

"So next Monday would be great! But before you go, look at the font on this website. Our client likes it, but we think it is hard to read and makes the site look a bit cluttered."

Abbey tentatively walked toward the screen to see what they had been discussing. In front of her was a website for children's toys, but from her experience, the font was wrong and hard to read. "In my opinion, the font should be changed. The current one is playful which gives it a great look for children but it is difficult to read. And the company is targeting the parents to buy the toys. Maybe the client's font choice could be used in the tagline of the site only?" There was a momentary silence, and Abbey held her breath. She didn't expect to be put on the spot like this, but she had total confidence to speak up.

"Great minds think alike." Zach smiled. "Thank you, Abbey, for validating what I have been saying for the last ten minutes. Except I like your suggestion for the tagline. I'll put that in and see what it does for the site. Then it's Randy's job, since he knows Bill so well, to sell him on the change."

"OK, OK, OK. I'll call him after you give me something to show him." Randy headed to a desk nearest the front window. "Nice to meet you, Abbey," he said, looking back at her before settling into his desk chair.

"I guess we will see you Monday. In the meantime, here are our numbers," Lance said as he handed her a business card that had the agency's information on the front and each person's cell phone number listed on the back. "If you need anything, any help at all getting situated around here, let us know." Lance smiled, and Abbey felt the last of the tension release. Then she saw the empty desk she presumed would be hers and secretly wished she could start tomorrow. But she still had things to do to get settled in, plus she wanted to take a little time to be a tourist in the Keys.

"Here is my number if you need me, and thanks again. I guess I will see everyone on Monday!" Abbey said as she turned to make her way down the stairs.

10

"So that's the new girl. Lance, you did good. She seems to know her stuff and sure is a looker, though you know she isn't my type," Randy quickly said. "Hope her designs are as pretty as she is."

"That's a sexist remark!" Everly said quickly.

"Everly, don't get your panties in a wad! You know I don't mean anything bad. She's just cute and seems real sweet. You know I still have my sights set on the guy across the street." Randy continued working on his computer as he talked.

Everly just shook her head and walked toward her desk. "At least now Zach can't complain about his workload."

Zach said nothing as he smiled, looking out the window, watching Abbey walk down the street. For him it was an instant attraction the moment he saw her. He didn't know whether it was her chocolate-brown hair, the beautiful green eyes, or the way her smile lit up the room. Maybe it was her outfit against her cream-colored skin that made her look like a long-time islander. Or it could just be a combination of all of it. Zach suddenly had a crush on a girl he basically knew nothing about. But as fate would have it, they would be working together, and he definitely intended to get to know Abbey—at work and hopefully off the job too. For Zach, Monday couldn't get here fast enough.

As she walked toward her Jeep, Abbey felt relieved. Not that she had been dreading meeting everyone, but there was always that anxiety at the beginning of an adventure, especially a new job. Everyone had welcomed her, once more giving her a sign that she had made the right choice moving here.

So the person she would be working with most was Zach. If he had designed the website she had seen, his ideas were really good. It would be nice to work with someone who appreciated graphic design and great websites. Plus, he seemed very friendly, not like someone that would feel threatened by another's opinion, especially a woman's. Abbey hoped her instinct was right about him. But more importantly, she couldn't forget how nice and cute he was! Not that she was looking for eligible men or a relationship, but she did seem to be bumping into some very good-looking men these first few days. Key West was feeling better with each passing minute.

With the most important "to-do" marked off her list, it was on to Key Plaza to the mattress store. After lying on one bed after another, she finally settled on a nice, queen-size, plush, pillow-top mattress that she couldn't wait to get to her new home. They would be able to deliver the very next day, and Abbey was more than grateful. Her couch slept fine, but to be able to stretch out on a nice, soft bed sounded luxurious. As for finding the perfect art desk, she had searched Craigslist before setting out this morning, hoping to find something nice and affordable, but there was nothing available. After doing an Internet search, her options were the local Home Depot or having a desk ordered. The thought of dragging a heavy package up the stairs was not appealing at all, so Abbey went to the local store and found a desk that would work, with some stackable plastic drawers she would fix up with either paint or decoupage to fit the style of her new home. The best part: they would deliver and assemble the desk for her. It was more than worth it to pay the extra for that service. Abbey was beginning to doubt her choice of a second-floor apartment but knew she would get used to it soon enough. Plus, she reminded herself that her legs were going to look great from her daily stair workout!

By the time Abbey was done, it was late afternoon. Even though she had grabbed an order of french fries while she was out, her stomach rumbled to let her know it was time for some dinner. Though she wanted to go out like she had the night before, she had to admit that all the excitement, moving, unpacking, and shopping had caught up with her. She was tired. Cooking dinner in and just relaxing with a movie sounded like perfection to her. Thankfully, her little place had come with Internet, cable, and phone as part of her monthly rent, something else that was already done for her.

Just as she pulled up to her little parking space, she spotted Josie walking toward the building. Abbey sat in the Jeep trying to decide what to do. Did she hurry up the stairs or wait till the woman went inside her own place? *This is ridiculous*, Abbey thought. *Remember yesterday how you decided to make friends with this lady? You can't do that hiding from her*, Abbey chided herself. So she took a deep breath and got out of her Jeep at just the right time so that she could greet Josie.

"Hi, Josie. Have a nice day?" Abbey said apprehensively but as cheerfully as she could as she looked at the woman, who stared back at her blankly. What was it about Josie that absolutely intimidated her?

"No" was all Josie said as she unlocked the door to her apartment, went in, and shut it, basically in Abbey's face.

Abbey stood, once again, in disbelief. How could this woman be so cold and unreachable? As Abbey walked up the stairs, she glanced back on the shut door below. She had to find a way to reach Josie. Granted, it had only been three days since she had moved here, but there was something deep inside that kept Josie distant from all her neighbors, according to the conversations with Garrett and Ella. Abbey hoped that maybe, just maybe, she would be able to help Josie in some way but it looked as though it would take time.

The next few days were full of activity that left Abbey tired but happy and content. As promised, her bed was delivered the next day, and that night Abbey felt like she was sleeping in the lap of luxury. It was perfect! The following day found her setting up her art and office area after the deliveryman had put the desk together and Abbey had arranged the plastic drawers, making it all come together for a cute little work area in her living room. Abbey couldn't help but smile as she looked around. Her little spot in her new city was actually feeling like home.

But she also played tourist each day. After picking up a city guidebook, she planned out activities to explore and check out the many attractions Key West had to offer. She decided to do one thing each day. Once she started to work, she would have to save these excursions for the weekends. It wouldn't be long before she would be able to play tour guide for her family and friends that would visit, something she was looking forward to. Maybe, if things worked out, Garrett would join her on some of her outings. She was beginning to think about him more and more. He was so sweet to help her that first day here. Add to that his smoldering good looks, and she couldn't help but look forward to him coming home. They already had a dinner date of sorts planned, and she would be able to learn more about the very single mysterious marine biologist that lived next door.

By the time Saturday rolled around, Abbey had visited the Hemingway House with its multitude of cats, enjoyed the beach at Fort Zachary, visited the Southernmost Point Buoy after borrowing Ella's bicycle for the trip, and of course, explored every part of Mallory Square. For now, the square was her favorite place, as she had been there every evening except one when they had a thunderstorm. Abbey watched the beautiful sunsets and talked to the different talented artists, secretly planning how her own little spot would look among the other artisans if she were able to secure a permit to sell her own artwork.

Abbey also saw Josie each day, and try as she might, her greetings and questions were all rebuffed. Josie answered curtly or sometimes not at all. But Abbey was not going to be derailed on her mission to break through to this woman. Maybe all she could do right now was be nice by at least acknowledging Josie each time she ran into her. Abbey did notice that Josie's presence was less intimidating the more she saw her and tried to talk to the older woman. She was getting used to Josie's short answers and hateful looks. But Abbey would smile each time, being friendly, hoping to reach this woman somehow.

11

OK, so what do I have to lose? Zach thought as he held the cell phone in his hand. He looked at the number already entered, waiting for him to press the dial button. It was Abbey's number he had gotten from Lance. They were all supposed to have each other's cell numbers, right? What if she thought he was some kind of weirdo, stalking her or something? No, she wouldn't think that. Zach had met her this week, and they were going to be working together. But Abbey didn't know that she had occupied Zach's thoughts all week.

Abbey was so different from the other women he had met since he moved to Key West. Since the day she came to the office, Zach couldn't quit thinking about her. He already knew that working with her was going to be great and challenging at the same time, because Zach couldn't deny he was attracted to her. But today, he just wanted to see if they could have lunch. That wasn't so creepy, right? The conversation continued to repeat over and over in his brain till finally he pushed the button. *Here goes nothing*, Zach thought as Abbey's phone began to ring.

"Hello?" He heard a cautious voice answer.

"Hi, Abbey. This is Zach. From work." His sentences were choppy, and he was sure that his nervousness was coming through his voice.

"Hi! How are you?"

"Fine. How are you?" He could hear his own awkwardness, something he had desperately wanted to avoid, but it was there.

"I'm fine." Abbey's voice was as cheerful as the day he had met her.

"Are you settling in OK?" he continued.

"Yes and very much looking forward to work on Monday. Think I'm all moved in, and I've been doing a bit of sightseeing. The first time I was here, I didn't get to see much at all, so I've been treating myself each day to a new adventure."

"Glad to hear that you like our little town. Well, I should say your little town now, too." He hesitated to ask the next question but finally found the courage. "Do you have plans today?" He had never felt this unsure of himself in his life! What was it about this girl that had him feeling like he was giving a speech to an audience of thousands?

"I have had several people, including one of my neighbors, tell me that Bahia Honda Beach is really nice, so I've packed a lunch and am heading that way shortly. I haven't been out for a swim or just relaxed since I got here, unless you count practically passing out each night from happy exhaustion," she laughed on the other end of the line. Zach smiled to himself. In his mind, Zach could see Abbey smiling, packed for a beach trip.

"Well they are right. It is a great park, and I'm actually going there today with a few friends. We go snorkeling there. I know the guy that runs one of the boats." OK, so it was a little white lie, he told himself. Zach actually had no plans for today except hoping to meet with Abbey somehow. Not a date, just a lunch or something, but the beach sounded a lot better. If he really had his wish, it would be a dinner date, but maybe going to the park and swimming would be better. He suddenly found his imagination soaring, wondering how she would look in a swimsuit. *Oh, man! Get a grip*, he told himself.

"Really? Maybe we can meet. I heard they have a picnic area. We can sit and talk if your friends don't mind. I would really like to know more about the office before Monday. That would help me out a lot." Abbey sounded just as sweet and friendly on the phone as she did in person, he thought.

"I don't think they will mind at all. So I'll look for you at the picnic tables. When you get to the park, there is a lot for parking on the other side of the gift store. It is right in front of the dressing area, and the tables are off to the side. Let's meet around one o'clock?" Zach amazed himself by pushing his nerves aside and being bold with his questions, something that usually didn't bother him. But Abbey had him feeling completely out of his element in a very good way.

"That would be great. I'm driving a red Jeep, and I'll be the one sitting by myself at the picnic table. I'll see you there!" With that, she hung up.

"Yes!" Zach said loudly as he pressed the end button on his cell. It wasn't really a date, but it would give him some more time with this girl that he found so intriguing. The problem was that he'd told her that he was going to be with friends, so he needed to find someone to go with him. But he wanted this time alone with her. What would she think if he showed up by himself?

Just so it wasn't a complete lie, he called a few of his friends asking them to tag along, secretly hoping they would all say no. And he was in luck. Everyone had already made plans for the day and wanted him to go with them instead. But Zach wasn't giving up this chance to meet Abbey—just him and her.

12

As Abbey closed the door to her apartment and headed down the steps, beach gear in tow, Josie stepped out of her apartment. She looked so different today, dressed in a bright-colored maxi dress and flip-flops. Her shoulder-length, honey-blond hair was tucked behind her ears, and she looked very relaxed. In her hands she had a book and a glass of what looked to be iced tea.

"Hi, Josie! It's beautiful outside today," Abbey said, once again trying to make conversation. But Josie continued to walk away, not acknowledging one word that Abbey said, and made her way to a pair of rocking chairs on the front porch that were separated by a small table.

That's it, Abbey thought. She was going to go sit with her right now and have a talk. She needed to find out if she had done anything to insult this woman. It had been a week, and even though Abbey had told herself to be patient, this would be the perfect time to find out if something was amiss, because right beside Josie was an empty chair.

Abbey walked up and took a seat beside Josie. After sitting there a few minutes just rocking back and forth while Josie read her book, Abbey proceeded to say what she had rehearsed in her mind.

"Josie, I don't know what I have done for you to be upset with me, but whatever it was, I apologize. I'm sorry if you didn't want anyone else moving in or if I was too loud or whatever. I just want us to be friends and neighbors." Abbey said nothing else while Josie continued to look down at her book.

"Please don't ignore me. Why are you so angry with me?"

The older woman slowly looked up, gazing across the street for a minute and then over toward Abbey.

"You haven't done anything. This is just who I am. I keep to myself, work, and try to enjoy the quiet life I have made for myself here on this island. I don't need any friends, so don't worry about me. If I had my way, I would be the only resident in this building, but that's not the way it works. If you keep to yourself, I'll stay in my own little space. Everyone will be happy." Josie said the words in that same monotone, icy voice as before. She wanted to appear fine, but Abbey could read between the lines. Josie was crying out for help, even though she didn't know it. Abbey's intuition meter was off the charts letting her know that Josie wasn't telling her the truth.

"Josie, everyone needs someone that they can talk to. A friend or friends that they can rely on. Why isolate yourself, making everyone dislike you? I find it hard to believe that is the person you truly are. I promise I'm not being nosy. I just feel we could be friends. I get that sense each time I see you. And I'm a great listener." Abbey waited anxiously after she finished, wondering if she was going to be kicked off the porch.

Josie looked up from her book, once again staring across the street. Why was Abbey being so persistent? Usually people just left her alone, but this little wisp of a girl was trying to talk to her all the time, always saying hello, always cheerful, no matter how Josie treated her. Everyone else just avoided her, which made her perfectly happy. But Abbey, the young woman sitting with her, had ignited an ever-so-small spark of desire inside her to have someone in her life that she could share things with. Abbey's persistence and just taking a chance to sit and talk with her, something no one else had done before, made Josie think twice about the young woman. Maybe there were good people in the world who valued relationships and friendships, even those that were loyal and honest. For so long, Josie felt that she could not trust anyone—to the point that she had built this cocoon around herself for protection. Her past still haunted her so many years after that horrible incident and she was afraid to let anyone in her protected, private life.

As Josie breathed a heavy sigh, she finally looked over at Abbey. "As I said, you have done nothing wrong. I've just always led a solitary life, and I like it that way. That's just the way I am."

Did Abbey detect a difference in Josie's voice? It almost sounded a little softer with some feeling—not by much, but Abbey could tell the difference, and she smiled inside.

"Maybe on the weekends, we can have tea on the porch, like we are doing now. We don't even have to talk, unless we see someone doing something crazy down this street, and that seems to happen just about every day in this city. Shocks me to pieces sometimes!"

Josie's laugh was minuscule, but Abbey heard it and smiled. She had chipped away a small piece of Josie's iciness. "I'm on my way to the beach. Enjoy your tea, and watch out for the crazies." Even though Josie wasn't looking at her, Abbey could see a slight smile on the woman's face, the first time since she had arrived here. Abbey's heart swelled at the sight.

13

The drive to Bahia Honda State Park was beautiful. The weather was gorgeous with a beautiful, blue sky dotted with puffy, white clouds and a temperature that was near perfect for the beach as far as Abbey was concerned. Everything around her was still so new that excitement pulsed through her body. She had to keep reminding herself that she lived here now. A resident of the Florida Keys. That thought made her happy. Plus the fact that she had actually seen a hint of a smile on Josie's face earlier.

It wasn't long before a large, brick sign announced the entrance to the state park. Abbey followed the winding road till she saw the gift shop that Zach had told her about then located the parking area behind it. When she stepped out of the Jeep, she was instantly in love with her surroundings. Again! To her left was a dazzling beach lining a pristine cove where children and parents were swimming and playing in the clear, blue water. To her right were trees, a building for changing clothes, and a wooden walkway to the beach that lead to the Atlantic Ocean. From where Abbey was standing, she could see the beautiful, clear water and couldn't wait to feel it against her skin. As quickly as she could, Abbey secured her tote bag to her small rolling cooler, grabbed her beach chair with its attached umbrella, and then headed toward the sand. As she walked across the wooden boards, she saw some picnic tables under shelters. Hopefully these were the ones Zach had mentioned. She looked at her phone and realized it was only 11:30 a.m., so she had plenty of time to enjoy the beach and take a swim.

Abbey found a great spot along the water, near the picnic area but not too close, and soon had her little area all set up with chair, towels, and cooler. All that was left now was to enjoy the scenery and go for a swim. She took a few minutes to sit and just relax, taking in all the beautiful nature around her. The park was indeed beautiful, just as everyone had described. White sand, clear water, trees for shade, and facilities that blended right into the nature of the park. She had even heard that people got married here along the shore, and she could see why. It was stunning, and at that moment, Abbey wished she had someone to share it with. A family member or friend. Instead she took pictures of just about everything with her phone so she could send them to her parents back home. But now it was time to enjoy the water.

As Abbey walked toward the ocean, she felt a wave of relaxation come over her. The combination of the sun, the temperature, the sea breeze, and the scene before her was intoxicating. With each step she took, the water was warm and inviting. Before she knew it, Abbey was swimming in waist-deep water, so clear that she could see the small fish swimming around her. It was so soothing, and she felt her body unwinding from the busy week of settling into a new place. As she floated in the water, she let her imagination soar and instantly saw herself as a mermaid. This was something she would do as a little girl when her family would take trips to the lake or the Carolina shores.

But this beach and this water were so different. Abbey could see to the bottom, making her feel like she was in one giant swimming pool. As she floated on the water, gently bobbing up and down with the waves and staring at the fluffy clouds above her, she felt so blessed. Not many people could just uproot their lives and take a chance like she did. So far she felt that her choice to move was turning out even better than she had hoped for. And though there were people all around, she felt like she was the only one floating in the waters of the Atlantic.

14

Zach saw her red Jeep as soon as he pulled into the parking lot. He parked in the space next to hers and took a deep breath. He was nervous but excited to see Abbey again. He couldn't wait to spend some time with her and hopefully find a connection between them. Zach couldn't remember having such a desire to get to know a woman as he had instantly felt the day Abbey had come by the office. But he knew they were going to be coworkers, and there was a fine line he had to walk. *Just take it one step at a time*, Zach thought, and this was a great first step!

Since it was almost one o'clock, Zach found a picnic table just in the nick of time, as it seemed everyone at the park had decided it was lunchtime. They would have a great view of the ocean, and it was a nice, shady area. Best of all, it was a little secluded, giving him Abbey all to himself. Zach put his stuff on the table and began to look out at the beachgoers along the shore. He suddenly saw her. Abbey was walking in the surf, looking as though she had just come in from a swim. He couldn't stop staring again. She was beautiful in her one-piece coral-colored bathing suit that had some sort of netting in the center, giving the illusion of a two-piece. Her chestnut hair was slicked back from her swim, falling just below her shoulders. To Zach, Abbey looked like a cover model. She was perfectly proportioned in every way. He watched her walk to her spot on the beach. As he continued to admire her as she toweled off while gazing back at the water, Zach was still feeling that this girl was different. And this was the perfect time and place to get to know her better.

As if on cue, Abbey turned toward the various tables along the beach, scouting each one to look for him. He waved as soon as she saw him, and she motioned that she would be there in a minute. Zach watched her gather her things and head toward him. The closer Abbey got to the table, the more he began to feel unsure of himself, wanting to make the best impression.

"Hey there! Looks like you enjoyed a swim. Great day for it," Zach said as he jumped up to help her with her beach bag and cooler.

"Thanks," Abbey said, putting her things on the table. "The water was fabulous. I think I could stay out there all day, but I would turn into a prune. Glad we could meet for lunch. Where are your friends?" Abbey glanced around to the other tables and people nearby.

"They all bailed on me at the last minute," Zach said, which he had to remind himself wasn't actually a lie and he took that as a sign that he was to have this time with Abbey all by himself.

"I'm sorry. You drove all the way here just to have lunch?"

"I love this park especially to snorkel at the reef. Do you snorkel?" he asked as she proceeded to get out her lunch. He grabbed the grocery bag that had his sandwich from the deli, a small bag of chips, and a fruit drink.

"I love to! I haven't been too many times, but each one was a wonderful experience. I can't wait till I get a chance to try it here. Each day I'm in the Keys, I find more and more things I want to try or do. It is amazing down here."

"Well, I know a few people who own boats that take people fishing, snorkeling, scuba diving, and more. Maybe we can go sometime," Zach suggested, hoping she wouldn't think he was being too forward.

"Really? That would be fantastic!" That was the exact answer Zach was hoping to hear from the beautiful girl sitting across from him.

As they both ate their lunches, Zach told Abbey all about work. She asked one question after another, and he wasn't tiring of the interrogation at all. She was so energetic, friendly, and funny. Add to that the fact that she was downright beautiful, and Zach was completely smitten. That instant attraction he had felt earlier in the week was growing by the minute. Most of the women he had dated weren't as sweet and kind as Abbey seemed to be. And he couldn't get enough of her Southern country accent.

"So you're from North Carolina?" Zach asked, trying to steer the conversation toward a more personal note.

"Born and raised. How can you tell?"

"That accent of yours gives you away. Plus, Lance told us. Everly couldn't believe that you would move away from the mountains."

"My accent is that bad?" Abbey said suddenly, very self-conscious.

"No, it's not bad at all. Actually, it's kinda cute. Fits you." Zach looked at her with a smile before taking a bite of his sandwich. She was smiling back.

"Yes, I've been told that I sound very 'country.' But you said something about Everly. Does she not like living here in the Keys?"

"Everly was born and raised here. At work she will tell us about how she can't wait till she can go on some adventure. She is determined to go to New York City."

"She sounds a bit like my brother, Drew. He wanted to be a journalist, so the day after he graduated from college, he packed up his car and headed to the big city. He is doing OK there, working for a small newspaper, but all we heard growing up was how he was going to be a famous journalist. I guess he is on his way." She continued to eat as he asked her questions about her family.

"Seems like all we have talked about is me. What is your Key West story?" Abbey asked.

"About me. Well, my name is Zach Isler, and I hail from the great state of Texas, the city of Galveston to be exact. Born and raised there. My parents and older sister still live there near the beach. We have always loved the water, and I do believe my mom had us in the ocean before we could even walk. Think that is one reason I gravitated toward the Keys.

"After I graduated high school, I went to the University of Texas in Austin. It was hard at first not being by the water, but I fell into the college life headfirst. My first two years weren't what you call stellar, so at the beginning of my junior year, my parents gave me an ultimatum: get serious, or get out and find a job. So I decided to go into graphic design, because I already loved to draw, and I was really good at computers. At school I was the geek everyone brought their computers to when they needed help. So that year I turned everything around.

"During spring break I came here with a bunch of guys, and we had a blast, at least what I remember." Zach laughed. "I went back home telling everyone that when I graduated, I was moving to Florida. No one took me seriously, and that strengthened my resolve to make sure I did it. I ended up graduating with top grades and was planning to get my master's degree when Lance called me about a job here. He was friends with one of my professors, and he was looking for a designer. That was nine years ago. I visit home a few times a year, and my parents keep threatening to move here since every time they visit me, they fall in love with the Keys more and more."

"So it doesn't get old, the island lifestyle?" Abbey asked with expectancy in her eyes.

"Hasn't for me. I love it here. I have said that someday I would like to live out on one of the outer keys and not in the city, but I'm saving my money now. I plan to buy my own place in the next few years. I have a little side business of writing guidebooks that I sell on the Internet that helps put some money into savings. For now, I love my little apartment in town." Zach couldn't believe how easy it was to just sit and talk with her. The conversation between them just flowed like the water they were sitting by. It was the most relaxed he had felt with any woman.

"You said the magic words for me. When people found out I was moving to the Keys, they first told me I was crazy. Secondly, I would hear 'It will get old within a year.' I would just smile, knowing that they were wrong. It's different down here. Kinda hard to explain." Abbey smiled at him, and Zach melted inside. This was so out of the norm for him.

"Can I ask you a personal question?" Zach looked at her seriously.

"Sure!" Abbey said with no hesitation.

"Did you leave anyone special behind in North Carolina? I'm sure there had to be a few broken hearts." Now he was flirting.

Abbey laughed. "No broken hearts, but I did have a boyfriend. The relationship was already coming apart before I told him I wanted to move to the Keys. We were moving in different directions but just didn't want to admit it. My decision to move here did it for both of us. What about you? There is no way you aren't attached." Now she was flirting with him, Zach thought as he watched her grinning at him.

"I was dating someone, but we broke up about five months ago. Right now, my life consists mostly of working and water sports when I'm not sketching or having lunch with a pretty girl at the beach." He looked over to see Abbey blush, and it wasn't from the heat.

"I'm sure the right girl is going to come along, and you will be forever changed."

Zach grinned back at her, thinking that the right girl might just be sitting in front of him.

Time seemed to stand still for Zach as they continued talking about everything from their favorite foods to all the gossip Abbey needed to know about work. It was like they had known each other much longer than just a casual meeting earlier in the week. Zach loved every minute of it, secretly hoping that Abbey was too.

"I'm really glad that you came today. This is my first outing with a friend. Now I can tell my parents I know someone in Key West. Maybe they will stop worrying so much," Abbey kidded him as they walked to their vehicles with their beach gear in hand.

"No, they will always worry. It's just what parents do. My mom and dad still drill me when we talk, but I know they just love me, so I don't say anything." Zach paused by the side of her Jeep, holding her things while she unlocked the door. "So I guess I will see you Monday?" Zach asked as they stood facing each other.

"Yes, and I can't wait. It looks like a nice place to work, and from everything you told me, it's much different from what I'm used to. Thanks again for coming, Zach. I had a really good time." He helped her put her things in the Jeep and watched her waving back to him as she headed out of the park. Zach couldn't remember the last time he had enjoyed such a great afternoon with an enchanting girl. Abbey was indeed everything he had thought about all week long since she had walked into the office that day to introduce herself.

15

Abbey drove back to Key West with a smile on her face, contemplating just how nice her day had turned out. She was able to enjoy the beach and take a wonderful, relaxing swim. Then she had lunch with a delightful, attractive guy. Zach had turned out to be much different than she had thought when she met him earlier in the week. With his good looks and charming wit, Abbey had been positive that he was in a relationship, but after spending the afternoon with him, Abbey concluded that Zach wasn't anything like she expected. He was so nice that Abbey could feel a little rush of excitement when she thought of him, wanting to get to know him better. But relationships with someone at work were usually not a good idea. So Abbey made herself a promise as she pulled up in front of her little building that Zach could be no more than a friend. That thought didn't sit well with her, but she had seen the devastating effects of an on-the-job relationship. Abbey had watched two people search for new employment when the couple called off their romance where she had previously worked. Abbey didn't want to go through that, but after the day she'd just had with Zach, it was hard to think of what could be. Abbey was attracted to him but kept repeating to herself, "Friend only." So now there were two men on her radar, and she had only been here a week. Abbey smiled to herself as she opened the door to her apartment. *Next time I talk to Hope, she is going to love this juicy bit of news*, Abbey thought.

When she woke Monday morning, her nerves were already set in motion. Abbey had met everyone, knew where she was going, and had even spent time with Zach over the weekend, so why all the jitters? She gave herself a pep talk as she got dressed, choosing to wear her favorite emerald-green tank dress with a short-sleeve, open-front, white summer cardigan. Her silver sandals completed her outfit, along with her silver hoop "lucky" earrings. As she examined herself in the full-length mirror, Abbey told herself the outfit looked appropriate given what she had seen others wearing last week. In fact, she could be overdressed, but she felt comfortable, and that was what she needed for this first day. Though she wasn't hungry, she ate a quick bowl of cereal and grabbed the small lunch bag that she had packed last night with some snacks and water for the day. Then she took a deep breath and headed out the door.

As Abbey reached the end of the steps, Josie's apartment door opened, and Abbey watched her walk out. She didn't acknowledge Abbey, even though she was sure Josie had seen her.

"Hey, Josie! Good morning!"

The woman just kept walking through the gate and down the street.

"Have a good day!" Abbey yelled, and to her amazement, even though her back was to Abbey, Josie waved as she continued down the sidewalk. She might not have said one word, but the wave of her hand was like a thousand to Abbey.

As she drove to work, Abbey's anxiety about the coming day was overshadowed by Josie's acknowledgment. Could she really be making progress with the older woman in just one week's time? It looked that way, but Abbey made sure not to get too excited. Even though she could already see relaxed conversations between her and Josie as they sat on the front porch, she reminded herself that this was a slow process. But the fact that Josie had acknowledged Abbey gave her more hope that one day they would be able to talk and maybe, just maybe, be friends. Something no one else, it seemed, had been able to do or for that matter wanted to.

As Abbey parked her vehicle, part of her wanted to just sit there, but she gathered her purse, tote bag and some courage then walked down the sidewalk to her new job.

"Hey, Abbey!" a voice said behind her. She turned to see Everly hurrying toward her.

"I thought I was going to be late again. Lance is great to work for, but he doesn't like it when I'm late, which is my only bad habit," Everly said, laughing. "Are you all moved in?" She fell in step with Abbey, walking the rest of the way with her.

"I think so. My house in North Carolina was big, so it is different living in an apartment, but I love it. Made me realize I didn't need most of the stuff I had back home. Moving definitely helped me simplify," Abbey said, grateful for the conversation and to have someone to walk into the building with on her first day. "How long have you lived here and worked for Lance?"

"I was born and raised here. And pitifully, still live with my parents. Seems like everyone wants to move down here, and I'm ready to move away! I'm trying to save my money to move to New York City. I have been there one time and can't wait till I have my own place there. Lance tells me when I'm ready to move, he will help me find a job, through his connections, but then he keeps begging me to stay. Plus, my family needs me here at the moment." With that last comment, Abbey could hear a shift in Everly's voice, sounding a bit downcast. She wanted to ask about it but also didn't want to pry. Maybe they would be able to talk later after they got to know each other better.

"I have a younger brother who lives in New York. He is a journalist there and loves it. When he heard I was moving here, he told me I had lost my mind. I'm the only girl, so both of my brothers are very protective."

"He is so lucky. I should have enough money saved to move in a year or so." Everly unlocked the door to the gallery, letting them both in before locking it behind them. "In the meantime, I think you are really going to like it here. Lance is a great boss. We will have to get you a set of keys today. Don't let me forget."

They walked upstairs to find their employer, the only person there so far, reading on his iPad with his feet propped up on the desk in his corner office.

"Hey, Abbey! Welcome! And, Everly, my dear, you are early—I'm so proud of you," Lance kidded as he got up and walked over to the two women. "Abbey, this will be your desk area." He walked to the empty desk she had seen last week. "As you can see, you have your own computer and all the supplies you need, but if you want to use your personal computer, that is fine. As long as there is no web surfing during work hours, unless you are researching a project. You can decorate your area as long you keep it tasteful. You can see we have white-boards everywhere, because sometimes that is the best way for us to brainstorm ideas. Whenever you need to use one, just pick your favorite, and your idea will stay up till you or we get it figured out. That's about it for work rules."

He began walking back toward his office, motioning Abbey to follow while pointing out another wall with white-boards, which were clearly in use. "We have a list of projects that we keep on this board along with this calendar to keep us on track. We pride ourselves on being about ninety percent early with finished projects. That is what has helped us grow, along with a very talented team of designers." Just then Abbey heard two male voices coming up the stairs rapidly.

"Wow, everyone is on time this morning. I'm impressed!" Lance said with a smile. "Zach, once Abbey gets settled, you need to go over the current projects we are working on, where they are in production, and their time frames. We will have our Monday morning meeting at ten thirty." With that, he turned and went back into his little office.

As Abbey walked to the empty desk, Zach quickly came up to her side. "Hi! How was the rest of your weekend?"

"Nice. I actually did nothing yesterday. Decided to be a bit lazy. What about you?" she said as she watched Zach put his things in the desk beside hers. He was certainly cute, and she'd had such a good time with him on Saturday, but they worked together. *Friends, friends, friends*, Abbey repeated to herself. But if Zach continued with his charm, it was certainly going to be hard. So she sat her things in her own work space, trying to take her mind off the sexy man who was to be her work partner.

"Yesterday I went boating with the guys. Did some water skiing, and my friend has some Jet Skis."

"Really? Jet Skis? I can just imagine what it must be like riding them here with this beautiful water." Abbey loved Jet Skis and her friend had one they would use at the lake. She could only envision what it would be like out on the ocean.

"Maybe we can go sometime. I'll let you know next time we are going out." Abbey could see herself on a Jet Ski flying across the aqua-blue water. Maybe even taking a ride with Zach. *Ugh! Stop that*, Abbey told herself.

"You OK?" Zach asked, as he looked at her, puzzled.

"I'm sorry. Kind of went off into my own little world. Promise I'm not that spacey. Just getting used to everything here in the Keys. It is so different from my hometown in the mountains." Abbey sighed as she put her things in her desk and arranged a few personal things on the top. "Let me know when you are ready to go over those projects," she said as she looked over at Zach getting settled for the day, turning on his computer, and getting out files. That brought Abbey back to work instead of the image she saw of her jet-ski adventure.

"I'm ready when you are." Zach motioned for her to come over to his desk. "Just roll your chair over," he added, motioning toward her chair. "We will go over the most important work right now. And, Abbey," he said, smiling at her, "I'm glad you're here."

Abbey's entire first week seemed to be a blur, one day running into the next. The project load was incredible, more than she imagined for an agency this size, but she loved every minute of it. And one thing was for sure—she was never bored. She and Zach worked together flawlessly, and even when they disagreed about a concept, they were able to come up with a solution by talking and using the whiteboards adorning the walls of the office. Zach was so easygoing and didn't have an ego attitude like some of the men she had worked with in the past. Every day the two of them ate lunch together, mostly discussing work, but personal stories usually found their way into the conversations. Abbey's friendship with Zach was growing each day, and she was glad that she had found someone with whom she could talk to so easily. He probably thought she was a bit chatty, but if he did, Zach never said anything. He was always the gentleman, which made her like him even more. Especially when mixed with his blond-haired, blue-eyed good looks. Abbey even told Zach about her determination to make friends with her very unfriendly neighbor, Josie.

"Sounds like a crabby old lady. Why the interest?" he said as he stuffed his mouth with a bite of his hamburger.

"First of all, that wasn't nice, and second, I think she is lonely. I feel sorry for her. She just needs a friend, and I want to help her."

"If anyone can do it, it will be you." And Zach meant it. Abbey was amazing, and every minute of each day he spent with her, he became more enamored with this woman. He had never looked forward to work as he did now. Each day, Zach couldn't wait to see her. Abbey made him laugh; he loved her stories, the accent— everything about her. He only wished he could figure out what she thought about him.

For Abbey, Zach was a lifesaver! He helped her learn everything she needed to know about work. By the end of the week her confidence was growing and she felt like part of the team. Actually, everyone at work had made her feel welcomed. Even though Abbey felt a little homesick at times, she was still so glad that she had made the move down here. It had only been two weeks, but she was starting to feel like this was her home.

Abbey had also made progress with Josie. Each evening, despite being tired, Abbey would sit on the front porch with Josie, even though the only words they exchanged were "Hi" and "Bye." They would sit for a while, Josie usually reading and Abbey just relaxing from her day. After about thirty minutes, Abbey would head to her place, leaving Josie alone with her thoughts. Maybe soon, they would be talking. These were baby steps, Abbey thought, and at least Josie wasn't pushing her off the porch!

16

As Abbey cleaned her little apartment, she couldn't believe that three weeks had flown by. Garrett was coming home today, or at least he was supposed to. She hadn't talked to him since the day he left, but Abbey had been watching her calendar. The handsome biologist would be here, and she had promised a dinner at home for helping her that first day she arrived. She had gone to the grocery store after work the day before to pick up the necessary ingredients for smothered steaks, one of her mom's classic recipes. Combine that with some creamy mashed potatoes and green peas, and she had a classic Southern dinner. Abbey even had a homemade apple pie in the oven now as she cleaned. She had no idea when he would want to come to dinner, but she was ready with the ingredients. Even the apple pie would keep in the freezer if he couldn't come in the next few days.

Though she didn't know much about Garrett, the way he had helped her that day she moved in was so endearing that she had thought about him often. But Garrett was like that elusive object that was just out of reach. Abbey even hoped that he might want to go out on a real date, even though originally she had decided that she wasn't going to date anyone for a while. She wanted to give herself some "free" time, especially after her breakup with Max. But something about Garrett made her want to throw her self-imposed rules out the window.

After everything was cleaned up to her standards, she decided to take a brave step. She was going to ask Josie to have coffee with her on the front porch. Actually knock on her door! For two weeks now, they had shared the downstairs porch in the evening after she got home from work, just sitting, no talking. Ella was even shocked when she rode up on her bicycle to find the pair in the rocking chairs. Later that evening, it was Ella who was knocking on Abbey's door.

"What's going on? Is Josie actually speaking to you?" The surprise in her voice was over the top.

"Not yet, but I'm determined to get her to talk. I think she just needs a friend."

"You have some patience, that is for sure. I'm just one that if you don't like me, so what. Your loss!" Ella said coolly.

"There has to be something that has happened to make her shut herself off from the world. Josie seems so unhappy, and maybe that is the way she wants to live her life. I don't know. What I do know is that I want to show her that she has someone here close by that she can talk to."

"Let me know how it goes. I've got to get to work. Good luck!" Ella strode out the door, shaking her head, and rushed down the stairs. Abbey wondered how Ella could manage two jobs as she watched her jump on her bike and race down the street. Abbey's one job was full-time and kept her more than busy.

Abbey had worked hard these last two weeks learning the routine of the office, and things seem to be getting easier a little bit each day. Everly and Randy seemed joined at the hip once work began each morning. Their desks were the closest to the windows overlooking the street below and right beside each other. This allowed them to slide back and forth between each other's desks for working quickly. Abbey found it amusing at times to watch them. Like bulldogs chewing on a precious bone, they both would get completely lost in their own computer world.

As for her and Zach, they were becoming a team too. They each brought different skills to the workplace, and they seemed to complement each other. They were beginning to put together some really good websites and pages for their clients. Zach told her repeatedly that he was glad that Lance had finally found someone with experience and creativity. He was always helpful, asking her if she needed anything. He would walk her to her car each evening and had even asked if she wanted to go for a boat ride with his friends. Abbey had turned him down as nicely as possible because, though there was a definite attraction to Zach, she couldn't help but feel that they should keep the relationship strictly professional. The lunch that day at the park was different because he was helping her get the lay of the land, so to speak. But Abbey couldn't deny that they were becoming fast friends or that the thought of taking the relationship out of the office had occurred to her. But then she would think of Garrett.

Abbey knocked on Josie's door a few times before the door opened. Josie was dressed in a T-shirt, shorts, and sandals, very different from anything Abbey had seen her in before.

"Good morning!" Abbey said cheerfully. "I was wondering if you would like to have coffee on the porch this morning."

Josie looked at Abbey with her stone face, and the next words just about knocked Abbey over.

"There is a little coffee shop around the corner. I was going to get some. Get your stuff, and let's go." Then Josie turned around to get her purse and started closing the door.

"Give me just a minute." Abbey ran back up the stairs, making sure the oven was turned off and grabbing her purse and cell phone before hurrying back down the steps. She couldn't believe that Josie had asked her to go to the coffee shop with her! The shock still had not worn off as the two women set off down the sidewalk.

As they entered the small café, they were met with a wonderful aroma of freshly brewed coffee. There were patrons scattered about sipping their drinks and reading or talking in groups. It was a cozy little spot off the main road, and the decor spoke clearly that it was of the islands. Josie ordered her "usual." Abbey had no idea what that was, so she tried a type of coffee with chocolate. Josie led them to a table near a window but out of the sun. The chairs were nice and soft with a cute, round, mismatched table between them.

"This is a really unique coffee house," Abbey said nervously, still a bit stunned by the invitation. They had walked the whole way there with only few words spoken.

"I love this little place. I found it the second day I was on the island and have been coming ever since." Josie stared into her coffee cup and then looked up at Abbey.

"Why have you been so nice to me?"

The question took Abbey completely by surprise. For a moment, she wasn't sure how to answer, but Abbey decided to tell her what was on her heart. "At first, I don't know. I was really excited about being here in a new city and wanted to make friends, especially with the people in the building I was going to live in. I have always had my own house, so living in an apartment is very new to me. But I'm loving it so far." She paused, wanting to carefully choose her words.

"I have to admit, the first time I spoke to you and you blew me off, I was shocked. I'm so used to people at least smiling or sharing a hello, but you seemed so angry or hurt, like I had done something to you or offended you in some way. I wasn't sure which. Honestly, from that point, I was determined to be nice to you and hopefully become your friend. I know that might sound crazy, but I believe that everyone needs someone. You seemed like you were always by yourself." Abbey paused again, trying to read the look on Josie's face, which had softened but still looked stoic. "Plus, I really like sitting on the porch after work, even though we don't talk. Learning my way around my new job has been fun but challenging—I think

I've got the routine now. Those few minutes on the porch each evening is a great way to unwind after the day. I was hoping that eventually we could start having evening conversations."

"What do you want to know about?" Josie asked in a monotone voice.

"About you. Why you moved here. Where do you work. What's your favorite color. Is there someone special in your life. I guess just talk." Abbey said all these things carefully, because this was all new territory with Josie. She was glad they were talking, but Abbey seemed to be doing all of it.

"Don't you think those are kind of personal questions to be asking someone when you have only been here for a month?"

"Not to me, but everyone is different."

"Plus, I'm much older than you. Why make friends with me?" Josie asked.

"Again, I don't know. Just because." Abbey paused, hoping Josie would take the lead and move the conversation along. And she was right.

"I moved here twenty-seven years ago on a whim. It was the furthest place I could go to basically run away from what had happened." Abbey watched Josie's face soften as she began to tell her story. It was the first time Josie hadn't looked tense or angry. Instead a look of sadness overshadowed her face.

"I was all ready to marry the man of my dreams. I had a wonderful job, and he had a cattle ranch in Montana. On the day of our wedding, he didn't show up, and I felt like my heart was broken into a million pieces. We had been together for three years. All of our plans for the future laid out in front of us. I'll never forget listening to my father telling our guests that the wedding was delayed and to enjoy the reception food.

"I found out that Michael, my fiancé, had just left town the night before the wedding, telling no one. When he returned home, he went straight to the ranch, not even coming over to see me to explain what happened. I was so depressed. I packed everything I could into two suitcases, and came as far south as I could. I told no one where I was except my parents, who in turned promised me they would never share the information. They passed away a few years after I came here, just one year apart, keeping their promise to me. They told no one, not even my friends." Josie inhaled deeply and then took a sip of her coffee.

"I've been here ever since. I work as an accountant for a private resort but just found out that they have been bought out. So now I don't know if I'll even have a job. So you see, that is why I don't get involved in relationships, friends or otherwise. I always seem to get hurt, so it is easier to just take care of myself and my dog."

Abbey was shocked at Josie's story but dared not show it openly on her face. She couldn't imagine being jilted at the altar and then losing her parents. Josie's fear of relationships was justified, even though it wasn't solving her problem. If Josie really thought about it, it only made things worse, but she wasn't going to say anything to her right now.

"Josie, I'm so sorry. I can understand why you want to protect yourself. Thank you for trusting me with your story." When Abbey looked at Josie, her face had softened considerably.

"Actually, Abbey, thanks for listening. You are only the third person that I have told that story. I'm not a mean person, but I know that I come across that way. I'm just scared of getting hurt again. The pain of being at that church with practically the entire small town waiting for you to walk down that aisle—it was humiliating. And the hurt once again when Michael wouldn't come and talk to me." A tear trickled out of the corner of her eye, and Abbey handed her a napkin.

"Josie, I can't begin to know what that was like. But if you ever need to talk, I'm here. I'm a really good listener, and if asked, I think I can give some good advice. But I do try to keep my mouth shut until asked."

"Well, I will give you that one. You have sat on the porch almost every evening, not saying one word. I thought at first you were a bit looney." Josie actually laughed at that as she looked at Abbey. Abbey knew then that she had finally broken through the wall that Josie had built so tightly around herself, and she smiled inside.

"I've told you my story; now tell me yours. Why did you move to Key West?"

Abbey told her about the wedding, her first trip here only a few months ago, and her spur-of-the-moment decision to sell everything and move. No life-altering event like Josie had been through. She'd just wanted a change of pace.

"Sounds like you had it made in North Carolina," Josie said as she turned in her chair to face Abbey.

"I will admit, from the outside it looked like all the pieces of the puzzle were there, but it was just a facade. I didn't realize that till I came here. There was just something about this island that felt right. Like I was supposed to be here. I don't know how to explain it without sounding like an idiot. And the art! It is everywhere, and I love it. As a matter of fact, the design agency I work for is above a gallery. My boss's wife is the artist, and I love her paintings. I'm hoping to get a permit to set up a table at Mallory Square and sell my paintings and miniature sculptures in the next few months. I just got my supplies in the other day."

"That must have been that big-ass package the UPS guy put at my door instead of yours. You will have to show me your work sometime," Josie said with a slight grin.

Abbey had a huge smile on her face. "I would love to."

"So you have been here a month. No guys knocking down your door?" Josie said again with a smile.

"No, I'm not looking for a relationship right now. Except I have to say, my next-door neighbor is a sight for sore eyes. You know, Garrett? He helped me move in the day I got here, so I promised him a home-cooked meal when he got home, which should be today or tomorrow. Plus, there is a guy I work with that is really nice—but working together and dating wouldn't be a very good combination. I had decided when I was driving down here that romance was off the table for a while, but depending on my dinner with Garrett, I might change my mind." Abbey was laughing, and in turn, so was Josie. She was actually laughing. This was what Abbey had wanted. To see a smile on Josie's face. She seemed more relaxed and so different than the woman Abbey had seen these last few weeks.

"Don't count on Garrett. He has been living upstairs now for a while. I've seen a few women, but I really think that man is married to his work. I will say he is a looker. I might be a crabby old lady, but a good-looking man will make me look twice!" She grinned. "What about at work? What do you do?"

"It's a small agency. Just me and four other people including Lance, our boss. Randy is a trip, and I love being around him, but I'm definitely not his type. He's gay but currently single. Then there is Zach, the guy I told you about. We work together on the website designs, and he is a sweetheart. We've become good friends. He has helped me a lot since I got here, finding all the ins and outs of the city. And I will say, he is quite charming! Then there is Everly, who is a computer whiz and a little younger than me. She was raised in Key West and can't wait to leave the island." Abbey paused before continuing. "Sorry to hear about your work situation. That's really tough. Have you thought about what you might do if the new owners do decide to downsize?" Abbey asked.

"I'm not really worried about it. If I lost my job, I would be OK. In fact, I probably wouldn't have to work if I was frugal enough, but I enjoy what I do. I've kept my license up-to-date and love working with numbers. I've just decided that I'm not going to worry about it or at least try not to. I'll have to wait and see. Ready to walk back?"

The conversation as the two women walked home ranged from being serious to both of them laughing. Abbey knew she now had a new friend, even though the age difference was more than twenty-eight years.

Josie couldn't believe that she was actually talking about her life to someone other than her landlords. And enjoying it!

It felt good to talk to another woman, even if she was much younger. To Josie, this girl, this woman, was sent to her like a gift to help her break down all the hurt she had surrounded herself with. Suddenly, she felt like crying, and tears began to run down her face. They were just about at the their little home, and Abbey didn't notice Josie's tears mixed with a smile till she turned to open the gate.

"What's wrong? Did I say or do something?" Abbey asked with alarm in her voice.

"No, you didn't. Just the opposite." Josie continued walking through the gate till she was sitting on the rocker on the front porch, their usual spot. Abbey followed her and sat, not speaking a word.

"No, I want to thank you. I was so mean to you when you moved here. My anger and hurt surrounding me still after all these years. I've been so bitter that I didn't care what other people thought, so I was just plain mean. I feel embarrassed now. But you, for some odd reason, persisted on talking to me. Thank you. Thank you for being kind to me and for listening today. I can't promise I won't be cranky at times, but you have shown me this last month that I don't have to carry around all this hurt inside. I might have been dealt a raw deal, but that was so long ago, and I need to just let it go. Move on. That's what I meant to do when I got here so long ago, but I can see now that I just carried it with me and let it insulate me from the outside world. Maybe little by little, I will be able to release it now. I know it will take time, but if it hadn't been for you, I wouldn't know what it feels like to have a little chunk of freedom inside me." Then she stood up and grabbed Abbey's hand, pulling her out of the chair, and hugged her, Josie's tears falling on Abbey's shoulders.

"Thank you, Abbey."

"You're welcome, Josie." This time Abbey had tears in her eyes, and they both smiled at each other, wiping tears that graced their cheeks.

"Hello there, ladies!"

17

They both turned around to see Garrett opening the gate and trying to drag three big tote bags in at once. They both wiped their eyes quickly, trying to hide the emotional talk they had just had, but Garrett was quick.

"Are those tears of happiness for my return from the sea? This must be what it felt like a hundred years ago when sailors returned home safely." Garrett definitely had a sense of humor. He laughed at his statement as he watched both women smile.

"We were having some girl talk," Abbey said, "and no, it wasn't about you. Hope that doesn't bruise your male ego." She smiled as she stared at Garrett. Even though he had been on a boat for three weeks, he looked mighty good. His tan had deepened from being in the sun for so long. His tank top showed taunt muscles, and a thick, dark stubble went across his lower cheeks and chin. To say he looked sexy was putting it mildly, Abbey thought.

"So how was your trip this time?" Josie asked, startling both Abbey and Garrett. Garrett was dumbfounded at first. He wasn't used to Josie actually speaking to him, so it took a second for him to respond.

"Actually very good. Got a lot of interesting information trying to target why the coral reefs are dying in some areas and thriving in others. I also got to tag more sea turtles, helping a fellow researcher. Tracking a few that are already tagged that like a spot here off Key West and then an area in Key Largo." He looked up to see both Abbey and Josie looking at him like deer in headlights.

"Sorry! I get a bit wrapped up in work. I think I should go dump these clothes in the washer and then put myself in the shower. Haven't had a decent one in a while."

Abbey decided this was her chance to remind him of the dinner. "Let me know when you want that home-cooked meal. Tonight or tomorrow would be great!"

"I'll take you up on it tomorrow, love. A bit tired today after unloading the boat and now unpacking my stuff."

"Tomorrow night it is." Abbey felt a fluttering inside as she thought of the next night, watching Garrett make his way up the steps.

"Abbey, don't get your hopes up. I can tell you from experience. That man is all about his work. You just saw he couldn't quit talking about it, and he just got home! I definitely don't want to see you get hurt. And I never want to see anyone go through what I did."

"Thanks, Josie. And I will be careful. Promise."

The next evening couldn't come fast enough for Abbey. She got up Sunday morning and went about making sure her apartment was clean. She also double-checked to make sure she had all her necessary ingredients for her planned dinner. Abbey wanted it to be a bit romantic but not over the top. It was difficult not to think of this as a first date when Abbey knew it was supposed to be her way of saying "thank you" for his very timely help the day she arrived in Key West.

A little after noon, she heard a knock at her door. A look out the small peephole showed that Zach was standing outside. "Hey there! Come on in," Abbey said as she opened the door.

"Sorry I didn't call first. I was in the neighborhood and thought I would stop by. Getting ready to go out in the boat again, and even though it is short notice, was wondering if you might be interested in going with me. And my friends, of course. We are going to find a sandbar and have a picnic of sorts. Maybe go snorkeling."

"I would love to, but I've already made plans. Remember the guy I told you about that helped me move in? Garrett? He got back in town yesterday, and we are having dinner here this evening. So I'm trying to make sure the place is all cleaned up, and then I have to cook. I'll take a rain check, though, if that's OK, because it sounds like fun." Abbey hated to disappoint him again

Zach was fast becoming Abbey's best friend. His help these last few weeks could not be measured. They were able to talk about practically anything and everything. Zach had come to her rescue more times than she could count since she had moved, helping her with all kinds of things, from fixing a small problem with her Jeep to telling her the best low-priced restaurants. And now, just the other day, he helped her find the information she needed to set up an artist table at Mallory Square. He had even offered to help her put her display together when she was ready to start selling her art. Abbey loved spending time with him, and they worked incredibly well together. But she also couldn't deny the attraction she felt for him but knew that taking their relationship to another level would complicate both of their lives.

"That is no problem. Didn't know Garrett was back." Zach did his best to hide his disappointment.

"Yep, he came in just as Josie and I got back from having coffee. Can you believe that? Josie actually invited me to coffee, and we had a wonderful time. I finally understand why she acts the way she does. She has had a hard life, but hopefully, she was able to let go of some of that hurt yesterday when we talked."

"Wow, that's good to hear." Zach was trying to sound cheerful and not think about the girl he liked having dinner with another man. It had been almost a month now, and it seemed Abbey liked him as no more than just a good friend. There had to be something Zach could do to make her see how he craved more than just a friendship, but he couldn't think of anything else that he hadn't already done.

"So, what are you fixing your mystery man?" Zach asked to keep the conversation going.

"What do you mean by 'mystery man'?"

Zach shrugged his shoulders. "Well, you only met him the day he helped you move your stuff upstairs and said good-bye to him the next day. Your words, not mine."

Abbey stood for a moment and realized that Zach was right. "Didn't really give it much thought. I guess you're right—I don't know him. But that is what tonight is for. I'm fixing one of my momma's finest recipes: smothered steaks, mashed potatoes, and creamed peas. Definitely not your typical island dinner."

"That does sound good. I'm sure he will enjoy it, especially after he has been around nothing but fish and on a boat for the last few weeks." Zach stood there looking around Abbey's little apartment, impressed. "You have fixed up your place really nice. Looks like you have been living here for a while, not just a month."

"Well, if it wasn't for you and the yard sales you took me to, plus helping me with some Craigslist finds, I'm sure it wouldn't be as presentable, so I have you to thank for making this place look homey." As she continued to talk to Zach, Abbey started getting out pots and pans to make sure her dinner was cooked on time. She knew the recipes by heart, so no cookbook was needed.

"I've got to go, or I'll be left at the dock. I hope you have a nice dinner. You'll have to tell me about it tomorrow at work. If he's not nice to you, let me know too, and I'll take care of him for you," Zach said with a smile while making a muscle pose with his arm.

Abbey couldn't help but laugh. "Promise I'll let you know." She went and gave Zach a hug. "Thanks for being such a good friend. You are really the only one I've got here, and you are the best!"

"Except now you have Josie too," he reminded her.

"That is still in the development stage. Remember, I have to take baby steps with her," Abbey said with a smile in her voice as they walked to the door.

"From what you have told me, the smaller the step the better. Enjoy your evening." It took everything Zach had inside him not reach over and kiss Abbey good-bye as they stood in the doorway. She looked totally irresistible, and he could feel his heartbeat quicken at the sight. Even just a quick peck on the cheek would be good enough for him right now. But after this conversation and knowing that Abbey was fixing dinner for another man, he would have to accept that the bond between them would only be one of friends, even best friends, as Abbey had said. It would be hard, but if that was the only way to have her in his life, friends it would be.

18

For the second time that day, there was a knock on her door. Since it was close to six o'clock, this time it had to be Garrett, and looking through the peephole again, she was right. Abbey looked down at the lavender sundress she had on with white sandals to make sure she hadn't accidentally spilled anything on herself while making dinner. A quick check in the mirror showed that she looked presentable, and she opened the door.

"Hello, love," Garrett said, standing in her door. "Smells wonderful from out here. I can definitely tell it is home cooked, and please tell me it's not fish." He walked into her apartment without even being invited in, and Abbey looked at him, perplexed. He was wearing an old T-shirt, faded blue shorts with holes around the hemlines, and a pair of flip-flops that had seen much better days. His hair was a mess but not too terrible, as though he had just woken from a nap, and his unshaven appearance was even more pronounced than yesterday.

"This looks like a totally different place than the last time I saw it. You have done wonders! So, how do you like the old house so far?" He quickly walked in and plopped down on her couch, putting his feet up on the coffee table with her still standing at the front door.

Taken aback by his appearance and lack of manners, Abbey shut the door and made her way to the small spot that was her living room.

"I really like it here. A lot different from North Carolina, but I'm finding my way around and made a great friend at work. My job is great, more—"

"Do you have anything to drink? I'm parched. Just came off the boat from gathering a few more things I forgot yesterday. Mainly some research papers I printed while we were at sea. Do you have any beer, by chance?"

Abbey hadn't even been able to finish her sentence. This was definitely not going like she had thought about all day.

"Sorry, no beer, but I do have some cola, sweet iced tea, or water."

"The iced tea sounds great!" Garrett was still sitting with his foot up on Abbey's coffee table and his head laid back on her couch.

"You can't imagine how good it is to be on land for a while. I'm actually glad it is time to turn in a report. I should be here for a while now, hopefully. I have enough research to keep me busy for at least a month, and I'm also going to help at the Turtle Hospital. Is dinner ready?" he asked as Abbey handed him the glass of tea.

"Yes, it is, unless you would like to sit for a moment."

"No, I'm starving. And whatever you fixed, it smells wonderful." Garrett got up and went into her kitchen, looking around at the pots and bowls with food just as she had sat down to talk to him.

They ate at the little table in the kitchen by the window. The sun was starting to set, but there was still plenty of light coming through. Garrett ate and talked nonstop about work—his research, the coral reefs, the turtles, the boats, the storm they were caught in, and more. Abbey could barely say anything but "Wow" or "That's too bad." Every time she tried to start a sentence, Garrett would take off in a different direction about something he had going on. She was beginning to think that Josie was right. Garrett did seem to be completely obsessed about his work. It was definitely a one-sided conversation, and she could tell by Garrett's demeanor that it wasn't done arrogantly. He was just excited about what he did and thought others would be too.

By the time dinner ended, Abbey was ready for him to go home. This whole evening had played so differently in her mind. Nice conversation. Slow, easy dinner. Maybe even a walk outside. But he hadn't even asked about her one time! Abbey's blossoming crush on this man had suddenly deflated, and she could feel the disappointment.

"That was a wonderful dinner, Abbey. Thanks for making it, even though you didn't have to. Consider the moving-in debt paid in full, even though I wasn't charging anything. You are a sweetheart. If you need anything, let me know. See ya!"

He opened the door and stepped out just as she yelled, "Thank you!" from the kitchen. He didn't even have the decency to let her walk him to the door.

As she did the dishes and cleaned up, she replayed the whole dinner scenario in her head. How had things gone so wrong? How had she misread this man that much? Granted, she only knew him from that first day of helping her, but she was usually a good judge of character. Garrett was nice and friendly but not a people person. Maybe that came from the type of work he did. Working on research vessels for extended periods of time didn't lend itself to developing friends, much less a girlfriend. She realized now that even though he may have seemed friendly and outgoing, he was a loner. Not like Josie but a happy loner. He was in love with his work. That was very evident this evening. As Abbey put the last dish in its place, she decided to call it a night. She took a shower and crawled into bed with her book but was fast asleep before completing the first page.

Abbey walked into work the next morning to find that she was the last to arrive. Zach was already at his desk, working on the website they had to finish by Friday. It was a complicated project that they had been working on now for two weeks. She sat her things on her desk, shaking Zach's attention from his computer screen.

"Hey there! So how did things go last night?"

"Well, it was interesting. Not quite what I expected." Abbey contemplated how much to share with Zach as she put her stuff away to get ready for the day. She would like to talk to someone about her perspective of the evening's events.

"Is that good or bad?" Zach already knew the answer to his question from her body language but didn't say a word.

"Just different. Maybe we can talk at lunch."

"Sure," Zach said, knowing that her date with Garrett wasn't a hit. Maybe this would work to his advantage in trying to get Abbey to see him as more than a coworker and best friend.

The morning flew by quickly, and Abbey was glad. This didn't give Zach a chance to ask any more personal questions and lessened her time thinking about the night before. At one thirty, though, they both decided it was time for a break. Abbey had brought her lunch, so they walked to the nearby outdoor café and found a table in the back. Zach ordered his food, sat down, and then looked at her with raised eyebrows to begin.

"What?" Abbey asked.

"We usually talk about our weekends, but you said earlier you wanted to talk about your date." Zach wondered if he really wanted to hear the details, but he knew he did.

"There really isn't much to say. He came over, we ate, and he left. End of story." Abbey nibbled at the salad in front of her, not looking up at Zach.

"That's all? Abbey, I'm your friend, and you know you can talk to me. I can tell you aren't real excited about whatever took place last night. I'm a great listener," Zach told her, smiling.

"Garrett showed up at the door in dirty work clothes. He basically barged in the house, went to the sofa, and propped his feet on my coffee table! No manners whatsoever but nice the whole time. While we ate dinner, all he talked about was his work. The boat, fish, research. I couldn't get a word in at all." Abbey paused for a moment and laughed. "Then all of a sudden, he said he enjoyed the food, got up, and walked out the door, barely saying good night. The whole evening from start to finish was just so strange. I mean, he was friendly, but it felt like I was having a meal with one of my brothers instead of the handsome, kind man that helped me move in."

"Sorry things didn't go as you planned," Zach said while excitement built inside him. He felt sorry for Abbey but was secretly glad that her date didn't go well. She deserved better than Garrett, and she needed someone who would be around, not always out to sea.

"It's OK. I think we will just be friends and neighbors. There are other 'fish' in the sea." When Abbey realized what she'd just said, she started laughing so hard that it was contagious, and Zach joined in at the pun she just made. As Abbey watched Zach, she began to wish that they didn't work together, because he was the type of guy she could see herself dating.

When Abbey arrived home that evening after working a bit late, she found Josie sitting on the porch and reading with her iced tea on the little table by the rocking chair. Abbey wasn't sure she should disturb her, but she wanted to tell her what had happened the night before.

"Hey, Josie! How was work?" Abbey walked onto the porch and slumped tiredly in the matching rocking chair.

"Same old thing. You're late this evening," Josie said without looking up from her book.

"This project at work is kicking mine and Zach's butts. I think we just about have it finished, but it's been tough." Then she was quiet for a moment. "My evening yesterday with Garrett was a bit strange."

"How so?" Josie asked.

"Well, we had dinner last night, and it was kinda weird. I guess I was expecting a 'date,' and he just wanted a meal." Abbey looked around before going on, making sure they were alone. Josie still wasn't looking up from her book. But when Abbey finished her description of her evening, Josie looked up.

"I told you he was wrapped up in work. Don't think he wouldn't know the difference between a date and a fish. Anyway, he is too old for you."

"Why do you say that? I'm twenty-eight. I don't see anything wrong with dating an older man. Except for Garrett, which is definitely not happening. Wait till I tell Ella what happened. Knowing her, though, she will still want to go out with him." Abbey giggled a bit, and Josie smiled.

As Abbey glanced out toward the street, she saw an older gentleman walking toward the house, checking house numbers as he walked slowly. As he approached the gate surrounding their little apartments, he paused, looking from the paper in his hand to the house number on the porch post, then back to the paper again as if to verify he had the right place. Abbey continued to watch him as he looked around, while Josie was still looking at the book in her lap. The man opened the gate slowly, walked up the sidewalk, and stepped up onto the porch.

"Hi. Can I help you?" Abbey asked the man, who was now staring at Josie who was still looking at her book

"Josie, is that you?" the gentleman asked softly.

As Josie looked up to see who had mentioned her name, her face displayed shock.

"Michael?"

19

"Josie? Is this really you?" the man said, not taking his eyes off her.

"What in the hell are you doing here?" The anger in Josie voice is palpable, and Abbey felt an instant, heavy tension all around them. Was this the Michael that Josie had told her about? The man that left her humiliated so long ago when he left Josie at the altar? If so, how did he find her after all these years? Abbey knew that if she had these questions rapidly filling her head, she could only imagine the turmoil that Josie was feeling right now.

"Josie, I'm going to leave so the two of you can talk," Abbey said as she gathered her handbag and tote to go upstairs.

"Abbey, you are more than welcome to stay. This *man* most assuredly won't be here long." Abbey knew that if words or looks could kill, the man standing on the porch would have been dead three times over by now.

As Michael walked slowly toward the two women, Abbey could see the distress in Josie's face and body. She was trembling and breathing so fast that Abbey was afraid that Josie might hyperventilate. But Michael was not being deterred.

"Josie, I know this is going to sound crazy, but I've been looking for you for a long time—years, really! Please let me explain why I'm here. Just give me a chance to talk. I know it's a shock for you—I understand. Maybe we can get together tomorrow? I know it's already late in the day."

"I'm not interested in anything you have to say. No explanations. Nothing. Just get the hell off my porch and leave. I don't want to see you again. I thought I made that extremely clear long ago!"

Michael didn't move but stood his ground. It was like he was taking in all of Josie's features, and he smiled. Abbey's first impression of this handsome older man was that he seemed very genuine and sweet, nothing like the man Josie had described to her. But Abbey knew Josie wasn't thinking the same thoughts as she.

"You haven't changed a bit," Michael said, still looking at Josie as though he had finally found a true treasure.

"Like hell I haven't. You have no idea how much I've changed. What you put me through was pure torture and left me forever a different woman. And seeing you now just brings back too many bad memories. *Leave. Now.*"

"I've come a long way and waited an even longer time to see and talk to you. I don't care how long it takes. All I want is some of your time so I can explain everything and make things right between us. But as I can tell that it won't be tonight, I'll come back tomorrow. Good night." With that, Michael walked off the porch and back down the street.

Abbey looked at Josie. She was sitting as still as a stone in the rocking chair with a look of fear and hurt on her face. Abbey could tell that she was in shock.

"Josie? Are you OK?" Abbey said softly.

"No, I'm not OK!" she practically yelled. "I can't believe that asshole found me! How in the world did he find me? And why? Why now?" Her voice softened a bit but was so full of hurt, anger, and bitterness. It was as though a floodgate of memories assaulted all of Josie's senses, and before she knew it, tears were falling from her eyes. Abbey got up and knelt in front of her new friend, and Josie's head fell to Abbey's shoulder as she sobbed. Abbey could only imagine the pain she was feeling, and there was nothing she could do to help Josie except be silent and let the tears fall.

How could he do this to me? Josie thought when she closed the door to her apartment, thoroughly drained of energy. After Michael left, she had cried till she had no more tears to give. Abbey had just stayed right by her side, not saying a word, letting her give in to her emotions and all the feelings she had stored up inside these many years. Once the shock had worn off, Josie told Abbey she would be fine, just needed some time to herself to process what she was feeling.

"Josie, if you need anything, you have my number, or better yet, come up to my place, OK?" Abbey said, looking at Josie's red-rimmed eyes, wanting to make it all better for her.

Josie looked at Abbey, seeing for the first time the daughter she had always wished she had. "You know, when you first moved in upstairs, I hated that someone else was already taking that place. Then when I saw that you were young, that made it even worse. I always feel like the old spinster lady when you young girls move in around here. But Abbey, you are different. You may be younger than me, but you have a beautiful old soul. I'm so sorry for the way I treated you these last few weeks, and thanks for not giving up on me. And I'm sorry I have soaked your shoulder from crying."

"I'm glad we were able to become friends, Josie. You are a beautiful lady. You just won't let yourself be who you really are. You've built this wall around your heart, and you have had good reason, but that is in the past. It's time to let it go. I know you are feeling vulnerable, but it will be OK. I also know it's not my place, so don't call me crazy, but, Josie, I think you ought to listen to what Michael has to say," Abbey had said as softly as possible.

Reliving the conversation with Abbey in her mind while she fixed herself a small dinner, Josie couldn't believe those words had come out of Abbey's mouth. There was no way she wanted anything to do with Michael. But now that the shock had worn off, her mind was letting her think about what could have possibly made Michael search for her and what he had to say. Josie couldn't deny that she was wondering what had brought him to Key West, but the biggest part of her heart wanted him gone, along with the painful memories.

She ate in silence at her kitchen table, the picture of Michael standing on the porch still fresh in her mind. Next it was a slow, hot shower, trying to work out all the tension that her body was holding on to, and this also brought on a new wave of tears. It was like an old wound had been reopened. All those feelings she had felt so long ago were assaulting her once again. Josie felt confused, fearful, worried, and embarrassed all at the same time. She didn't realize how long she had been under the hot water till it started turning cooler. She quickly dried off and went to bed even though it was early but sleep eluded her. She wondered where he was, what he was doing. Josie pictured Michael in her mind, and she did have to admit that the years had been very kind to him. Even though he was older, he was still the good-looking man that had taken her breath away all those years ago. He was tall and still muscular, which meant that he must still be working on the ranch, she surmised. His dark hair had turned mostly gray but made him look just as sexy as he did when they were dating. Physically, he still seemed to be the Michael she knew. But why was he here, and what did he have to say? How would she know if he was different from the person who had broken her heart so long ago? Maybe she would give in and take Abbey's advice by talking to him. Now that the jolt of seeing Michael again had lost its initial punch, Josie was starting to feel more calm. But the questions still filled her worried mind till she finally fell asleep from exhaustion.

Abbey's night was also a bit sleepless over what had happened on the porch. Her heart was heavy for Josie, but she wondered what Michael was doing here. Not that it was any of her business, but Abbey really wanted to know. Hopefully the former couple would be able to talk, if Josie let him near her again. That would be a game of wait and see. She would be there for Josie for support, someone Josie could talk to if she felt the need. Abbey could only imagine how she was handling the news that her former love was not only here in her town but also wanted to talk to her again after many years apart.

The next day at work, when they went on their lunch break, Abbey filled in Zach with all the details that had happened the night before.

"I hope she talks to Michael, but I'm not going to push her on the subject. Lord knows it has taken this long for her to open up to me. Just not sure how she is going to handle all this mentally." The worried look on Abbey's face told Zach it was time to switch gears.

"Let's change to a happier subject. Something a little more fun, and I'm telling you right now—I won't take no for an answer. We are going snorkeling this weekend, and you are coming with me," Zach said, smiling broadly. Abbey couldn't help but grin. She had to give Zach credit for persistence, and she couldn't deny that a huge part of her did want to go. She truly loved spending time with him—so what if they worked together? They were just friends, right? Going snorkeling would be fun. She had been so focused on Garrett's homecoming that every time Zach asked her to do something, she always had an excuse. For some reason, Abbey had acted as though she and Garrett were in a relationship even though it was only a dinner, which had been a total flop. And the truth was, she loved the time she spent with Zach. She just had to be careful not to give the wrong impression about their relationship.

"You know, that sounds perfect. I haven't been out on a boat since I got here, and it's been so long since I've snorkeled, so I would love to go with you," Abbey said as she watched Zach's smile get just a bit bigger.

The rest of the week flew by as the workload was heavy. Abbey and Zach worked feverishly on the website that had to be completed the next week. After work, it seemed she always ran into Garrett, good-looking and charming as ever, but he talked nonstop about fish, algae, coral, and boats. Abbey would listen and just smile, realizing that even though Garrett did lack some people skills, she still couldn't help but love his enthusiasm about his work. But any romantic notion she had thought about of this man her first day in Key West had completely disappeared. He would be a good friend and neighbor, nothing more. And Abbey was perfectly OK with that.

Every evening, she would check on Josie. She hadn't sat out on the porch anymore that week since the night Michael showed up, afraid he would catch her outside again.

"So you haven't talked to him at all?" Abbey asked.

"He certainly has tried. He found out where I worked and came by to ask me to go to lunch. I told him no, of course. He has come by here every night, a few times before you got home, but I haven't even opened the door. He keeps talking as though we were sitting on the porch, always asking for a little time to just 'chat,' as he says. And he makes sure to remind me every time before he leaves that he is staying in Key West till I agree to talk." Josie was pacing back and forth in her living room as she spoke, while Abbey sat on the couch. This week was the first time she had been in Josie's place. It was so quaint, and Josie's dog, Jewel, seemed to be a permanent fixture on Abbey's lap as she listened to Josie. If only she could help Josie make that all-important decision to give Michael a chance to tell his side of the story.

"You need to just go ahead and talk. Get it all out in the open. Tell him exactly how you feel. Get it over with."

"Abbey, I'm not ready. I don't know when I will be, or if ever! I just don't know. I'm so torn, and on top of all of this, I found out today that I'm not going to have a job when the new company takes over the resort. There is so much happening at once. I even went to my doctor today and told him what was going on, because I'm a nervous wreck, and my stomach has been churning. He gave me some medicine that has helped. I feel like the peaceful little life I created has been turned upside down."

Abbey looked at her friend, seeing the pain and confusion on her face. "You know, Josie, sometimes change is a good thing. It's all on how we look at it. I know it's hard right now, so maybe take some time this weekend for yourself. Think about the good that could come out of both situations."

Josie looked at her incredulously. "You got to be kidding! There is *nothing* good about either situation!"

"That is your anxiety talking. Don't be so quick to jump to conclusions. Michael might be a totally changed man, but you won't know till you allow yourself permission to talk to him. Everything happened so many years ago, and a lot has probably changed during that time. You won't know unless you talk to him. Anyway, he seems to be pretty persistent, so I doubt he is going anywhere till you give in.

"As far as the resort goes, your résumé is excellent, so finding a new job shouldn't be a problem. There are so many businesses here that could use your skills. You also said that you had saved a substantial amount of money to live on through investments. Do you really have to work, or do you just want to? Josie, there are so many possibilities, good ones, but you have to be willing to change. Accept that things aren't going to be the same anymore, which, believe me, I know is hard. You made a major change once before when you decided to move here without anyone knowing. If you can do that, then I know you can handle it now."

Josie had finally stopped pacing and sat beside Abbey, her eyes again filled with tears. "Thank you, Abbey. I know you are right, but it's so hard. I had my routine, all nice and neat. It feels like a tornado has suddenly ripped through my life. Thanks for being here for me." She hugged Abbey tightly then Jewel jumped in Josie's lap, licking away the tears, which made both women smile. "I had truly forgotten how nice it was to have a friend I could talk to. And by the way, I have noticed that you also have had a visitor almost every night," Josie said, raising her eyebrows, changing the subject to focus on Abbey.

"You mean Zach? He is a sweetheart, and we've become great friends, nothing more. We work together, so friends it is. It's almost like he is my big brother!" Abbey smiled at Josie as she continued to watch Jewel snuggle with her owner.

"Maybe he should be more than a friend. He is nice look-ing and very polite. Always says hi and seems very sweet." Now Josie was sounding like her mom, and she laughed just a little.

"Yes, like I said, he is great, and we are going out on the boat this weekend with his friends. I finally said I would go. But we are just *friends*."

"It's about time. He has been asking you to do something practically every weekend since you moved here. Why did it take so long for you to say yes to that boy?" Josie was trying to lighten the mood by talking about Abbey's love life instead of her own.

"Honestly, I really thought there might have been some-thing between me and Garrett. He was so sweet and helpful that first day I was here. Kinda flirty! But that isn't happen-ing. I thought maybe that first dinner was just a fluke, but I've learned that Garrett is just being himself. He is sweet and nice, but truthfully, he isn't my type. Except as a friend. Zach and I talk about everything and have so much in common. But *we are just friends*," Abbey said to Josie and secretly to herself.

"Then you need your eyes examined. You can tell by the way he walks to your door that the boy wants to be more than just your *friend*. And I think the feeling is mutual if you would admit it. You have a way of always emphasizing the word 'friend' as though you are trying to convince yourself."

Abbey smiled. "Have you been spying on me?"

"It takes my mind off the mess that seems to be swirling around me," Josie said.

20

Despite Josie's protests, Michael continued his daily visits to the house. Josie eventually returned to her nightly routine of sitting on the front porch, even though Michael showed up every evening only to be rebuffed. Abbey definitely had to give him the award for persistence. She did notice by the third week that Josie's defenses were starting to crumble just a little. Josie didn't immediately order him off the porch or not answer her door. Apparently, Michael was true to his word: he would take all the time needed to be able to talk to her, and by the looks of it, he was justified.

Abbey could already see the daily routine. Michael always seemed to show up a little after Josie got off work and would come to the porch. Josie's reaction and words were practically the same each evening: a stone-faced look and a "Please leave." But Abbey noticed small changes taking place within Josie. Michael's constant visits were breaking down Josie's defenses.

Abbey hoped, for Josie and for Michael, that they would be able to talk soon. Her words to Josie were the same almost every day: let him tell his story, and give him a chance to explain.

Abbey went on that first boat ride with Zach and immediately fell in love with the clear, blue waters surrounding the Keys. All his friends made her feel so welcome, and she instantly felt like part of their little group. The first weekend was snorkeling on a little reef not too far from land. The next weekend it was water skiing in Florida Bay. Abbey decided she would leave the skiing up to everyone else and enjoy the scenery from the boat. She could have sworn all of Zach's friends were born with gills, because almost every activity they did had to do with the beautiful water surrounding Key West.

When they weren't spending time on the boat, Zach showed Abbey all the special little places of Key West that made it so unique, like small-town restaurants with great key-lime pie, little-known but great bands where they would just go and listen to the music, and of course, always checking out the artists on Mallory Square, admittedly Abbey's favorite thing to do.

Now that she was settled and had a routine, Abbey started her mixed-media acrylic paintings using all the unique places around the city as her muse. As for her small sculptures she enjoyed crafting, she found herself making dolphins, sea turtles, sea horses, seashells, and colorful fish. Abbey even made a palm-tree sculpture with a hammock, which she envisioned in her own backyard one day.

"Come on in," she said as she heard the knock on the door. She knew it was Zach because he had texted he was on his way over with sandwiches and a surprise. *If he's brought me more pie, I'll be buying a new swimsuit shortly, if not a whole new wardrobe*, she thought.

"Um, that smells so good. But I've got to start cooking my own dinners again. When I came here, I was eating whole, unprocessed food, and my body thanked me for it. If I keep eating all the treats this island offers, I'm going to be big as a house!"

Zach smiled as he sat the dinner on the table. He could glance over and see the newest painting Abbey was working on. It was going to be beautiful. Her artwork was amazing and, in his opinion, rivaled the boss's wife's work that hung in her own private gallery. That was why he couldn't wait to show her the paper he had in his pocket.

As Abbey sat down at the table, the food smelled and looked so good that she started eating right away. "I didn't realize how hungry I was! I came straight home and started working on that painting. The sculptures are drying, so I can probably start painting them tomorrow. Sorry, I'm talking with my mouth full," she said, trying to smile at him apologetically.

"Glad you like what I picked out. I wasn't sure what kind of sandwich you like, but I knew you liked their spicy fries."

"Thanks again for dinner. You said something about a surprise on the phone? Please tell me it's not more food!" Abbey looked at him anxiously.

Zach pulled the paper out of his pocket and laid it on the table. "Here is all the info you need to be able to set up your own artist table at Mallory Square. I got all the details and found out that you have to 'audition' at Bayview Park first, and if they like what they see, you are in."

Abbey about choked on her food. Her own table at Mallory Square? Excitement coursed through her, and she jumped up, reaching over to Zach to give him a big hug and nearly knocking him and his chair backward. Even though her excitement was over the top, Abbey felt a rush of electricity pulse through her as her arms reached around Zach's neck, touching his skin. She wondered if he felt it too. She looked at him to see him staring at her with a smoldering twinkle in his eyes.

Suddenly feeling self-conscious, she quickly pulled away. "I have to audition?" Abbey sat back down, trying to concentrate on the news instead of the feeling still clinging to her.

"They have to see what your artistic talent is, how you create what you do, and make sure there aren't too many people already selling your type of craft. But this is the best news. You remember Joey? He went snorkeling with us a few weeks ago. His dad is on the commission for picking artists for the park. I already talked to him and his dad. Told them all about your sculptures and painting. From the way he sounded, you are a shoo-in." Zach waited to see excitement exude from her face, but instead she had a look of terror. Abbey suddenly forgot her feelings as she concentrated on this bit of news.

"I can't do that! I'm not ready! My work isn't nearly as good as what I see there each time we go. Why did you do this?" Abbey's mind was in panic mode. Yes, she wanted to show her work there. It was her dream she had thought about when driving down here. But now that the possibility actually existed, her insides felt like jelly. How could she measure up to the artists she saw every time she went to the square?

"I thought you would be excited. You talk about it every time we go to the square. I thought for sure you would be excited. I'm sorry if I was out of line by talking to Joey's dad, but it's perfect for you. If you don't feel ready, don't do it. But, Abbey," he continued, gazing at her with admiration, "all of your work is beautiful. Your paintings are wonderful, and if I remember right, no one displays or sells these little sculptures that you make. I've seen how you work, and it is amazing the way you take a piece of clay and make it into a stunning piece of art. You need to give yourself some credit, and don't compare yourself to anyone else. Everyone's art is different, and in my opinion, yours is extra special." Zach took her hand because he could tell Abbey's nerves were creating anxiety about this piece of good news, but to him she looked so beautiful. He wished he could just scoop her up in his arms to give her the comfort and confidence she was lacking. Zach had thought that over time, he would see Abbey as a best friend, but instead his feelings for her continued to move in the direction of a romantic relationship. This was the woman he had always wanted. *If only she felt the same way*, Zach thought.

Abbey was starting to calm down, her heart beating a little slower. Maybe she had overreacted, but she suddenly felt very exposed. She had sold paintings and more in North Carolina. Why was this so different? Maybe because back home were the people that she had known since she was a little girl. But here on this tropical island, it was different. She was stepping out on her own, no support except Zach's unwavering confidence in her abilities. She wanted desperately for people to like her and her artwork. And what if they didn't? What if she didn't sell anything? This was the first time since moving to Key West that she felt like she couldn't breathe. Then she looked at Zach and suddenly felt calm. He seemed to have a way about him that made her see things differently, and all the anxiety that had overcome her started to melt away little by little.

"I'm the one who should say I'm sorry. You're right. I do want a table down on that square. I used to sell my art pieces back home, but for some reason it feels so different down here. I feel vulnerable." She took a deep breath and was finally able to take another bite of her sandwich. "So, when is the audition?"

"Vulnerable?" Zach asked, a bit taken aback by her statement. "You know I'm here for you."

"I'm sorry—again! That's not what I meant. In North Carolina, I was surrounded by lots of family and friends, people I have known my whole life. Here, I'm starting fresh. I'm just now feeling like a real resident, so taking this next step has me anxious. But you are right—I have you. That's what best friends are for!" Abbey reached over and gave Zach a kiss on the cheek. Once again she felt the sizzle of electricity that washed over her but tried to quickly erase it from her mind. This was one feeling that she knew she could not act on

"Like I said. You have my support, one hundred percent. Now tell me. Why do they call this panel of people a 'jury'? Kinda odd, don't you think?" Zach smiled, trying not to show how the kiss she had just given him was like a gift. He had wondered many times what it would be like to feel her lips on his but a kiss on the cheek was the next best thing.

"That's the terminology in the art world. They are a group of people that decide on or judge your work, especially in competitions. Sounds like this jury is going to make the decision whether I'm a capable artist and if I deserve a spot on the famous Mallory Square. Though it sounds like I'm going to court." Now she laughed a bit, which eased her nerves even more. Abbey suddenly knew she could do this and how much Zach had done for her. He believed in her, so why shouldn't she believe in herself?

"If I am going to do this, I have to get to work. I certainly do not have enough art to sell."

"Well, the 'jury' is next Monday at ten o'clock. You need to talk to Lance tomorrow and ask for the time off," Zach reminded her.

Abbey's panic button set off again. What would she tell Lance? That she was taking on a second job? "What do you think he will say? Has anyone ever done this before since you've worked there?" she asked, looking over at Zach.

"No, but I don't see why he would get upset about it. It's not like you are working on his time, and you're selling at the square, not in a gallery. Does he know about your artwork?"

"When I interviewed, I told him I did different types of artwork since I was an art major, but that was about the extent of the conversation. Just need to get up enough nerve to talk to him tomorrow. I haven't asked for any time off since I came here. Hopefully the process won't take that long." She sat there contemplating everything, thinking through what she would need to do, using the paper that Zach had given her to help her make a plan.

"Once you have talked to Lance, I'll let Joey's dad know whether you will be there or not. That should make things go more smoothly for you. Wish I could go with you," Zach said softly as he watched her, still seeing the bits of stress showing through her body language. He really wanted this for her but wondered now if he should had taken the initiative to help her achieve this goal of hers. Zach only wanted to see Abbey happy—something best friends always wanted for each other.

As they finished dinner, Zach continued to help Abbey decide what she should make for the committee. Then the conversation changed to the current project at work. Even though both tried not to talk about work outside of the office, this particular website had both of them excited, because they were designing a site that was specific for children to be able to have their own small community. Zach saw it like a Facebook site for children, with lots of protection to keep the kids safe from online predators. It was also a learning center. It was a big task, but at least they had plenty of time to work on it. The whole agency was excited when they got the bid on the site. Now the ideas were flowing, and part of the fun was picturing themselves as little kids. What would they want to do on a website that would be fun, and they wouldn't know that they were actually learning something new at the same time? Each time they started talking about the project, all the stories of their childhood came up. Both Zach and Abbey were usually laughing so hard, they couldn't breathe half the time at the crazy antics they both had pulled. Especially since they both had brothers and sisters.

"I gotta go," Zach said as he got off the couch where they were sitting, the TV on but neither of them watching. Abbey walked with him to the front door.

"Zach, I can't thank you enough for getting the information about Mallory Square, and the more I think about it, the more excited I am. Still nervous, but I know I can do it." She reached up and hugged him tightly, once again giving him a kiss on the cheek. As she pulled away, the tingle on her lips gave her even more to think about.

"It was really no problem. I have confidence in you, Abbey. I know you can do it, and I just wanted to help make your dream a reality. You deserve it." He smiled at her as he opened the door. "I'll see you tomorrow at work," Zach said and then he was gone down the steps. She continued to watch him till he was away down the street on his bike. The kiss on the cheek had unnerved her a bit. It had left her with more to think about than the possibility of her own artist spot in Key West.

Two kisses! Yes, it was only on the cheek, but that doesn't matter, Zach thought. Oh, why had she done that? If she only knew how hard this was for him. He longed to hold her in his arms and give her not a kiss on the cheek but one on her lips, so gentle and deep that it would take her breath away. And probably his too! He wanted to walk the street holding hands with this woman. Cradle her in his arms. Brush away tears if they should fall down her cheeks and cheer her while she accomplished her dreams. He wanted so much to be more a part of her life than just a friend. Even though he was happy as he rode his bike home, a little depression set in with the fact that what he wanted was just a fantasy. Would he ever be able to be with Abbey without thinking of her as his very own? He hoped so, because if they couldn't be together as a couple, Zach certainly didn't want to lose her as his best friend.

21

The next day, Abbey made a point of going to work early because she knew she could talk to Lance before the day began. He was always at the shop early, reading his papers on the iPad and drinking his plain, black coffee. All morning Abbey had rehearsed the speech that she wanted to give to Lance about taking time off and her desire to have an art show at Mallory Square. She just kept her fingers crossed that he would understand and know that it wouldn't affect her job at all.

Talking to Lance about her plans for a little artist table turned out better than she could have imagined. He was all for her selling her artwork and was actually excited for her. The time off next Monday was no problem, and Abbey was smiling from ear to ear. As soon as Zach walked in, she gave him the thumbs-up, and he smiled.

"If I get this gig, I'm going to need assistance figuring out how to set up my area. Can I impose on your wonderful ideas?" she asked, leaning into him, so close that she didn't realize what she was doing till she had practically wrapped her arm around his.

"No, I think I've done enough. Time for you to do the rest on your own." Though he tried to sound nonchalant, Zach just couldn't do it. It wasn't long before everyone was making suggestions for her opening debut as a street artist. But they also noticed how Zach and Abbey were so close, touching each other and acting as though they were a couple. Everly and Randy exchanged glances with eyebrows arched high as they watched from a distance.

"I still have to get through the jury process next Monday, so say a prayer for me," Abbey told them all. As she turned to go back to work, it was hard with all the art ideas swirling in her head about her potential upcoming show. Abbey kept writing ideas down in her notebook as they would surface in her mind, but she really needed to concentrate on the web design facing her on her laptop.

As she pulled up to her apartment building that evening, Abbey was tired, but the excitement from yesterday and today still had her adrenaline running on high. She was going to use the evening to make plans after she told Josie the good news. Josie was always waiting on her, since she got home first. Sometimes she even had a glass of sweet tea waiting for Abbey. But as she got out of the Jeep, Abbey immediately noticed that her rocking chair on the porch was occupied. Michael was sitting in the chair beside Josie, and they seemed to be actually talking. Abbey couldn't believe her eyes! His persistence had paid off—what she wouldn't do to be a fly on the wall to hear that conversation. Abbey wondered what Michael had done to finally win a small amount of Josie's trust.

"Good evening," Abbey said as she walked through the little gate and up the sidewalk.

"Hi," Michael said, standing up, walking toward Abbey, and extending his hand. Abbey shook the older man's hand and smiled. He was handsome in a rugged way. And so polite. She imagined how he must have looked and been so long ago when he and Josie were supposed to get married. "I'm Michael, a friend of Josie's. It's nice to meet you, Abbey. Josie has told me you live upstairs."

"Nice to meet you too. Hey, Josie," Abbey said, opening her eyes wide and smiling at Josie so only she could see Abbey's expression of excitement.

"Hi" was all Josie said in response, sounding almost like the woman Abbey remembered from when she'd first moved into the building. This wasn't the Josie she had come to know these last few weeks, so she decided now wasn't the time for more pleasantries.

"It was nice meeting you, Michael, but I have a lot of work ahead of me this evening, so I best be going. Josie, I have some news that I would like to share with you later. I'll call you in a bit, because I would like to get your opinion. Enjoy the evening!" Abbey hurried up the stairs, saying a little prayer that things would go well between the pair of estranged lovers sitting on the front porch.

22

"She seems very nice. Looks like you have good neighbors." Michael was nervous as he tried to make small talk to start the conversation. He had only just arrived five minutes before Abbey pulled up, and this was the first time in over three weeks that Josie hadn't run him off the porch. Michael hoped that Josie would talk to him. So much had happened over these many years, and he wanted—no, needed—to explain everything. To tell her about his life and how much he realized the mistake he had made so long ago. Maybe, just maybe, she would give him a chance to make things right between them once again.

"She is a real sweetheart. Almost half my age, but we have become friends since she moved here over two months ago. Abbey is completely different from the others who have lived in this building. Most that have been here like to party, live here for a while, and then head back to wherever they came from. Abbey is kind, caring, and patient. Lord knows, I wasn't her biggest fan when she showed up as the newest tenant, but she was pretty persistent on being nice to me. I hadn't had that in such a long time." Josie fell silent. She didn't know what else to say, and she certainly wasn't sure she wanted to hear the speech she was sure Michael had prepared. But Josie finally couldn't sit any longer without telling Michael exactly how she felt about his arrival in Key West.

"Michael, I don't know what possessed you to find me and come here. And I really don't want to know. The only reason you are sitting that in chair right now is so I can tell you to please leave and stop coming to my home. I have found my life here in this town. I like it just the way it is. You showing up out of the blue has disrupted just about everything for me, and I just want things to go back to normal. I've got a lot on my plate right now, and you are complicating matters more. Please, for the love of God, leave. Tomorrow if not sooner. I don't want to see you anymore."

There. Josie had finally said the words she had been rehearsing in her mind for over three weeks. The problem was that Josie did want to know why he was here and to explain what happened, as he put it, but her intuition told her that things would get messy if she let Michael speak more than a sentence. It would change things for her, she knew it, and she wasn't ready for or desired anything different in her life right now. So it was better to push him away. Hopefully, Michael would accept her decision and take the next flight off the island.

"Sorry if I have come at the wrong time, but I'm not leaving this city till we have talked. And I mean more than 'Hi' or 'Bye.' I've been here for a while now, and if I have to stay longer, so be it. The length of time I stay is up to you, Josie."

She finally looked at him, in the eyes. Those familiar eyes that she remembered from long ago. Those eyes that had once mesmerized her as Michael told her he loved her for the first time. Even time couldn't erase the twinkle Josie had always seen in those eyes of blue. His dark hair now with a heavy mix of gray, along with the subtle lines on his face, showed that he had aged, but he was still as handsome as before, maybe even more so.

As she looked at him, actually studied him for the first time since his arrival in Key West, Josie saw the man she had once hoped to grow old with. To have children and grandchildren with. Suddenly, her feelings were all over the place as she let herself look at him and remember the past. The good and the bad. Josie had to admit that Michael still made her feel weak inside, and she felt the smallest spark of happiness as she finally gave herself permission to realize that he was really here on her porch, determination radiating from the words he spoke.

Josie sighed heavily. "I will listen if it will assuage your guilt. You embarrassed me, Michael, in front of all our family and friends. You lied to me. You broke my heart. So many promises you made to me, and even though time has passed, a very long time, that pain still rears its ugly head now and then. I thought I was healed till you showed up. Now you've put more upheaval in my life that I don't need right now, because there are other things I'm dealing with. So say your peace then leave. Please, just leave." Josie could feel the tears stinging the corners of her eyes but was determined not to let them fall down her cheeks. It was proving to be not such an easy task.

"After you let me talk and you really listen to what I have to say, if you still want me to leave, I promise I will be gone. I will never bother you again. All I ask is that you listen—with your heart, not the past hurt. I know that's hard and probably not fair of me to ask, but please try." Michael looked at her with pleading eyes, and though Josie couldn't find her voice to answer, she nodded.

"Well, I guess I should start at the very beginning. First of all, I'm sorry about the wedding. I should have never run off and not showed up at the church. I should have talked to you the day before when all of a sudden, I had this feeling that everything around me was crashing down. I felt like I was suffocating, and I got scared. We had started the ranch, the cattle were doing fine, but we weren't making any money yet. Then I kept thinking about how I was going to be someone's husband and own my own business. It felt like there was no way I could support both of us, not like your daddy had made me promise when I asked for your hand in marriage. He scared the daylights out of me! But I loved you so much that I told him that I would never hurt you and always make sure you were cared for. I truly believed that and felt like I would always find a way." Michael took a deep breath and sighed, turning to glance across the street before looking back at Josie.

"Anyway, the day before the wedding, at the bachelor party, everyone kept coming up to me saying crazy things like 'Last day of being single' and stupid shit like that. And suddenly that was all I could think about. I panicked. I went home that night, grabbed the suitcase that I was packing for our honeymoon, and took off in the farm truck. I headed west like I was running from a mad bull. Had no idea where I was heading except away from everything I knew. I felt like I needed air. Like I just needed to breathe. Josie, it was the stupidest thing I've ever done, and I've lived with that guilt since. Instead of talking to you, letting you know how I was feeling, I ran. I know that I can't say sorry enough in this lifetime, but I am truly sorry for what I put you through."

Josie sat listening to each word that Michael was saying. She didn't realize how tense every muscle in her body was till she noticed her hands were curled into tight fists as though she wanted to punch something—maybe Michael!

"Do you have any idea how humiliating it was to be waiting at the church, family and friends sitting in the pews, wondering what was the delay? My parents asking me if anything was wrong? Your parents too! They kept asking where you were, and I had no clue. When it was evident you weren't coming, people came up to me one by one telling me how sorry they were and proceeded to call you every name in the book. It was awful. Just thinking of it now makes me nauseous. And when you did show up a week later, you went straight to the ranch! You didn't even come to see me. Michael, we lived in a very small town. I felt like I was getting slapped in the face again. I trusted you with my heart. All you had to do was come and talk to me." There was no holding back the tears now. They flowed down Josie's face, leaving wet streaks across her cheeks.

"I was embarrassed. I knew that you must have hated me by then, and I didn't blame you. I had screwed up royally, and I knew it. If I had thought things through instead of acting impulsively, I would have realized I had a bad case of cold feet. But I was still in love with you. The only thing I could think of as I pulled into town was to get back to work. The whole debacle would just blow over. But it didn't. I had more hate messages on my answering machine than you can imagine."

"No, I can imagine quite a few," Josie said coldly.

"It seemed the only people that didn't know what had happened were the buyers of a large corporation that came the next week. They offered me a great deal for the ranch to be one of their suppliers of beef, one that I couldn't refuse. So I threw myself into work. I promised myself that I was going to come and see you the next week, hopefully so we could work things out. I kept telling myself I needed time. In my mind I finally had this plan for the future, for you and me that sounded right in my head. I felt like I was more in control of things around me. That's when I got the courage to come and see you. It had been over three weeks, and I was hoping that you would have had time to be less angry with me. At least, I was hoping." Michael stopped, closing his eyes briefly as he relived the very painful memories.

"I decided to go to your house, unannounced, which is probably not the best thing in Montana, where it seems everyone owns a gun. I'll never forgot the look on your daddy's face with the shotgun in his hands, your momma in the background with tears in her eyes. I thought I was gonna be dead for sure. But your momma calmed him down quickly. They didn't let me in the house but came outside to talk. I asked where you were, and all they would tell me was that you were gone, and it was all my fault that they had lost their little girl."

At Michael's words, more tears were falling from her eyes. She could see the picture in her mind—her parents defending her on the front porch of their home. Her parents who were gone. They had supported her decision to leave, but she'd had no way of knowing that she would lose them so soon. Josie blamed Michael for that too.

"I couldn't believe it when they told me you had packed up and moved. No matter how hard I begged, they wouldn't tell me where you had gone. I asked everyone or at least tried. Most people wouldn't talk to me for a long time, and your friends were especially pissed—at me for what I had done to you and at you for leaving, not telling anyone where you went. I can understand the reason you left, but why keep secret where you moved to?" Michael looked at her, pondering.

"Because I didn't want to see you. I didn't want to have to deal with the heartache all over again if you ever found me. I didn't want you to say you were sorry and not mean it. I wanted to get away from everyone I knew because it seemed everywhere I went, all I saw were eyes that pitied me. Poor Josie! What will she do now? It was hell, Michael, and I couldn't take it anymore. So I ran. Yes, I ran away from home. You cost me my life, my parents, everything I had in Montana. I came the furthest south I could. On the bus ride here, I had a lot of time to think about how I wanted my new life to be. And when I got here, I found my own place and a little job. I figured this was what I needed to heal. I thought that horrible fiasco was completely behind me till you showed up." Those memories were threatening to break her down to her core once again. But she had to keep it together while she was here with him. Later, Josie told herself, she would allow herself to feel the emotions, as painful as it may be.

"I can see your point. Josie," Michael said with a pause, looking her directly in the face "I really am sorry. I will never be able to tell you that enough, but it is true. All these years I've thought about you. Where you were. How you were doing. If you ever got married and had a family." He paused and looked at her.

"What about you? Did you get married? If you are and you are down here, that's going to be the icing on the cake. You probably haven't changed one bit." Josie's voice was angry now just thinking that he could be cheating on his wife.

"I did get married. No one you knew. I met her on a business trip about two years after you left. We got married, lived on the ranch, and things were nice for a while. I also have a son. He is twenty-two years old, and I couldn't be prouder of him. As far as his momma goes, we are divorced. Have been for over ten years now. She thought she would like living on a cattle ranch, but it wasn't for her. On a trip home to Seattle to see her parents, she met her old boyfriend from high school. They had an affair that I was completely oblivious to until she asked for a divorce. Seth, my son, lives with me now. He loves the ranch and helps run it. I insisted that he get his degree first, which he did." Michael's revelation about his marriage and son took Josie by surprise. Somehow she had thought he would have stayed single just as she had.

"Seth was actually the one that insisted that I come and find you. And if I did, to make things right."

"How does he even know about me?"

"Because I told him. Right after Seth graduated from high school and much to my ex-wife's chagrin, he moved straight to Montana. He wanted to live with me before, but his mom was adamant that he stay in Seattle, saying they had the best schools and culture. Little did she know that her son wanted to be a cowboy. Anyway, about six months ago, he found an old box on a shelf where I had stored some photos and a few other things. He asked about the woman in the picture, and I told him all about you."

"You kept pictures of me?" Josie asked quietly.

"I kept a lot of things that reminded me of you. So once I answered Seth's questions, he got kinda hateful with me. Told me I was a dumbass, and I couldn't really correct the boy, because he was right. He actually started searching for you online and found out that you were working at a resort here in Key West. Not a lot to go on, but from the information the resort listed on their website, along with company pictures, he was sure it was you. Once he showed me, I was so happy to finally see you that I had tears in my eyes. Seth told me I was an idiot if I didn't go after you, and I knew in my heart he was right. I may have married another woman; I may have a successful company. I have a great son. But my life has never been complete. I screwed up so royally, Josie, and I want to make it right. I know that we don't know each other like we did before, but I want to get to know you all over again. I want to be in your life, and I certainly want you in mine. I've waited so long, and I know it was all my fault. Please, I'll do whatever it takes to prove that I won't hurt you ever again. I want to be the man I should have been for you long ago. I just need you to give me a chance. I won't even begin to tell you what Seth said I should do."

"I have to hear this. Tell me," Josie said.

Michael sighed heavily. "He told me that even if you told me to eat shit, I should do it just to prove how much I'm still in love with you. But, please, if I have to eat shit, could you please put it in some kind of pie?"

Josie couldn't help herself. Even with tears spilling down her face, she started laughing. Seth was one smart boy, she thought. And Michael's sincerity seemed genuine. He had been here for over three weeks now. He had been patient. But how do you trust someone that hurt you so badly? Josie had read the books, been to therapists. They all came to the same conclusion: let the past stay in the past. But in reality that was so much easier said than done.

"Tell Seth thank you for the suggestion. But, Michael, I don't think you realize the scope of how bad your betrayal hurt me. It has taken these many years for me to build a life again. I've had a hard time trusting anyone. And now, you share your story, tell me you still have feelings for me, and I'm just supposed to fall back into your arms because you say you love me? Trust has to be earned. You stripped away every bit of that long ago, and the road back is long. If I were to even *consider* talking to you again, we would have to start from scratch. Right now, I need time to digest everything you have told me. And it's late. I have an early workday because our resort is being sold."

"I know," Michael said.

"How do you know about that?"

"Remember my computer-genius son? When he was looking for you, he found out about the sale. He was a business major with a minor in computer science. A very smart one at that. He finished college in three years. He would have graduated high school faster, but his mother refused, holding him back. What are you going to do? Will you be able to keep your job?"

"I don't really want to talk about it right now. I need to go. We will talk more later," Josie said as she walked to her door with Michael right behind her.

"Tomorrow night, here on the porch again?" Michael asked hopefully.

Josie looked up at the face in front of her, wanting to trust the man more than she wanted to admit.

"OK" was all she said as she went in her apartment, shutting the door, with Michael standing right on the other side.

23

For the next hour, Josie sat on her couch, replaying the conversation with Michael. He still loved her after all these years. And he had an ex-wife and a son! That hurt. If he had loved her all this time, how and why did he get married? Apparently his son was OK with his dad finding her, because Seth searched and found her. Most children, even as adults, didn't like it when it came to their parents being with someone new. But Michael had said Seth was smart, and it sounded like he was compassionate too. Still, there were unanswered questions. First, was Michael being truthful about his story? Could she ever trust him again? And the most important one of all—did she really still love him?

The knock on her door startled her and brought Josie back to reality. She looked through the small hole in the door to see Abbey standing there in her pajamas.

"Goodness, girl," Josie said as she opened the door. "What are you doing traipsing around in your PJs?" She opened the door, and Abbey hurried in.

"A really long day. I had already taken my shower and didn't feel like changing to come down to see you. I wanted to make sure you were OK. To say I was shocked when I pulled up and you were actually talking to Michael is putting it mildly. And he was sitting next to you, which was a huge change from the last few weeks. He usually is standing while you completely ignore him." Abbey wanted to ask more but knew she had to let Josie tell her what had happened on her own terms.

"I'm OK. Just a little shocked and confused." Josie wasn't sure what she wanted to share with Abbey at the moment, but when she began telling her about the conversation on the porch, the whole story spilled out. And honestly, it felt good to be able to share it with someone whom Josie felt that she could finally trust after all these years.

"I could see where you could feel a bit lost right now. I can't say I know how you feel, because I've never been in that situation. But, Josie, one thing is for sure. That man still loves you. He tried to find you but couldn't. He got married, but it didn't last. He says his ex liked the city life, but I'm sure his feelings for you didn't help, whether she knew about you or not. Obviously, his son could see his dad still thought fondly about you after all these years when they were looking at those pictures, or he wouldn't have done all the detective work to find you. Put all that together with the fact that he has been here for weeks, coming to see you each day, waiting patiently. Men just don't do that unless they are in love. Or maybe when someone owes them money," Abbey said with a laugh, trying to bring a smile to Josie's face, which she did.

Josie leaned back on her sofa and closed her eyes. So much information at once that she felt completely overwhelmed. "I want to agree with you, but I'm scared. I don't want to go through that hurt and pain again, but I have to admit—I know that I still love him. It might be buried under a lot of hurt right now, but that first day he showed up, I knew. I was mad and angry but happy too. That's what makes this all so damn confusing. My emotions bounce from one feeling to another. It makes me feel like I'm going to snap. I told him I had to give some thought to everything he shared with me tonight. We are going to talk more tomorrow."

"That's a great start! You have to remember that it's going to take time. What the both you of have been through doesn't repair itself overnight. Michael seems patient enough. The question is—are you?"

Before Abbey left Josie with her thoughts, she shared with her what Zach had done by helping her possibly get a table at Mallory Square. Abbey could tell the news helped take her mind off the evening's talk with Michael, because Josie actually gave her a hug before Abbey walked out the door. Abbey was so excited that her persistence was paying off. Josie was coming out of her shell and facing the things she had run away from all those years ago.

"I keep telling you that he is a good boy and that you need to snag him while you can," Josie said with a smile on her face as she talked about Zach. This sounded like Josie giving Abbey motherly advice but also, finally, the talk from a true friend.

"Josie, you are right. Zach is great, and I love spending time with him. But we work together, and office relationships just don't work. I want to keep my job and my friendship with Zach. But he does make it hard at times," Abbey said as she walked out the door.

"Don't wait too long. Time is precious," Josie said as she shut the door.

"Is she finally talking to you?" A whisper came from behind Abbey, startling her so much she about jumped out of her skin.

"My goodness, Ella! You scared the daylights out of me!" Abbey's racing heart started to calm down. "Yes, she finally is. I told you she was a nice woman. Just needed a friend to talk to."

"Well, you have the patience I will never have. I also heard that you had dinner with Garrett again," Ella said, pouting.

"What? I don't know who told you that, but it's not true. Once was enough. He is a sweet man, but he is all about his work, Ella. I already told you that. Who told you we had dinner again?" Abbey was curious.

"Garrett did! I talked to him two nights ago!" Ella was mad now.

"Well, I'm not sure what his motives were, but if I were you, there are plenty of nice men here on this island. Ones that aren't obsessed with fish and turtles." Both women laughed as they said good night. As Abbey stood and watched Ella walk to her apartment, she then glanced back at Josie's door and felt blessed to have such good neighbors. But a talk with Garrett was indeed warranted next time she saw him. He could not use her as an excuse because he didn't want to go out with Ella. That was the only thing Abbey could think of as to why he would have told Ella such a lie. Garret was sweet, but they were only friends. The fantasy that had played in her head that first day she arrived here had completely vanished.

Abbey worked hard over the next few days, making her sculptures each evening and a few paintings to be able to take to the jury selection committee. Zach brought over dinners when he could and even helped her while she was hard at work by getting things she needed and baking the tiny figures. Their conversations were filled with childhood memories, the goals they wanted to reach, places around the world they wanted to visit, and sometimes work, as they would try to figure out issues on their latest project. Abbey enjoyed being with Zach more than she wanted to admit and she sometimes wondered if Josie was right. Abbey still remembered the way she felt when she kissed Zach on the cheek. There was a tenderness that passed from him to her and she couldn't deny that she had a desire for the man that stood across the room with pot holders on his hands, helping her bake the little treasures everyone told her would be a success at the square.

Her evening routine of sitting on the porch with Josie had changed now too. Each evening when she arrived home from work, it was Michael sitting on the front porch with Josie, but now the former couple were talking. Michael had taken Abbey's spot on the porch, and she prayed Josie could make amends in her heart and with her emotions. Even if Josie didn't reconcile with her former love, maybe she would be able to let the hurt stay in the past and move on in her life. Abbey knew that the talks they were having had to be healing for both of them, so she left them alone as much as possible.

On Sunday, as she was coming back from a grocery run, she saw Michael and Josie walking down the street. She wanted to follow them to see where they were heading, but she would wait on Josie to tell her any news. She hoped that they were going out for lunch. If so, this meant they were making progress. Excited, Abbey couldn't wait to ask Josie what was happening. She hadn't talked to her much this week between getting ready for her presentation for the Mallory Square audition and trying to leave them alone to talk on the porch. Plus, Abbey knew by now that Josie liked to be alone with her thoughts, and she didn't want to intrude.

As she grabbed the first bags to haul up the stairs, Zach appeared on his bike.

"Need some help with that, ma'am?" he said, smiling at her. She felt a rush of excitement as she watched him secure his bike and walk toward her. *Ugh, he is so cute*, she thought. *Friends, Abbey, just friends.*

"You are just in time. Guess what? I just saw Josie and Michael walking down the street. They are actually doing something together besides sitting on the porch. They have been talking all week."

"You are really rooting for this guy, aren't you?" he said as he took the rest of the bags out of the Jeep and some from Abbey's hands.

"He seems really nice. Can't say what he did to Josie was acceptable, but he seems genuine in his attempt to make amends.

But we both know how Josie is extremely stubborn. We'll have to wait and see how this plays out. Hopefully with a check in the 'Win' column."

"Are you ready for tomorrow?" Zach asked as they sat the groceries on the table.

Abbey looked over at her growing inventory of figurines and paintings. If she didn't get to sell them at her own artist table, she was going to have plenty of Christmas gifts this year, she thought.

"I think so. I'm getting a bit nervous, but I've already put together what I need to bring to the selection process and to show how I produce my art. Since I won't be able to bake the figurines there, of course, I took pictures on my iPad to show them." She displayed for Zach the presentation she had put together.

"Well, since you are all prepared, why don't we go do something fun today? Let you relax a little. What about going back to the beach? Say for another picnic?" Zach asked hopefully.

Abbey wasn't sure. She felt torn. She certainly would have loved to take a break from all the hard work of the week, both at work and at home. But at the same time, she felt like she should still be preparing or practicing her speech before the committee.

"You know what? That sounds like a great plan to me, but I have a request. Do you mind if I ask Josie and Michael to come? I'm sure she will say no, but it couldn't hurt to ask. Maybe get them out doing something different." Abbey looked at Zach expectantly, and being the sweet guy that he always was, he agreed.

"Calling a bit early. Whatcha need?" Even though she and Abbey were friends now, Josie was still Josie. She had that hard edge when it came to her people skills, but Abbey could see it soften just a tiny bit each time they talked.

"Sorry, but I saw you and Michael walking down the street, and I wanted to catch you before you got too far. Zach and I are going to go on a picnic to the beach. Why don't you two come with us?" Abbey felt like she was walking on eggshells as she asked the question.

The silence on the end of the phone had Abbey thinking that maybe this wasn't the best idea she'd had, but Josie told her to hold just a minute. "OK. We will go. You picking up the food?"

"I sure will. How does one o'clock sound?" Abbey asked excitedly.

"We will drive separate and meet you there." Josie's voice was icy, but Abbey was learning that for Josie, that didn't mean she hated you. It was part of her personality that was still bitter after all these years.

"Perfect! We will see you there!" Abbey turned to Zach with a smile on her face. "I can't believe this! She and Michael are actually going to meet us at the beach. Do you realize how monumental this is? Must mean that they are getting along somewhat. I've been so busy this week that I haven't really had any time to talk to her. Plus, when I got home from work each evening, Michael has been here every night, sitting on the porch, both of them talking, looking friendly. I can only imagine everything they have to talk about after all these years of being apart."

"I'm surprised she hasn't ripped him a new one! That was pretty low, what he did to her!"

"Don't you say anything today. She didn't swear me to secrecy about what happened between the two of them, but I would rather she think I didn't go telling her story. Michael seems to be a good man that made a bad decision. From the bits and pieces Josie has told me, he has loved her this whole time despite getting married and having a child."

Zach looked surprised. "He is married and down here looking for her? That takes some balls!"

"No, he's divorced now. Michael's son actually found Josie for him on the Internet by chance. To me, something like that doesn't just happen. When you are meant to be with someone, things will work out." Abbey looked wistfully out the window and then went back to packing the things they would need for the day. Zach already had the beach chairs and cooler. Abbey grabbed her bathing suit, towels for both of them, and some picnic supplies. All they needed to do was get the food.

"I hope this was a good idea," Zach said as he loaded up Abbey's Jeep. He had intended to spend the day alone with Abbey and was finally going to let her know how he truly felt about her, whether she felt the same way or not. He didn't want to make her uncomfortable, and if things didn't turn out like he hoped, at least he had tried. He kept thinking that if he told her how much she really meant to him, maybe she would see him differently. That was his prayer.

"I guess we shall see how it goes," Abbey said with a smile as they headed down the street, windows down, letting the breeze flow through the Jeep.

24

To say the ride to the beach was tense for Josie and Michael was an understatement. Michael offered to drive, and Josie accepted. From the minute she sat in the passenger seat, more memories from the past flooded her. This reminded her of how they would picnic in the nearby mountains in Montana, just the two of them, where it was simply beautiful. The memory made her smile. Now they had a somewhat agreeable arrangement. Their talks each evening had become more about what they had been doing the years they had been apart. Most of the time, Josie could only see more mistakes Michael had made as he shared his past with her. Her hurt and anger caused her to only see the negative instead of anything good Michael had to say. But he sat there taking every bit of Josie's hurtful remarks and frustrations. This patience was beginning to win her over, but she didn't dare let him know. A small part of Josie was beginning to see the Michael she had known so long ago. The Michael she had never forgotten, if she was truthful to herself. The Michael she wanted back in her life. At times it was hard for her to embrace the feelings that were bubbling to the surface for the man sitting beside her in the car. Even through all the anger and hurt, that love she had felt so long ago for him was starting to seep into her life again, in subtle ways. And though it scared her, it also made her feel alive.

"You will have to tell me where to go." Michael was driving and looking for the sign to the state park, from one side of the road to the other.

"I've already told you where to go once, and you didn't listen, so maybe you will this time." As much as Josie wanted to sound irritated at his request for help, she found that she couldn't help but grin at him. Michael just looked at her, smiling while shaking his head.

"It is coming up here in a minute on the right. You'll see a brick wall sign with the name Bahia Honda State Park." Almost as soon as Josie uttered the words, the sign came into view.

"Turn here and follow the little road around toward the beach, past the gift shop. There will be a parking lot on the left. I'm sure Abbey and Zach are at the picnic benches by the beach."

"Do you come here often? This is beautiful!" Michael said as he drove along the winding road to the parking lot, looking at the scenery.

"When I first moved here, I came often. It's so peaceful here, and I needed time to be by myself. Not that I couldn't find it in the city, but there has always been something about this beach that calls to me. That's why I was glad that Abbey invited us. I wanted to share it with you." Oh, crap! Josie couldn't believe that those words had just left her mouth. She looked over at Michael slowly, and he had a smile on his face. It was one thing to think these thoughts, but to say them aloud, she suddenly felt so exposed.

Josie suddenly wanted to rebuild that wall that she had surrounded herself with in her mind for protection, but she couldn't. It had been way too long. It was time to let go of the hurt and the past. Michael had been patient for over a month. He had explained what had happened. They had gone over it again and again, as much as Josie needed to help her understand. Michael didn't care how much they talked about it. He only said that he wanted to make everything right and be a part of Josie's life again. He had waited too many years, and he was determined not to waste any more time. Josie had felt like the words were all fluff at first, but Michael was good on his promise. He didn't push her. He didn't beg her. He had been a gentleman the entire time since he arrived in the Keys. And he had also told her that since he had given her an account of everything, if she didn't want him there, he would leave. But at least he would leave knowing that he had done all he could to win back the love of his life. Michael really did love her, and nothing would change that. Even though Josie finally admitted to herself that she still loved him, she needed more time.

As soon as they were parked and out of the car, Josie spotted Abbey at the table, waving her hands widely to signal where they were. She smiled again and realized what a wonderful friend she had in the young woman. Josie actually had a friend, she thought. Had it not been for Abbey's persistence, Josie never would have opened up to her, and their friendship wouldn't have blossomed. It had been a long time coming, but maybe Josie's luck was turning around. But that thought scared her too. *One thing at a time*, she told herself as they made their way to the picnic table.

Abbey hugged Josie as soon as they reached the table. "I'm so glad that you guys were able to come. Hi, Michael," Abbey said. "This is my friend, Zach Isler." The two men shook hands.

"Nice to meet you. How are you liking the Keys so far?" Zach asked Michael.

"Starting to like it better and better," he answered as he looked over at Josie. Abbey noticed immediately that something was different between the two people standing before her and had a hard time suppressing a smile. They seemed so right for each other, even though Abbey didn't know Michael very well. But what man would spend over a month just waiting to talk to a woman as stubborn and angry as Josie had been? Abbey had to give him credit for not giving up.

"Hate to ask this, but is there a restroom nearby? Had a bit too much coffee this morning." Michael looked around, trying to see if he could find what he was looking for.

"I'll show you. The food should be fine for a few minutes. We'll be right back," Zach said, giving Abbey a wink.

As the two men walked away, Abbey couldn't wait to start flooding Josie with all the questions swirling around in her head.

"Sounds like you two are getting along! Care to tell me any details?"

"No."

"Ah, come on, Josie. You know you can talk to me. Please?" Abbey was desperate to find out what was going on between the two. She might have been nosy, but she was a hopeless romantic.

"You are a little busybody, aren't you?" Josie said, making sure the food was covered till everyone was back at the table. "Things are better. We've done quite a bit of talking. He has told me that he loves me, always has, and always will, no matter whether I decide to give our relationship another try or not."

Abbey was shocked. "Wow! That's fantastic! You are going to try again, aren't you?"

Josie sighed and stared back at her. "Abbey, it's not that easy for me. I'm scared. All I can remember is the hurt. Being lied to. Humiliated."

Abbey gently grabbed both of Josie's hands, looking her in the eyes. "Josie, let it go. It's in the past. Hanging on to it is only making you unhappy. You deserve some joy and peace. You are a beautiful woman with a caring soul. Let someone who loves you pamper you, take care of you, and be a part of your life." Abbey could see tears starting to well up in Josie's eyes and she didn't want to make her cry. "Besides, he is damn good-looking and very sexy!" That statement had both women laughing when Michael and Zach walked back to the table.

"What's so funny?" asked Zach.

"Girl talk!" Abbey said, looking at Josie and giving her a smile.

The lunch turned out to be much more pleasurable than Abbey had anticipated. All four of them talked about everything, enjoying the food and the nice weather. Before they knew it, two hours had come and gone.

"Are we going swimming before we go home?" Zach asked Abbey, hoping to get some alone time with her.

"It's getting kinda late, especially with my audition in the morning."

"Audition?" Michael asked.

"Abbey is going to be the next great artisan at Mallory Square. She paints and makes figurines. She meets with the judging panel tomorrow to see if her work qualifies. I have no doubt she can do it," Zach said, sounding proud.

"I love it down there. It seems like a different sunset every time I go. The street performers are wonderful, and a few would make great comedians! And there are some mighty talented artists," Michael said. "I'm sure if Zach thinks your art is some of the best, it is," he added graciously.

"When I moved here, being able to show my artwork was one of my first big goals I wanted to accomplish in Key West. Zach helped me by getting the info I needed, and his friend's father is on the jury committee. Maybe this time next week, I'll be a street artist!" Abbey said with her fingers crossed.

"Well, good luck. Your personality will win them over for sure." Michael smiled sweetly at Abbey. *Josie, you are crazy to let this man go*, Abbey thought. But then she hadn't been through the painful circumstances that Josie had endured.

Abbey looked back at Zach. "I'm going to skip the swim today. I'm really sorry."

"No worries. Maybe we can come back in a few weeks, depending on your work schedule. Little starving artist here." Zach gave her a smile and a wink, nudging her in the arm.

"We are going to head back to town. Thanks for the invite. It was nice to come here again. It's been a while since I have visited, even though it is so close by," Josie said as she gathered her things. Michael also said his good-byes, and soon Abbey and Zach were watching the couple leave.

"That turned out much better than I thought. They actually seem to be getting along. Josie was even nice to everyone. I meant that in a good way," Abbey said.

Zach chuckled. "I know what you meant. Guess it's time to get you home so you can rest up and make sure you have everything ready for tomorrow." Zach grabbed the tote bags and rolling cooler before they made their way to the Jeep.

As he walked by her side, Zach so wanted to hold Abbey gently in his arms and just blurt out how he was feeling for her. Maybe he could talk to her on their ride home, but as each minute ticked by, he seemed to be losing his courage.

25

"Thanks for helping me get everything upstairs and also for a wonderful day," Abbey said as they sat the last of their beach things on her floor. Zach suddenly felt a wave of courage. This was it. *If I don't tell her now, I'll just chicken out again and again*, he kept thinking. As he turned to leave her place, he stopped with his hand on the doorknob.

"Abbey? This is probably bad timing, but I have to talk to you." Zach turned to look her in the eyes and took a deep breath.

"I've wanted to tell you this for some time, but when I'm around you, I just seem to lose my nerve. So here it goes." As he continued to look into her eyes, he took one of her hands into his. "You are the best friend I've always wanted. I love spending time with you, being with you, working with you. You are absolutely perfect to me, and I think I am falling in love with you." There. He finally said the words he had rehearsed every day for the last two months.

Abbey stood there looking at him, dumbfounded. She didn't know what to say. Zach was her best friend, and being with him always made her happy. Was she attracted to him? Yes, that was for sure. But she was unable to admit that what she was feeling could possibly be true love though she remembered the tingling left behind from the kisses she had given him on the cheek that day. Zach was basically the perfect guy, but she was afraid to give in to how she felt.

"Wow," she said as he stood there looking down at her. "Zach, you are a terrific guy, and I love spending time with you. You make me laugh, working with you these last months has been a dream, and you are my best friend. But I don't think my feelings match yours. I'm sorry."

Zach stood there looking at her, his beautiful Abbey. He had known that this would be her answer. Even though he could feel the rejection throughout his body, he was glad that he had finally told her.

"I just wanted you to know. I don't want this to change our friendship, OK? You are my best friend, someone I can talk to, and every time we are together, we have so much fun. I don't want to spoil that, and I hope I didn't by telling you what I did. Please, still friends?"

Abbey watched Zach, her wonderful Zach. "Definitely, still friends. Thanks for understanding." She hugged him tight. "One day some girl is going to take you away from me. I hope when that day comes, I will still have my best friend."

"I don't think that will be for quite a while," Zach said with a smile on his face, though on the inside there was no happiness to be had. "Will you be able to get all your stuff to the park in the morning? I took the time off from work so I could help you. Lance actually asked me to, if you can believe that."

"He did?" Abbey said in disbelief though she was still in shock by Zach's declaration of his feelings for her. "I've got it, but I'll meet you at the park, and maybe you could help me get set up."

"I'll be there at nine thirty. See ya, Abbey, and thanks for a fun day at the beach." Zach headed down the steps, and she watched him go. She couldn't quit thinking about what he had told her. He loved her. He was probably the best guy she had ever met. Why couldn't she figure out her conflicting feelings? There was that part of her, body and soul, that wanted a deeper relationship with this man, but another part of her was warning her to stay just friends. Why? As Abbey shut the door to her little piece of the island, she prayed that she wasn't making a mistake with this terrific guy..

Abbey was at the park almost an hour before she was due to be there. She sat in her car rehearsing the small speech she had written for the committee that she would stand before and what she had to present to them. But her thoughts kept wandering back to the conversation with Zach the previous night. He said he was falling in love with her. Though her sleep had been restless thinking about Zach, her concentration had to be on her audition right now. Abbey had gotten up very early to double-check that she had everything she needed for her presentation. But all the excitement and anxiety was taking its toll on her physically, as Abbey felt the nausea set in. *Take some deep breaths*, she told herself as she shut her eyes. The knock on her window made her jump so hard that she was shaking, but then she looked out the window to see Zach standing there, all six feet, two inches of him. For some reason he looked very sexy to her this morning with his blond hair still a bit damp from a morning shower, she supposed.

"Sorry, I didn't mean to startle you, but I thought you would be here early. Let's get you set up and checked in."

As Abbey got out of the Jeep, she gave Zach a hug. "Thanks for being here today. It really means a lot to me." There it was again. That electric feeling when Zach put his arms around her. Between the audition and the feelings Zach was giving her, her anxiety was in high gear.

It didn't take long for Abbey to have everything ready for the jury committee before her. There were ten other artists applying for the chance at a table on the square, and as she surveyed the competition, no one else was making sculptures and figurines. That was a plus for her. When it came time to show the jury panel her artwork, she suddenly was quite calm as she presented how she made her little works of art and did a quick acrylic mixed-media painting of a beach with shells. It wasn't complete, but the committee was able to see the quality of her work. They all thanked her, said she would be notified of their decision within a week, and moved on to the next artist.

"That wasn't as bad as I thought, but I couldn't read their faces or body language. I really don't have a clue as to what their decision will be," Abbey said as they packed up her supplies and artwork.

"I'm sure you will get that permit. Just need to plan your first day on the square so all of us can celebrate," Zach said as he helped her put her inventory in the Jeep.

"Let me find out the verdict before we go planning anything. Right now I think we best get our butts back to work. We have to finish that website by the end of the week. To say there are a few bugs is putting it mildly."

"That is something I have to agree with you there." Zach's voice sounded more monotone and cool today, Abbey noticed. He was nice and basically his usual self, but something was a little off. It had to be the conversation last night and right now there was nothing she could do about it but act as if nothing had happened, and hopefully things would smooth out.

Waiting to hear if she had passed or failed at her audition kept Abbey nervous the rest of the week, each night rushing to the mailbox when she got home, hoping to see a letter from the city. She also noticed that Michael was there every night now, and not just on the porch anymore but spending the evenings with Josie. In the short time since she had moved to Key West, things were already changing. She had finally made friends with the "hateful woman" downstairs, and the best friend she had on the island had made a profession of love to her. Now she was hopefully getting to jump into the unknown but exciting waters of being a professional artist. She wanted someone to talk to, but things were complicated now.

After getting her mail and seeing there was not a letter, Abbey looked over to see that Josie was sitting by herself for the first time in a while, so she headed to the porch to speak to her friend.

"Wow, a little unusual to see you here by yourself," Abbey said with a laugh as she sat down in the rocking chair. Josie didn't laugh or say anything.

"Is something wrong?" Abbey asked quickly, not wanting to upset her.

"No, everything is really fine, actually. I'm just thinking." Josie's tone was a bit unsettling, and Abbey knew something had changed.

"Care to share any thoughts? Been kinda curious about what has been going on with you and Michael."

"Well, my last day at work is in two weeks," Josie began. "And Michael has asked me to move back to Montana with him."

"Whoa! What? Back to Montana?" Abbey couldn't believe her ears. "And your job is gone? What are you going to do?"

"As far as the job, I'm not worried about it. I'm going to rely on those investments I told you about. Not that I would be living in the lap of luxury, but I would be fine. I've been working for thirty-seven years straight, so a little time off sounds good to me. As far as Michael and Montana, I'm still thinking on that one. I'm definitely not moving back north, at least not now." Josie stopped and sighed as she looked over at Abbey.

"I have come to realize that I'm still in love with Michael. I guess I always have been," she said, reaching for Abbey's hand. "But I'm still frightened. Michael wants us to rediscover our relationship again after all these years. My heart is screaming yes, but I feel paralyzed with fear. That is why he isn't here tonight. I told him I needed some time to think. And I wanted to talk to you."

"Josie, no matter what you do in life, you take the risk of getting hurt. Whether it's your job, falling in love, or walking down the street. Choose to be happy. You've let this hurt rule your life for so long, but like I've said before, it's time to let it go. It's time to be happy. I would say you should set some boundaries to make sure his intentions are true and make sure you truly want this next step."

"Like what?" Josie asked.

"Maybe he has to live here for a while. Date all over again as though you just met. Start from the beginning. I know you said you love him, but learn about him like you did all those years ago. Just a few suggestions." Abbey didn't want to be too forward, but she knew that was what she would do.

"I had already thought of the idea of him living here. His son and manager are taking care of his cattle ranch back home, so that shouldn't be a problem. At least here, we are away from everyone that knew us as a couple. It would give us time to see if this is real love or just infatuation."

"See, you are already thinking without fear. I know that you will do the right thing for you."

"And what about you, Abbey? What about Zach?" Josie looked at her with curious eyes.

"What do you mean?" she said as she started going through her mail nervously one more time.

"You know what I mean. Anybody that has eyes can see that that boy is in love with you, and you feel the same way. Admit it. I can tell every time you two are together." Josie sat rocking in the chair, staring out toward the street as usual while saying the words Abbey wasn't sure she wanted to hear. Abbey couldn't believe Josie's uncanny ability to read people.

"Josie, we are just good friends. Best friends, actually...but he did tell me last night that he loved me."

"Well, what did you say?"

" I see him as a great friend, someone that I can fully be myself with, no judgment. Even a shoulder to cry on if I had to. I'm not sure about the 'in love' part but I can't see myself without Zach in my life. I've never felt such conflict with my feelings for someone. My last boyfriend, Max, I knew the moment I saw him that he was the one I wanted. Or at least I thought so. We were together two years, and the love thing was more just 'because we are together' than that true soulmate love. He was so good-looking, and things started out great. He was treating me like a princess, and then we just got in a rut, and things went stale. I don't want to do that again."

Josie stopped rocking the chair and looked Abbey in the eyes. "Sounds like you need to take some of your own advice, young lady. You might be happy, loving it down here, but you are afraid too. Maybe not like me. I've had more time to let things stew, but you are afraid of risks also. That man loves you. He's fun to be around, has a wonderful personality, makes you laugh, listens to you, helps you, cares for you. And if you would allow yourself to step off this so-called perfect path you have so carefully planned for your life, you'll admit it to yourself—you feel the same way about him. You are in love. What was it you said to me one day? I had built a wall around my life to keep myself protected? Looks like you have built a wall around your heart for some reason. Now all you have to do is ask yourself why and start tearing it down."

Abbey sat back in the chair, feeling like she had been punched in the gut. Josie was right, but why? Why was there a fear of a relationship? Just because things hadn't worked out with other men she had dated didn't mean they all would be like that. As she was thinking about what Josie said, she looked through her mail one more time. Suddenly, she saw the envelope.

"It's here! I must have passed it over the first time!"

"What? The letter from the city?" asked Josie. "Open it!"

The smile that flashed across Abbey's face told Josie what she wanted to know. Abbey had gotten the permit to sell her artwork. She was happy for the younger woman but hoped this news wouldn't replace their earlier conversation.

"So when is your first day on the square? But more importantly—when are you going to tell Zach you love him?" Josie smiled at her.

Abbey heard Josie's words, but all she could think about was the letter in her hand. "I was accepted! I've got to call Zach!" She reached for her things, and before she left the porch, she bent down and gave Josie a hug. "Thanks for the talk. I won't forget about what you said. But don't forget about what I said about love. You deserve it, Josie."

"You do too, Abbey."

26

Since she had enough inventory between her figurines and paintings, Abbey decided that her official opening day would be the upcoming Saturday. She had never thought that after living here a little over three months, she would already be an artist selling in Key West. In the plan Abbey had made while driving down here, her goal was to be there on the square within one year. She really had to give Zach all the credit for finding out the information and helping her. He truly believed in her. Even though she was scared, Abbey had done the first part, auditioning. Now to see if the islanders and the tourists would really love her work. She would find out on Saturday.

When she called Zach that night to tell him about the letter with the enclosed permit, he was more than excited for her. "There was no doubt in my mind" was the first thing he said. He offered to help her set up her booth with its display, but Abbey felt a bit awkward accepting his assistance after he had expressed how he really felt about her. Actually, the whole week had been a little odd, even though they both tried to act like nothing had happened. Their working relationship and friendship had felt strained. They still talked and worked great together, had lunches, spent time with each other after work almost every night. But it felt different for Abbey.

Was she feeling guilty, or was it something more? She kept thinking about her conversation with Josie on the porch about giving Michael a chance. Should she give herself a chance? When she thought about Zach, Abbey felt this rush of excitement pulse through her. Why wouldn't her mind let go of the "plan" she had in place for her life? Zach was the kind of man every woman dreamed of, and he was right there on her doorstep. But it was too early in her new town to even entertain a relationship, Abbey thought. It would be too many changes at once so for now she would put Zach's words out of her mind.. Her event on Saturday was just around the corner, so Abbey put all her energy into making sure her first show on Mallory Square was going to be perfect.

Abbey made a list of the things she needed and went shopping the next evening after work: a sturdy folding table, a pale-colored tablecloth that would showcase her sculptures well, and a folding screen to place behind her for her artwork display. She also wanted to get a small, battery-operated, portable fan, because the days were getting warmer, and she would be in the sun for a portion of the time.

She had a rolling tote bag that would store her money, snacks, water, and iPad. Since time was of the essence, she quickly printed her own business cards on the computer. She applied for her Florida tax license online, which gave her permission to sell after she printed up the temporary form. It seemed like she had everything in place for her first show.

Everyone from work, even Donna, Lance's wife, was excited for her, and they were coming to her opening-day celebration, which made Abbey feel even more excited about the upcoming weekend. Garrett wasn't in town, being out on the boat again for a week, and Ella had to work. But Josie and Michael were coming. As Abbey took a minute to try to relax on Saturday morning, she couldn't believe all the friends she had made in the short time she had lived here. They were her cheerleaders, with Zach leading the charge. They were going to help her celebrate tonight, and she felt so blessed that she had found good people to surround herself with.

When Abbey called to tell her parents, they were so excited and proud. They wanted to come to see their baby girl start her new venture, but there was no way to get there in time. Abbey promised them a FaceTime call once her display was set up, giving them a tour of her booth. It was only a few months before they were coming for a visit, and she couldn't wait. Her parents were staying for a whole week. Abbey wanted them to stay with her, but they insisted that they were going to stay in one of the hotels downtown. Her mom and dad had decided that their visit to their only daughter was going to be a second honeymoon, since Abbey had to work during the day. She couldn't blame them. The resorts off Duvall Street were beautiful, and one day she wanted to treat herself to a weekend of luxury even though she lived in the city.

Everything was packed and ready. She really needed a nap, Abbey told herself, but as she lay down to close her eyes, her excitement kept her awake. Instead, she took her shower and got dressed for the evening. Just as she pulled her bright-pink maxi dress over her head, she heard a knock on the door. A look at the clock told her that it was too early for Zach. He was coming to help her get everything to the Jeep and then set up on the square. She looked through the peephole in the door to see Josie standing on the other side. This was the first time she had ever visited Abbey's little place.

"Hey there! Come in! Sorry everything is such a mess. I usually keep things pretty orderly, but I've been flying around here trying to get everything together and organized. I probably should have waited till next week for my first show." Abbey was talking nervously. She had wanted Josie to visit several times, and now her apartment looked like a train wreck.

"Don't worry about all that. I know you have been pretty busy. Not like you have something big going on tonight," Josie said as she smiled at Abbey.

"Have a seat," Abbey said as she motioned to the only empty chair in her living room. "How are you?"

"I'm fine. Looking forward to tonight, and I have something for you." She pulled out a small box wrapped beautifully with a silver bow and presented it to Abbey.

"Oh, Josie, you shouldn't have. Thank you," she said as she unwrapped the small ribbon tied around the box. When she opened the lid, inside was a beautiful silver dolphin on a chain. It looked as though it were jumping out of the water and had a small blue stone for an eye. It was gorgeous.

"This is beautiful! It will go wonderfully with my outfit tonight." She quickly removed the little dolphin from the box and put it around her neck, where it fell just below her collarbone. She went over to the mirror and looked. It was perfect. She turned and quickly hugged her friend.

"I wanted to give you this for a couple of reasons," Josie said as they both sat back down. "First, it is your artist debut, and I feel like I need to stand in for your parents tonight since they couldn't be here. Secondly and most of all, it's a thank-you.

"You have become the friend and daughter I never had. I was so hateful and mean to you when you first moved here. It is hard for me to believe that I'm sitting here with you giving you this pendant after the way I treated you. Most people would have just ignored me, and to tell you the truth, that is what I was hoping you would do, but I'm glad you didn't stop pestering me. Your parents raised a wonderful daughter, and I plan on telling them that when they get here. Thanks for being my friend, Abbey. You don't know how much it means to me. You have helped me to start living my life again. Until you moved here, I just existed. I really didn't know how stuck I was in so much self-pity and anguish. I was miserable but thought I was fine. I definitely wasn't happy, but it didn't matter to me. Now it does. I want to be happy. I want to have new experiences, even though sometimes it feels like I have waited too long. I can't get those years back, but I can start where I am now. Seeing you achieve your dreams has ignited some old dreams of mine. Now that I'm going to be without a job, maybe it's time to give them a try like you are doing tonight. So thank you."

Abbey was glad she hadn't applied any makeup just yet as tears slipped down her face as Josie talked. She was thinking back to that first day when Josie had brushed her off so hatefully, and now here they were, sitting across from each other, crying happy tears.

"Josie, thank you for being my friend. We might have had a tough start, but you are helping me too. You mean a lot to me, and I knew that day I met you that we would be friends. Just wasn't sure how long it would take!" They both laughed as they wiped tears. "And I want to thank you and Michael for coming tonight. Speaking of Michael, has any more progress been made on that front?"

"I'm actually seeing him for the first time tonight since last Wednesday. We have spoken briefly on the phone, but I think it may be time to have a heart-to-heart talk after your big celebration." Abbey watched as Josie talked, and she could tell her friend was tense. Josie was wringing her hands back and forth.

So here they were: Abbey stressed about her first art show along with the conflicted emotions about Zach, and Josie's anxiety coming from the talk she was going to have with Michael. At least they both had each other to lean on, Abbey thought as she considered their situations.

"Going to give me a preview about what you are going to say to Michael?" Abbey asked hopefully.

"No, I'm going to talk to him first, but I promise to let you in on the details later. Right now I need to let you go finish getting ready. Won't be long before your Prince Charming will be here to help you." Josie looked at Abbey with her eyebrows raised, while Abbey just shook her head.

"Josie, not now. All I'm focused on is tonight's show."

"Don't wait too long, Abbey. You might not get a second chance. Take it from an old lady who waited so long because she was stubborn and wouldn't give in to her true feelings. If I had long ago, we probably wouldn't be sitting here having this conversation. I just don't want you to look back and wonder why. Zach is a good man. And besides that, he's very easy on the eyes!"

"Josie!"

They both laughed before she left, while Abbey twirled the little dolphin on the silver chain around her neck.

As Abbey continued getting ready for the evening, Josie's parting words had her thinking about Zach again. In her mind, things felt so complicated where he was concerned. She couldn't sort her feelings about what she should do—was this part of her plan, or should she just be spontaneous and see if a relationship with Zach would work? Abbey couldn't remember a time in her life where she was so unsure of a situation, which caused her so many uneasy emotions. Maybe she was afraid of getting hurt like Josie did. She could never see Zach doing that, but she had already made a terrible assessment of Garrett, even though he was a sweet man.

Once again, she had to clear her mind and focus on her task tonight: to have the best first showing on Mallory Square. She would have to put these thoughts about Zach and her feelings on the back burner for a little while.

27

This time Abbey knew the knock on the door was Zach. He had arrived to start loading her Jeep with all she would need for this special night. She had bought convenient plastic tubs to store her artwork in that she positioned on a rolling luggage cart. The cart would also hold the wire rack that would display her artwork behind the table with her figurines. Everything else she needed fit right into her rolling tote. As she looked around one more time at the items on the floor and looked over the checklist she held in her hand one more time, Abbey felt like she was as prepared as she would ever be.

In no time flat, Zach had everything down in her vehicle. There was just enough room for the two of them.

"Are you ready?" he called up to her as she was walking out the door. Abbey suddenly felt uneasy, questioning why she was doing this. Was she good enough? Would people like her art? Would she sell anything? Was it worth the stress? *Stop it*, she yelled to herself. *You've come this far, and there is no turning back.*

Her goal was to be completely set up by five o'clock. Sunset wasn't till 7:35 p.m., but she wanted to be there early for the nightly lottery that determined the spot among the rest of the artists. It was based on seniority, and with her being one of the newest people there, her location was unknown. But she felt that no matter where she was, it would be OK. Abbey was just excited to be there!

Abbey knew some of the artists already there, because since moving to Key West, she had become a regular visitor. She loved the square, and Zach was with her most of the time. They would watch the sunset and usually talk about some of the "costumes" they saw people wearing. And it seemed the two of them always had an ice cream before heading home. But tonight was a different ball game altogether. She was on the other side of the table tonight, being a vendor instead of a visitor or tourist. As she climbed into the Jeep, her nerves were still on edge, and she could feel a panic attack coming on.

"Are you OK?" Zach said, looking at her. Abbey had suddenly turned very pale.

"I think so. Just feeling extremely panicky. Almost like I can't breathe." Abbey knew she was hyperventilating.

Zach looked around the vehicle but couldn't find anything like a bag for her to breathe into. "Abbey, cup your hands like this." He showed his hands put tightly together and placed over his nose. "Put your hands over your nose and mouth. Then take some slow, deep breaths." Abbey did as he instructed, watching his face the whole time for reassurance.

"You've got this tonight. I know you're nervous, but just remember this is what you wanted to do, and your artwork is phenomenal. I can't wait for you to share it with the world. This is just the first step to 'Creations by Abbey Wallace.' How is that for a business name?" He kept talking, trying to take her mind off the waves of uneasiness until she finally calmed down. Zach could see the color pouring back into her face.

"Now, let's switch places," Zach said, getting out of the Jeep and walking to the driver's side. "I think it would be better for me to drive right now."

Still trying to calm down, Abbey nodded as she got out and slowly walked to the passenger side.

She felt much more relaxed now as they made their way toward the water and the pier. Anyone would be nervous, she told herself. But Abbey couldn't quit thinking about how Zach had completely erased the jitteriness that was threatening to consume her earlier. She looked over and watched him as he drove, thinking about the wonderful man sitting next to her. Now her pulse quickened, but not because of the art show. Abbey was slowly embracing the realization that what she felt for Zach was more than mere friendship. Maybe she was even in love with him. But she had to think about this later. There was too much going on right now to give this new emotion the time it deserved. Abbey knew now that it was something she had to face, but instead of uneasiness, it made her happy inside. She felt a little giddy, and a smile graced her face unknowingly as she watched Zach.

"What's wrong? Are you OK now?" Zach asked as he stopped at the red light and realized she was looking at him strangely.

"I'm OK. It was just an intense moment of high anxiety. But I'm calmed down now. Thanks to you! I don't know what I would do without you, Zach." Abbey reached over and kissed him, not on the cheek this time but on the lips. She pulled back, startled at her actions, and she could tell Zach was shocked too.

"I'm sorry! I just—" She was stammering around for the right words to say, but nothing was coming to her brain. What was wrong with her? And a kiss on the lips? Now? The best thing about it was that it felt so right.

A honk from the car behind them brought them both back to the present. Zach stared at her for a moment but then acted as though everything was normal as he stepped on the gas. "It's about time to get everything set up. We want it looking great before everyone shows up to celebrate."

"Yes," Abbey said slowly, still thinking about the kiss and how it had sent shivers through her body.

As they set up her little spot, Abbey was more than happy with the mobile cart she had decided to purchase—and with Zach's help. She probably would eventually get the hang of doing this by herself, but she was so happy to have Zach's help tonight. As they set up her display, she kept glancing at him, studying him. His hair. His eyes. The muscles of his arms. His denim jeans that fit him so well that, to her, he had the body of a toned athlete. Even the way he moved as he put the backdrop rack behind her table was sexy. She felt like she was looking at a different man tonight. The realization that her feelings for Zach were stronger than she had admitted to herself was dawning on her little by little as she watched him. She also replayed over and over in her mind, the kiss that had taken place in the car.

"Grab your phone. Let's get some pictures before everyone shows up. Your display looks awesome." Zach grabbed her up in a bear hug and swung her around. "OK, go behind your table, and let me get some pics!"

He took what seemed like a hundred pictures, even though it was only a few. But before Abbey knew it, people were already coming by her table, asking all sorts of questions. Most importantly, they were buying! They bought her little sea-creature sculptures and one painting. Suddenly, she looked up to see Donna, Randy, and Everly arriving with Lance, who was carrying a sizable insulated bag with a smile on his face.

"Your display is fantastic! Abbey, you look right at home. I brought a little celebration drink to toast your first day as an artist at the square," Lance said, holding the bag up. Inside were plastic cups along with a bottle of champagne and a bottle of wine. "Thought I would bring both, since I wasn't sure what everyone liked. As long as we can make a toast to you."

"Do you mind if we wait till Josie and Michael get here, my neighbor and her friend?" Abbey asked tentatively.

"Of course. We are going to walk around just a bit, because it seems you have some more customers, young lady." Lance glanced over her head at the people standing in front of her table.

Zach couldn't help but watch Abbey as she interacted with the people. She was warm and friendly, telling them stories of her art and why she loved what she did. They were drawn to her like bees to flowers, and the proof was the sales she was making. At this rate, Abbey wasn't going to have much left to sell, but she had already planned that she wouldn't be back till next Saturday. This weekend was more of test to see if this was something that would work for her and to gauge how people reacted to her artwork. As Zach continued to watch her, he knew even more deeply that he loved this woman. And the small kiss they had shared on their way here had him even thinking of her more. He wished he could interpret what had happened in the Jeep only a few hours ago.

"Looks like you are sort of a hit tonight," Josie said as she and Michael suddenly stood before her table. Abbey came quickly around the table and hugged her friend tightly. Then she reached over and hugged Michael too. Abbey could tell he wasn't expecting it, but he didn't shy away from it either.

"Thank you both for coming. I'm still overwhelmed about this whole thing, but it really has been so much fun. My artwork is actually selling!" she said excitedly, and Josie couldn't help but smile.

At Josie's prompting, she remembered that she was supposed to FaceTime with her parents, so Zach grabbed her iPad, and Abbey dialed in. But all she had time to say was "Hi" before there were more people standing before her table.

"Hi, Mr. and Mrs. Wallace. I'm Zach, Abbey's friend. I'm going to zoom back just a bit and show you what your daughter is doing. Abbey is a hit with the tourists and locals tonight. I think she might sell out of everything she made!" Zach gave Abbey's parents a quick little tour of her space and then showed them a bit of Mallory Square.

"Abbey tells me that you are coming down in a few months. This is a fun place every night, so I'm sure she'll be bringing you here, but not while she is in work mode. Oh, here is Abbey. Nice to meet you!" he said quickly as he handed the tablet back to Abbey.

"I'm so sorry, but things have been much busier than I expected, in a good way. I sure wish you were here though." Abbey looked lovingly at her parents on the screen and suddenly had a twinge of homesickness.

"Not much longer," her mom said. They quickly said their good-byes as Abbey wiped a small, happy tear from her eye.

By now the sun had set, and all her friends were gathered around her table. Lance had dispensed a drink for everyone. Then he began.

"Here's to Abbey! May you have the best success out here, my dear! You deserve it!" Everyone cheered in agreement, clinked their cups together, and took a sip of their drinks. Abbey was on an adrenaline high.

"I want to say something," Abbey started. "I want to thank each of you for coming out here tonight for the support. You believed in me and gave those nudges to give this a try, especially Zach," she said, glancing his way. "I couldn't have done this without all the encouragement. Thank you from the bottom of my heart." There were hugs from everyone before they left the square, leaving just her, Zach, Josie, and Michael.

"I'm proud of you. Like I told you this morning, I feel like a proud parent even though you aren't my child. But if I had a daughter, I would want her to be just like you," Josie said as she hugged Abbey and gave her a kiss on the cheek. Then she whispered in her ear, "Now it's time for me and Michael to have a little talk. Say a little prayer for me." Josie pulled away and smiled mischievously at Abbey, who grinned back at her friend.

Abbey and Zach watched as the couple walked away. "Do you think they will get back together?"

"I think we might know after tonight. Josie said they are going to have 'a talk' tonight."

"Whoa, that sounds ominous. Hope Michael is prepared for the ride," Zach said sarcastically. Abbey punched in the arm and laughed.

"Ready to pack this up?" he said, looking at the table before them. There wasn't much left, and they both stood in front of the table grinning. She was so excited to know that people really loved what she was creating. She didn't even have a clue how much money she had made, and right now it didn't matter. She was happy that it had been a success, but more importantly, she had stepped out of her comfort zone. Abbey had really done something she had always dreamed of. And she couldn't have done it without Zach.

Suddenly, she knew and she was sure. A feeling came over her and warmed her from head to toe. Abbey was in love. That tingling love she had dreamed about that made someone shiver just to be near that special person. The revelation didn't surprise her because she was finally accepting what she had known in her heart all along. It was like she was seeing him with fresh eyes. The growing feelings she had for Zach were now free. She wouldn't hold them back any longer. But would he believe her when just a week ago she denied what she felt, claiming to be only friends? She hoped so, because if his feelings had changed, she would dread to deal with the heartbreak. But that was a chance she was willing to take, because she couldn't wait to tell him.

28

Josie and Michael walked down Duval Street, not talking but watching the people around them. Josie didn't know where to start, but a crowded street wasn't the setting she had imagined during these last few days of thinking. They finally found a little restaurant with an outdoor seating area that would give them some privacy. Also, it was in a public place that would give her a little more courage. Josie had taken the time to plan what she wanted to say to Michael, but now as she sat across the table from him, the words felt jumbled in her head. He looked so handsome tonight. Michael had completely adopted the island life, clothes and all. When Josie looked at him, she could remember the twenty-something guy she had fallen in love with. Through the bad memories, some of the more happy times were beginning to surface. Even though they had both aged, Michael still was rugged and sexy like he was thirty years ago. At fifty-seven years old, he still could turn the heads of most women he happened by.

"What are you thinking about so intensely?" Michael said as he looked across the table at her.

"A lot of things, but first, thank you for coming to Abbey's big opening tonight. If it wasn't for her, we wouldn't be sitting here at this table. You might not know her as well as I do, but I'll let you in on a little secret. She is your number-one supporter on this island." Josie took a sip of her sweet tea and continued to look into Michael's eyes.

"Here I was hoping you would say you were my number one," Michael countered, leaning back in the chair.

"Michael, we need to talk."

"I thought that is what we have been doing for weeks now."

"No, I mean a serious talk. About my future and yours. I needed these past couple of days to sort out all the emotion and memories you brought back into my life that day you walked on the porch and startled me. I still can't believe your son was able to track me down so easily."

"Oh, it wasn't that easy. It took him a few months, remember? I kept telling him to give up, but he is very determined when it comes to some things. I guess we became his 'project.' Hopefully one day you will be able to meet him. I know he sure wants to meet you." Michael sat quietly, waiting for Josie to make the next move in this tense conversation.

"This is so complicated. I had this whole speech planned out in my mind. Things I wanted to say, and now as we sit here, I'm more confused and have completely lost my train of thought." Josie sighed, closed her eyes, and took a deep breath. *I can do this*, she told herself.

"Michael, I won't deny the fact that I still love you. Even though you hurt me the way you did, I finally found the courage to admit that I have always loved you. I've missed you each day. But I didn't realize it till the day you showed up at my home. I had put you on a shelf in my mind and tucked you away. You were a part of my past, a bad part, and since it was over with, I moved on—or at least I thought I had. I came here. I built a life for myself. I have, or should I say had, a good job and made some good investments. I only have one more week before I'm unemployed, but they have offered me a great severance package, and with my other accounts, I actually can live here and not work for a while. I have had dreams of doing something different for some time now. Things I had thought about trying when I was younger. I think it may be time to pursue those dreams, since I'm about to be jobless. But when it comes to you and me, I'm torn about letting you back into my life. How do I know you won't hurt me again? Run off? Get scared? A person's basic personality doesn't change."

Michael leaned forward and took Josie's hand in his. At first she wanted to pull away, but the feel was comforting and her hand fit perfectly in his. Like two magnets that were finally connected. "I have changed. Do I get scared? Hell yes! But I've grown up. I was an idiot. I already told you about my craziness around our wedding day. I just got cold feet. And I took for granted that you would always be there when I was ready. When you left and I couldn't find you, it was sheer torture for me. But as the months went by, I realized my mistake and did my best to move on, just like you did. There was nothing else I could do. Yes, I got married, and I did love her, but it was different from the love I had with you. I can't explain it. The best thing that came out of my marriage is my son. Seth is wonderful, and I feel so blessed that he wants to work with me in Montana. He loves the ranch and actually reminds me of myself at that age, except I don't think he would leave the love of his life stranded at the altar.

"I want us to start over again. Just as though we are dating for the first time. I want to be with you, Josie, only you. Please give us a chance. A lot of time has passed, and I don't want another minute to go by without you by my side."

Josie could feel the last of the ice melting from around her heart with each word Michael spoke. They were exactly what she wanted so desperately to hear. "I want to be with you again. I can't believe I'm saying this after all these years, but I do want to be by your side. But I can't move back to Montana. My life is here in Key West, at least right now. If we are going to give this a second try, it would have to be here. Away from where we started last time. I know it would be hard to make a relationship work long-distance, but I can't go back to Montana right now. I have to know that this is real and know your feelings are true before I can think about changing things in my life. I'm sorry."

Josie watched as Michael's smile grew so big within seconds. He quickly brought Josie's hand to his lips and kissed it. "That's all I need to hear, and there is nothing to be sorry about. I'll move here. I'll rent an apartment, and we will date, just like teenagers. We will start from the very beginning."

"Are you serious? What about the ranch and Seth? What about everything back home? Are you running away again?"

"Josie, you got to start thinking a bit more positive. I'm not running away from anything. I have a general manager that runs the ranch for me. I also have a small farm store I own with its own manager. Seth handles the books for both businesses and reports in to me. How do you think I've been able to stay this whole time here waiting, hoping for you to come around and give me a chance?"

Josie was a bit stunned by his news, but one sentence caught her attention. "Waiting for me to come around? That was a bit assuming and arrogant, don't you think?" This was it. This was what she had been waiting for. A remark or something to let her know that letting her guard down with this man was a mistake.

"Sorry, I used the wrong words. I'm really sorry! I was sure hoping you would come around, so I was prepared to stay for as long as it took. I love you, Josie, and I'm not going to take no for an answer. I want to be with you for the rest of my life, and if that means moving here for now, dating again, then that is what I intend to do. I made plans with Seth and my general managers before I left. Seth is really the only one that knows all the details, and every day when we check in, he bugs me about what is going on. His girlfriend, Leah, keeps telling him to leave me alone."

With that last statement, Josie couldn't help but laugh. She looked at Michael and smiled. "Well, Mr. Garner, I would love to get better acquainted with you. I think this is a very promising first date, wouldn't you agree?"

Josie could see Michael's happiness as it shone through his entire face. More importantly, it was the first time in so long she had felt excited about something in her life.

"I think it is the best first date I have ever had."

29

"So, how do you think it's going with Josie and Michael?" Zach asked as they were putting the last storage box into Abbey's Jeep.

"I don't know for sure, but I think Josie has softened up quite a bit where he is concerned. She still loves him, you know. He might have hurt her pretty badly, but it was long ago. Plus, Michael is pretty persistent. He keeps telling Josie he isn't leaving till she agrees to go out with him again. He claims that he is still in love with her."

Like I am with you, Zach thought as he watched Abbey put her small tote in the backseat. "Wouldn't that be difficult unless she moves back to Montana?"

"Or he could move here. You never know." Abbey shut the door and leaned against the vehicle. She was tired but exhilarated too. But most of all, now that the crowds were thinning out, basically gone from the beautiful square, Abbey wanted to talk to Zach, just the two of them by the water of the pier. She saw a perfect place for them to sit and enjoy the nice breeze blowing off the water as they watched the lights from passing boats.

"You want to go sit by the water before we head home?" she asked as she looked at Zach. "Unless you had something else planned."

"Nothing else for me tonight. I was just going to help you unload your stuff when you got back to your place, then head home. Going skiing with the guys tomorrow, at least they say skiing. Probably end up on a sandbar somewhere playing Frisbee. You want to come? You know you are always welcome." He was being so matter-of-fact that Abbey was losing her nerve about telling him how she felt. Last week she had said she wanted to be friends, and now she wanted to tell this wonderful, caring man standing beside her that he was the love of her life.

"Let's go sit on the side of the pier. I love listening to the water."

They walked side by side to the edge by the water. There were very few people around, which gave them more privacy but also helped her gather the courage to express her feelings to Zach. But she hadn't given much thought to how she wanted to tell this man she was crazy in love with him. Why she had waited, she didn't know and right now didn't care. She only knew that the closer they came to the spot where they would be sitting, the more excited and nervous she became.

They sat on the edge of the pier, their legs dangling over the edge but still high above the water. Abbey looked over at

Zach as he watched a lighted sailboat go by. "It is beautiful tonight. I can't thank you enough for all your help. None of this, my own spot on the square, the sales, my artwork being shown—everything wouldn't have been possible without you, Zach."

"I'm just glad to be of service. I aim to please," he said jokingly.

"Seriously, you have become such a great friend. You are one of the most caring people that I know. You are great with everyone, and they all love you. Your personality makes every person you come in contact with smile. You are always quick to help out anyone. You are really special."

"Thanks. That means a lot coming from you."

OK, Abbey, you can do this. Just tell him, she told herself. Her thoughts kept repeating in her mind, as there was silence between them.

"I love you, Zach."

"I know. You already told me, and you are my best friend too. I can talk to you easier than any of my other friends," Zach said, continuing to gaze out over the darkened waters.

"No, Zach, you don't understand. I'm in love with you." Abbey sat there looking at him as he slowly turned his head to stare at her.

Zach couldn't believe what he heard. As he looked at her, she was smiling, and her eyes seemed to sparkle. She was beautiful, sitting here in the low light of the streetlamps and the moon up above. He was hoping, no, praying that she meant what he thought.

"But you said—" was all Zach could say before Abbey leaned over and kissed him softly on the lips. As she pulled away, she finally knew what she wanted to say.

"I'm in love with you, Zach Isler. You are my best friend, but you are also the man I love. When you told me last week that you loved me, I was taken aback. I didn't plan on getting involved with anyone once I moved here. I had this grand scheme of working, just enjoying life a bit slower and simplifying everything. Then I met you. We became coworkers and, before I knew it, best of friends. You have shown me more in the last three months what a friend is than I think I've ever known. But when you told me you loved me, I was confused. I had these rules in my mind: no dating at work, and stay single for a while. So I wouldn't allow myself to give in to the feelings I knew were there. But this whole week, every time I saw you or we did something together, even talking on the phone, it all felt different. I could see and feel that our relationship was moving in a different direction. Then I got some great advice from Josie."

"You're kidding. Josie?"

"Yep. That I would be crazy if I let you slip away from me. She said that she didn't want to see me go down a similar path as she had, being lonely and not having anyone to share life with. She thinks you are the best guy around. Except for Michael." Abbey laughed as she looked out at the water.

Zach looked out into the dark harbor once again in silence. Abbey wished she could get inside his head and find out what he was thinking. Suddenly he stood up and reached his hand down toward Abbey. She grabbed it and stood, facing him.

The happiness Zach was feeling was indescribable. As they stood facing each other, he looked at her, tucking a loose strand of hair behind her ear that was blowing in the wind. "Abbey, I think I have loved you from the day you stepped into the office. I even watched you out the window as you walked back to your Jeep that day. I have never felt this way about another woman. I have dated others, but until you came along, I never felt real love." He put one hand sweetly on her cheek, wrapping his other arm around her waist, pulling her gently toward him. As he kissed her tenderly on the lips, a surge of love for this woman coursed through him. "I love you, Abbey. More than you can imagine."

This time Abbey wrapped both her arms around his neck, bringing him even closer to her and the kiss that ensued was long, deep, and full of passion. Neither of them cared if anyone was around. It was a kiss that solidified their relationship. He continued to kiss her. On her cheeks, down her neck, and back to her lips. Every part of her felt like she was on fire, sizzling from head to toe. There was no indecision in her heart now. Zach was hers, and she was his. Everything felt right.

30

Josie and Michael watched the Jeep pull up and park right outside the gate. They were sitting on the porch and talking with no lights on, enjoying the bright, moonlit night. They agreed that this had been their first "official" date and decided that they would take it slow, not planning anything, and learn about each other all over again.

As Josie watched Abbey and Zach get out of the vehicle, she put her finger to her lips to signal Michael to be quiet. And what she witnessed made her smile. Zach couldn't get around to Abbey's side of the car fast enough before they were both embraced in a steamy kiss. Josie looked over at Michael and mouthed the words "I told you so" to him, and he just smiled along with her.

"Hello, lovebirds!" Josie said rather loudly.

Zach and Abbey were so startled that they almost tripped through the gate. "Goodness, Josie, you scared me!" Abbey said, straightening her dress to make herself look presentable.

"Hey there, Zach," Josie said slowly and cheekily.

"Hi," he said, sounding a bit embarrassed.

"Looks like Abbey wasn't the only one to have a good night," Josie continued, teasing the couple like they had been caught misbehaving. She noticed that Abbey and Zach had the happiest, silliest looks on their faces. They both seemed to glow, and Josie couldn't wait to find out more details from Abbey about what had taken place after she and Michael had left this evening.

"I guess I could say the same for both of you," Abbey said to the couple sitting in the rocking chairs. "Sitting outside, under the moonlight, porch light off. Do you need a chaperone?" Abbey giggled as she talked. "I want to thank both of you again for coming tonight. It meant the world to me to have all my friends there. I can't wait to do it again, but it will have to be next Saturday, because I have a lot of inventory to make."

"Did you make any money?" Michael asked.

"I don't know. I haven't had a chance to check it out. I know I'm out there to bring in extra cash, but I had so much fun meeting the people, the atmosphere, and finally being able to say I'm officially a street artist. Wonder what my college professors would think of me now!" Abbey said with glee in her voice.

"It doesn't matter. You are doing what you love, and it looks like you have a great support system," Michael said, nodding his head toward Zach.

"That she does," Zach said as he hugged her from behind so they could both continue talking to Josie and Michael. "Well, we will leave the two of you alone. But, Josie, Abbey said you have some space in the downstairs storeroom for her stuff. Think we might be able to put it in there tomorrow? It should be OK in the Jeep tonight."

"No problem. We will work something out. Good night, you guys," she said as she watched the couple walk up the steps to Abbey's apartment.

"I'm so glad to finally see them together. That boy has been patient with her while she figured out what she really wanted."

"Sounds familiar," Michael said as he looked over at Josie.

"Don't you start on me!" she said jokingly as she got up and suddenly sat in Michael's lap.

"Well, I think I've been pretty patient. But you know what? You have definitely been worth the wait!" Michael brought his lips to hers, kissing her tenderly as though it were the first kiss ever between the two of them.

"I think you are worth it too!" she said as she hugged him and then pulled back to look into his eyes. "Please, Michael, don't break my heart. I'm putting my trust in you." Then Josie laid her head on his shoulder as they rocked back and forth in the single chair.

As she opened the door to her apartment, Abbey couldn't wait to wrap her arms around Zach again. It was like she couldn't keep her hands from touching him, wanting him to be with her every second. They kissed from the door to the couch, where they plopped down, and Zach cuddled her in his arms.

How many times he had dreamed of this exact scenario, Zach couldn't count. But having the girl that had consumed his thoughts for the last three months actually snuggled up next to him was priceless. Even though they were both exhausted from the long day, they sat as close as possible on the couch talking about the evening when they weren't touching lips. Before he knew it, though, Zach looked down to see Abbey's eyes closed, her head resting on his shoulder. This beautiful girl with a wonderful soul had told him she loved him tonight. The happiness Zach felt inside was like nothing he had dreamed. He slowly scooped her up in his arms and carried her to bed, tucked her under the sheets, and kissed her good night, even though she didn't know he was there. He wrote her a quick note, leaving it on her nightstand so she would see it upon waking, and left to go home. But he could have stayed the whole night just holding her in his arms.

When Abbey woke the next morning, she realized she was still in her clothes from the night before but comfy in her bed. Happiness radiated from her face as she remembered everything from last night. The artist show and finally letting go. Letting herself admit she was in love with her best friend. She glanced over and saw the note propped against her lamp on her bedside table with Zach's handwriting. The last thing she remembered was being wrapped in his arms on the couch. She must have fallen asleep, and he put her to bed. She smiled at the fact that as far as she was concerned, he could have stayed all night. Nothing would have happened, because they were so exhausted, but having him there would have been a big treat for her. She got up and dressed quickly to get to Josie's place for their usual Sunday coffee on the porch. Abbey couldn't wait to tell Josie she had taken her advice. She slipped on a pair of shorts, a tank top, and flip-flops before grabbing the coffee beans Josie liked and headed downstairs. She knocked on the door a few times before she heard her finally coming to the door. But the person greeting her wasn't Josie. It was Michael!

Abbey stammered through her shock of seeing this man—dressed but definitely as though he had just woken up. "Ah, good morning. Is Josie here?"

"Hi, Abbey." Josie looked like she had thrown on clothes quickly and tried to make herself as presentable as possible. She also had a distinctive blush to her face as she stood beside Michael in the door.

"I'm sorry if I interrupted anything. We just usually have coffee every Sunday. I should have called you, but I was a bit excited from last night." *Not just about my show but Zach*, Abbey thought. But it seemed Josie had her own happy news to share.

"I'll leave you two to talk. Nice to see you again, Abbey. Congratulations again on your show!" he said as he walked toward the kitchen.

Josie came outside and shut the door. "Abbey, I'm really sorry about this morning. Ah, things just progressed a bit differently last night than I expected." She looked down at the doormat they were standing on.

"Oh, I can see that." Abbey laughed, and the red on Josie's face became much deeper. "I guess you two are going to start over again?"

"Yes. He is actually going to move here for a while, and we are going to date. Kinda like we just met for the first time."

"Looks like you had a heck of a first date." Abbey couldn't help but tease her friend.

"Honestly, it was wonderful, and now I'm going to go inside to eat breakfast. I'll have to skip our morning coffee. How about lunch later?" Josie asked.

"I'll have to take a rain check on that. My *boyfriend* is picking me up for a surprise around noon. At least that is what he said in the note he left for me on my bedside table. But I do have to admit, I fell asleep on him while were we cuddling on the couch last night."

"Boyfriend? Young lady, it's about time. I'm so happy for you!" Josie said as she gave Abbey a big hug.

"I could say the same for you. Let's promise each other that sometime this week, maybe lunch or dinner, we will sit down and give each other details of what is going on."

"Sounds great! I have short workdays all week because Friday is my last day."

Abbey had forgotten about the resort being sold. "Oh, Josie, I'm sorry. I totally forgot. Is everything OK?"

"Remember, I already told you I'll be fine. And I'm thinking about doing something I always dreamed about, but we will talk later. Smells like scrambled eggs and toast are waiting for me." She smiled widely and went back inside to join Michael for breakfast.

31

Abbey read the note again that Zach had left her. "Be ready at noon. Bathing suit and towels are required. We are spending the afternoon together. I love you!" As she read the note again, she began to wonder where he was taking her. Maybe they were going back to the beach? She loved the park, but they had just been there last weekend. But she didn't care. They could have stayed inside for the whole day, watching movies and having pizza delivered. Right now, the time couldn't pass by fast enough for her.

Abbey had everything ready to go, eagerly watching out the window for any sign of Zach and his bike. Her concentration was broken as an unfamiliar car pulled up to the front gate. She might not have recognized the vehicle, but she knew the man in the driver's seat. She watched as Zach got out of the blue Honda, and she reached her front door just as he did.

"Is that your car?" she said as she opened her front door. But no answer came, because suddenly Abbey was swept up into Zach's arms. He kissed her eagerly then smothered her with more kisses as his hands caressed her back from the nape of her neck to the small of her waist.

Finally Zach let her go, but not too far, just enough so he could see her face. "Good morning, sleeping beauty, or should I say good afternoon. It was very hard to leave you last night looking so beautiful, sleeping in my arms on the couch. You were exhausted, but you had one busy day. I have to say that yesterday turned out to be a pretty good one for everyone, it seems. I just saw Michael leaving Josie's apartment." He raised his eyebrows as he looked at Abbey.

"I went down for morning coffee like I always do on Sunday, and Michael answered the door. Looked like he had dressed in a mighty big hurry," Abbey said with a grin on her face. "Josie came outside and told me that she and Michael were going to try dating again. It seems their first date was pretty good!" Zach laughed and thought that would have been a hell of a first date for him and Abbey too.

Zach had imagined many times what it would be like to hold Abbey next to him with no barriers, but not till last night did the desire become so strong that it was hard to resist taking her in his arms and carrying her to the bedroom, but not for sleeping. Dating came first and then a commitment, he reminded himself. They already knew each other so well but now they would be learning about a whole different dimension to their relationship. Building a trusting, soul-mate bond was the direction they were moving toward. A place where he could share both body and soul with this amazing woman standing in front of him.

"So, what is the big surprise? Bathing suits and towels? Are we going back to the beach?" Abbey asked, so eager to know what he had planned.

"Nope. You have to wait a bit longer, but get your stuff, and we will head to our destination."

Abbey could barely contain her excitement, reaching up to meet his lips with hers one more time. "I'll be right back." But before she could walk two steps away, Zach grabbed her waist and pulled her back to him, both of them enjoying one more hot, steamy kiss that left Abbey weak all over. Why had she waited so long to give in to these feelings? she thought as happiness flooded her body. If she had known it would feel this good, she never would have hesitated.

"You keep that up, and we won't be going anywhere," she said.

"I can cancel the surprise. I don't care where we are today as long as I'm with you."

"I feel the same way, but you have piqued my curiosity—I love surprises. Let me get my things." This time he let her go get her tote and lunch bag. Then they set off for the unknown destination that Abbey still couldn't figure out.

It wasn't long before they arrived at the dock where the boat that belonged to one of Zach's friends was moored. Abbey had been out on the boat with everyone a few times and recognized it immediately.

"If we are going out in the boat, where is everyone?"

"Today, it is just the two of us. Josh is letting us borrow it. Maybe we'll find a sandbar or just anchor and go swimming. Whatever we decide, it is just the two of us spending the afternoon together. I've got a great picnic lunch packed in the cooler, extra towels, a blanket, the iPad, and portable speakers. And of course, some drinks. We are celebrating today, my love." He helped her onto the boat like a servant would treat a princess. As he looked at Abbey and how she seemed to glow today, sometimes he wondered if this was all a dream. It still didn't feel real, but it was, and he thanked God that this wonderful woman wanted to be in his life.

"Just you and me? This day is getting better and better!" Abbey said excitedly as she looked at all the preparation he had done. "Where are we going first?"

"I figured we would head out to the sandbar, then decide if we want to picnic there or anchor close by. With it being a Sunday, there could be a lot of people. We'll just wait and see."

"As long as I'm with you, anything sounds perfect," Abbey said as she stood beside him, her arm around his waist as they steered out of the marina, heading for the open water of the Atlantic Ocean.

32

"That was a bit awkward," Josie said smiling at Michael. She had forgotten all about the weekend routine she and Abbey had. Every Sunday, coffee on the porch, weather permitting, going over their week, and talking about life in general. It was where some of their deepest conversations had taken place, ones that had helped Josie come to grips with her past in favor of a better future.

"Well, it might have been awkward, but I can't say I didn't love the look on Abbey's face when she saw me at the door. Think she might get the idea that I'm in love with a wonderful woman?" Michael said as he pulled Josie into an embrace.

"We haven't talked about the 'L' word just yet, so let's keep that way. You wouldn't have told me that on a first date years ago," she said looking up at him.

"I also wouldn't have been here the next morning either. Wasn't my style, and if I remember correctly, yours either.

Things just happened last night, and I don't regret it one bit. I know it's only going to get better from here on." He pulled her close to him once again causing Josie to literally drop the plate she had in her hand. At least it didn't break, but it wouldn't have mattered. Josie was in love. Last night might have been their first official date for their renewed romance, but he had been here for the last six weeks, courting her, as the old-timers would say, by his patience and persistence, showing up every day whether she spoke to him or not. He had worn her down and stolen her heart once again. Now Josie was seeing Michael in a new light altogether. Her "rugged mountain man," as she used to call him a long time ago, was here before her, but now he looked like her "laid-back island guy." She liked that. Both names suited him well. Josie just beamed as she gazed up at the man before her.

"What are you smiling about?" Michael asked as he stared into her eyes.

"I'm truly happy. All this time I thought I was happy here, but I can tell now I was just content. I made a new life for myself, totally different from Montana. I made a few friends; at least, I thought so till Abbey moved in. She showed me I really just had acquaintances all these years. Then you show up, and I realize I've never really loved anyone but you. I dated a few times here, but nothing was ever right. I just feel different, and that 'different' feels good."

"Did I just hear the word 'loved'?" Michael asked.

Josie realized she did just say it: she basically told Michael she loved him. But she just grinned as she went to get another plate so they could eat the breakfast they had made together.

It consisted of scrambled eggs, bacon, toast, and juice. They were both starving, but not just physically. This was a whole new chapter in their lives, getting to know each other once again. For Josie, it was rekindling a past love and learning to trust again. Building new friendships and moving on from a career into the unknown. There were lots of changes, and Josie normally didn't handle change well. But for once she felt like she had a support system in her friends and now Michael. She couldn't say that in the back of her mind there wasn't a small, nagging voice that kept reminding her of the past, but it was becoming more faint as time passed.

"So, this is your last week at work. What are your plans now? You told me before you had it all handled, but that was when you weren't talking to me like you are now," he said from across the table.

At first, Josie wanted to revert to her old self and tell him it was none of his business. It was an old habit to change, so she took a deep breath. "I've been investing my money in some stocks over the years. It became a hobby of sorts, but I never told anyone. I have a really good portfolio, so I will be able to live off the interest with no problem. I guess that's one good thing that came from being an accountant all these years."

"Wow, good for you. But what are you going to do? Sit at home all day, or try something new?" Michael asked.

"This might sound crazy, but I think I might write a book. A fiction novel. I have had some ideas for years about writing stories about Montana. I've kept a list of notes as I thought about them, and they range from mysteries to love stories to a memoir of living there as a child. I have to admit, I love

Montana, but the Keys have become my home. My brother is in Hawaii, as far as I know. When he left out of high school, he didn't come home except for my parents' funerals. I guess that goes for me as well. I haven't heard from him since but then, he didn't ask where I moved, and I didn't offer any information. You would think that we hated each other, but we are just so different. My brother wasn't born to live in a small town. I was surprised he went to Hawaii, but he did tell me he loved it there and was married. But so much was going on when he was home that we didn't talk much, and as soon as everything was over, he left on the first flight out. He even let me settle all the estates and money. He didn't care. So, basically, I have no one in Montana. My life is here in these islands."

"You have me in Montana. Some of your friends are still there. There are people who still love you back there. We are all older and wiser now. And there are some that are gone. Maybe one day you'll consider coming back." Michael looked over at her and could see a small tear in the corner of her eye. Going back home would be hard for Josie, and he didn't want that for her right now. They were fine right here. This was where he wanted them to rebuild their relationship again. His business was in fine hands. He could tell by the daily reports he received from Seth. They would just have to take it one day at a time.

"I think you would make a great author. You were the straight-A student in school in every subject. Always put me to shame!" Michael said as Josie blushed a bit. She had to admit school had been easy for her, and then she had breezed through college. That was why learning the stock market had actually been fun for her. Josie was good with numbers, and right now that was turning out to be a huge blessing.

"School or no school, you've done well for yourself. From the pictures you have shown me, the ranch looks like it has quadrupled in size. The big corporate deals you have for grass-fed beef are amazing. I'm glad you are keeping it real and treating the animals humanely. Too many people out there are only in it for the money. You were never that way. I'm happy to see you haven't changed in that respect."

"I'm still a cowboy at heart, but this little city is growing on me. It is so relaxed. Might be hot as hell sometimes, but I think I could get used to this." Michael reached across the table and took hold of her hand. Then he stood up, leaned over, and kissed her on the lips. "I know I could definitely get used to this every morning."

"I think I could too," Josie said softly. The feel of his lips on hers had left her wanting more of him.

Abbey loved standing by Zach as he steered the boat into the open water. The ocean was beautiful today. No choppy whitecaps, just swells that the boat easily skimmed over. Every now and then, Zach would look over, giving Abbey a quick kiss before looking back over the bow of the boat.

It wasn't long before they spotted the sandbar they usually went to with their friends. As they expected, there were already boats anchored close by the small, white island, with people carrying picnics through the water to claim their spot on the sand.

"Let's anchor here instead of going to the sandbar. I have a feeling it will be pretty crowded before long, and I really want you all to myself today," Zach said as he wrapped his arm around her waist, looking at her so tenderly. *This is a perfect spot,* Abbey thought as she looked around at the other boats and people enjoying the gorgeous water on this bright, sunny day. They were far enough away for privacy and for some swimming in the clear, blue water.

"Sounds like a great idea. Plus, I'm starved," she said, looking for the cooler he had brought on board earlier.

"I went to our favorite little café, bought sandwiches, chips, and fresh fruit with a chocolate dipping sauce. Drinks are water and fruit juice. No alcohol, since we are here by ourselves."

"OK, now I'm really hungry. When can we eat?" Abbey said anxiously. But as she looked at Zach, she could tell that food wasn't on his mind.

"So am I, but not for food," he said as he walked slowly to her, once again gently putting his arms around her. Zach pulled her as close to him as he could, kissing her gently but with much passion. Abbey felt like she was becoming part of him, every fiber of her being set afire just by his touch. This gorgeous, sexy man wanted her and was in love with her. Abbey's mind was still trying to compute all that had happened in the last twenty-four hours.

"I love this too," she said as she gently ran her hands across his chest and then down around his waist. "But my stomach is growling a bit. Sorry to spoil the mood," she apologized.

"You didn't spoil anything. Actually, I'm a bit hungry too, but having you all to myself and this close—it is hard to resist your charms. Let's spread the blanket out under the canopy, and I'll get the cooler."

As she set up a place for them to eat, Abbey decided she would rather sit in the seats under the canopy, watching the other boaters and people while they ate. There was no telling what would happen if they laid that blanket out. Instead of just eating a nice lunch, it might turn into something else. As much as Abbey wanted that intimacy with Zach, she was taking it slow. Yes, they had been friends for quite a while now, but this new, beautiful turn in their relationship changed things. She wanted to learn even more about the man who had stolen her heart.

"Ah, this is as good as when we eat at the café," Abbey said as she took a bite of her turkey sandwich. The chocolate that was to be part of the dessert was sitting out in the sun, melting so they could drizzle it over the fresh fruit. Since they both had an intense love for chocolate, Abbey was sure there would be leftover fruit and no sauce. Zach had thought of everything, and it was perfect. She was enjoying this beautiful day with her wonderful boyfriend. As the word "boyfriend" twirled in her head, she sat watching Zach, so glad she had finally come to her senses and realized that what she felt for him was a true, real love.

"I'm ready for a swim. Do you want to snorkel or just enjoy the water?" Zach asked, reaching for the masks.

"I think today I just want to enjoy swimming with you. Haven't done that before, because we are always with someone." Abbey gave him a sly smile and took off her cover-up, and before Zach knew what was happening, she dove into the water. It was a few seconds before he joined her, swimming straight to her.

"This feels amazing," she said as she treaded water and he swam up to her. He reached for her in the water and Abbey wrapped her arms around his neck, giving him a salty kiss. But she continued from his lips, to the tip of his nose then his neck. Even a little nibble on his ear. Zach groaned till he could take it no more and pulled her into a sweet, longing kiss where they started to sink under the water.

"We will have to finish that in the boat," he said, coming up for air.

"I'll be sure to remind you!"

They swam around the boat, splashing each other back and forth, playing like two little kids in a swimming pool, except they were able to watch the beautiful schools of fish swim by. But the thing that took Abbey by surprise was the female manatee and her calf that swam so close. As Zach came up behind Abbey, reaching for her hand, Abbey was amazed, trying to be as still as she could as the manatee moved by, so close she felt like she could reach out and touch her. Before long, they both were watching the pair swim out toward the Atlantic.

"I've never been that close to any sea creature before. That was awesome! They are so graceful, and the baby was beyond cute," Abbey said excitedly as they climbed the ladder back into the boat.

"I think you are beyond cute. Actually, I think you are downright beautiful!" Zach looked at her once they were both on deck. Abbey suddenly reached over to Zach, slowly drawing him close to her. "Remember, we were going to finish that kiss where we almost drowned," she said with an impish look on her face.

As Abbey glanced up at Zach, it was like nothing else existed around them. It was just the two of them, enjoying the moment and each other. He tasted salty from the ocean water, but she didn't care. But just then a boat came by, hooting and whistling at both of them. They suddenly looked over to see Zach's friends in another boat, pulling alongside of them.

"Thought we might find you guys near the sandbar. We have been on the other side all day. Looks like we have been missing the show!" Josh called out. Before either Zach or Abbey could answer, Josh and the others waved and went on, leaving Abbey's cheeks red, and not from the sun. Zach just shook his head and smiled.

"I guess it is time to get back. We have work tomorrow, and it has been one busy weekend. But," he said as he hugged her tightly, "one of the best weekends of my life."

"For me too. I love you, Zach," Abbey said softly.

"I love you too, Abbey."

33

When they arrived at Abbey's apartment and everything was put away, she didn't want Zach to go, but they both had things they had to do before the start of the week. After a promise of an evening phone call and another fiery kiss, Zach left. This whole weekend had been pure magic for her—the artist show that turned out better than she could have hoped for, then her sudden realization that she was genuinely in love with the most wonderful man on this island, as far as Abbey was concerned. Her feelings for Zach were like nothing she had experienced and felt so good. Her weekend had been perfect!

Then Abbey remembered her shock when Michael had answered Josie's door this morning. Maybe she wasn't the only one that had a fantastic weekend! When Abbey had left Josie that morning, she was surprised to see that Michael had spent the night. She didn't blame Josie, but what a difference six weeks could make. Abbey knew she would get the rest of the story one evening this week during her and Josie's porch time. Right now, her bed and a pending phone call were waiting for her.

When Abbey went to work the next morning, she met Zach outside at the little café where they ate lunch.

"I would like to give you a more proper good-morning greeting. You know—me kissing your lips, cheeks, neck. But we don't know who might be looking," Zach said before he gave her a quick gentle kiss on the lips. But just the thought of what Zach had described made Abbey's pulse quicken as she imagined the scenario.

They had discussed how they would handle their working relationship last night when Zach called her, but now seeing him in person, Abbey knew this would be tough. Lance had never mentioned that interoffice dating was not allowed, but Abbey was sure they would have to talk to him. She didn't realize how nervous she was till Zach walked up beside her, gently touching her hand and telling her that everything would work out. Their work as a team had been praised since she got there, and she wanted it to continue. They worked very well together despite butting heads on a few ideas. Even in those times, they always came to a greater solution by combining their designs. Lance had praised their work, but all four members of the team worked so well together that this place honestly didn't seem like a job to her.

"Do you think it might be best for us to talk to Lance and tell him we are seeing each other? He never said anything about dating people we work with, right?" Abbey asked, sounding worried and a bit concerned as they walked up the steps.

"It has never been an issue. Randy is gay, I'm straight, and Everly has always been like a little sister to me. But I think you are right. He will probably be OK with everything as long as we are professional on the job. That might be difficult for me, but I can do it. Just have to look forward to those lunch breaks and evenings. And weekends will be the best." They didn't realize it, but their heads were almost touching, as they talked, oblivious to the person who had walked into the room.

"Well, what do we have here?" Everly's voice boomed through the office space. Abbey and Zach pulled away so fast that Zach almost lost his footing and fell backward, causing Everly to laugh.

"Wow, looks like this was a big weekend not only for Abbey but for some others too!" she snickered as she put her things away at her desk.

" Mine was pretty good, but who are you talking about?" Randy asked as he came around the corner, overhearing the conversation.

"Ask Zach. Maybe he can fill you in on the details. I know I wouldn't mind hearing them." Everly sat on the corner of her desk, arms folded with a grin on her face, looking from Zach to Abbey, both of whom looked like two kids who got their hands caught in the cookie jar.

Randy looked back and forth between the two. Immediately he knew what was going on.

"Way to go! It's about time. I was wondering when you two would get together. It was just so obvious." He gave his commentary as he set up his laptop and got some papers out for the day's work.

Abbey and Zach both stood still, shocked that their actions had given anything away. Was it that obvious? They were wondering what they should say or do next, when Lance came in.

"What's going on?" Lance asked casually as he entered the workspace and poured himself a cup of coffee.

"Zach and Abbey are dating—finally!" Randy said, not even looking up from his computer.

Lance looked at the two standing by their desks, who were trying to comprehend everything that just had taken place in a span of a few minutes. How had everyone come to a quick conclusion, seeing their budding romance?

"I was wondering how long that would take," Lance said. "Can I see both of you in the office for just a minute?" Abbey and Zach looked at each other, wondering what he would say. He didn't look upset. In fact, he acted as though it was no big deal, but they both were wondering as they walked gingerly toward his office.

"Listen," Lance began as they both sat down, "I'm not against you dating just as long as while you are here in this office, you are working. No making plans, no displays of affection, no talking about personal stuff. You get the drift. Your work is first and foremost while you are here. But I have to say I'm glad you are finally seeing each other. Been waiting to have this conversation with both of you for a while. Had it all planned out."

"We will keep it strictly professional at work, promise," Zach started. "And our work standards will still be the best as they always are."

"Lance, thank you for understanding. We will keep our personal life out of the workplace. Promise," Abbey said confidently.

"I know when I've hired good people, and you two are some of the best I have ever had working for me. Just keep up the good work."

They both walked out of the office feeling better now that everything was out in the open, even though that wasn't quite how they'd planned it. But then as soon as they sat at their desks, the workday progressed as usual since the day Abbey had started working at the little design agency.

As they left work for the evening, Abbey was excited as she was going to Zach's place for dinner. She had never been to his apartment before and knew it was a "bachelor pad" as soon as she walked in. It was cleaned up but very sparse, with a little furniture and a huge TV in the middle of the living room. *Typical for a guy who loves sports the way Zach does*, she thought as she smiled to herself. She had to give him props for keeping it clean though. After living with two older brothers and visiting Drew's place in New York, which looked completely unorganized and cluttered, she wasn't sure what to expect. Abbey could now say that as far as apartments go, Zach's place was nothing like her brothers!

His apartment was located on the bottom floor of an old house that had been renovated to create two separate living quarters: one upstairs and the downstairs one Zach rented. It was a cute house painted white on the outside with a small porch on the front. No rocking chairs for relaxing but beautiful all the same.

"I made sure the place was cleaned up just for you," Zach said as they walked in.

"It's nice," she said as she continued to look around his place. "How long have you lived here?"

"Since I arrived on the island. Found it the second day here, thank goodness, because the hotel prices were pretty steep. Thought I might find myself sleeping in my car if I hadn't found it so quickly."

"Our places aren't really that far apart. No wander you can get to my apartment fast. I thought you were a speed biker," she laughed as she joined him in the kitchen, wondering what they were having for dinner. Standing on her tiptoes, she looked over his shoulder while he grabbed some covered containers out of the refrigerator. But she also had her arms wrapped around him, distracting him so much that he quickly put the containers down. He turned, put his arms around her, picked her up off the floor, sitting her on the kitchen counter and kissed her so sweetly. Zack couldn't help himself when he was near her, and apparently Abbey couldn't either.

"I have to warn you. I'm not the best cook, so I prepared this ahead of time," he said once they both came back up for air. The opened containers revealed grilled chicken, roasted asparagus, baked potatoes, and a bowl of fresh melon, because he knew Abbey loved fruit for dessert.

"Wow, you did all this before work?"

"I went to the store last night after I left your place because I really didn't have much in the fridge. That might change a little now that you will be coming over more often. At least I hope so. But to answer your question—I prepared most of it last night. I know how I am in the morning, and this would have never been cooked. I hope you like it," he said tentatively. "I've lived here for six years, and you are the first girl I have fixed dinner for."

"Then I feel very special."

"You are very special to me." Zach reached over to kiss Abbey one more time before they began filling their plates.

He didn't have a kitchen table in his place, so they settled for eating on the floor around the makeshift coffee table he had made out of wooden crates. There were blankets on the floor for seating and a candle to give light to the little table. To Abbey, Zach had created the most romantic mood as they both ate dinner by the flickering candlelight.

"We made it through our first day at the office. I was a little nervous this morning, wondering if we would be able to make this work. Then knowing we would have to talk to Lance. I couldn't believe they had been waiting for this all along. Were we that transparent?"

"I don't know, but I do have a question," Zach said as he looked over at her. "You have no idea how happy you have made me. But I have to know—what changed your mind? You were so adamant about us staying only friends. To say you shocked me Saturday night is an understatement."

Abbey put down her fork and stared at her plate for a moment. How could she explain this when she wasn't sure what had happened herself? She only had an inkling of why.

"To be honest, I'm not sure exactly. I've never been in a relationship where something terrible happened like what Josie went through. But my past relationships were blah, for lack of a better word.

"When I was driving down here during my move, I kinda promised myself that I was starting fresh. New job, new atmosphere, and I wanted to find me. Enjoy this new freedom. I wanted for once to do things my way, not following what others said I should or shouldn't do. When I thought about it, I had always been in a relationship, it seemed, never taking time for myself. So I decided that I was going to put romance on the back burner of my life for a while and just be with myself." Abbey took a sip of her water and a deep breath.

"But I arrived in Key West, and the first person who was nice to me was Garrett—a guy. Then I met you at work. You were so cute and helpful. You were the sweetest guy I think I ever met. You know, like someone who is too good to be true? And we had a working relationship that was great. We had fun at lunch. We talked like best friends. You were and are my best friend here, so that was all I allowed myself to see. I really thought that was how you saw it too until you told me you had feelings for me. That broke into that little, selfish bubble I had put around myself. I knew there were feelings for you all along, but I had convinced myself that they were friendship only. And you, being the wonderful guy you are, said you were OK with that, so accepting of what I told you.

"But something in me changed the other night. I couldn't quit thinking about you and what you said. What it would be like to share all my life with you. To be held in your arms. About being kissed by you. Then Josie sat me down on the porch and basically told me to get my act together and snag you because if I didn't, someone would, because you were a prize."

Abbey took a sip of water and continued, watching Zach look so sweetly at her with nothing but kindness on his face. "But when you helped me put up my art display, it just hit me as I watched you. You had no vested interest in my show that night but you helped me anyway, caring so much about me and my happiness. Suddenly, I thought: *I love this man. I really love him.* But then I was scared and felt strange because I had told you that we were just friends. I was afraid at first to tell you how I really felt because I didn't want you to think that I was crazy. But I had to let you know."

Zach had sat quietly while Abbey explained the best she could, but as she finished, he had a slight smile on his face.

"Why are you looking at me like that?" she said.

"When I told you I loved you, but you said you wanted to be just friends, I knew that I needed to keep pursuing you. I felt like I was being told to keep at it; don't give up. And that if it was meant to be, it would happen. If not, eventually someone else would show up in my life. I guess I was taking an idea from Michael's playbook. I have watched him be persistent and patient with Josie, and look where it has led him. Granted, it took a little longer for us. And you did shock me when we were sitting on the dock. I wasn't sure what you wanted to talk about, but boy, you made me the happiest man the other night."

Even though there were dishes still on the little table, they got up and sat on the couch, Zach holding Abbey in his arms as they watched the flickering candlelight.

"I've dreamed of this since the day I met you. I knew then and there that you were the one for me. That week before you started work, I kept asking Lance all kinds of questions about you. I think that is one reason he wasn't too surprised by our little announcement today." They sat there together for a while in silence, listening to each other's breathing as they sat as close as they could, just relaxing in the moment.

Abbey was the one to break the silence. "I really don't want to do this, but it's probably time for me to go home. I have artwork to finish by Saturday, and as much as I want to stay right here," she said, resting her head fully into Zach's shoulder and chest, "I'm getting tired. It's been a long day. Actually, it's been a long few days. But they have been absolutely wonderful, and I wouldn't trade them for anything." She reach up and glided her hand along the dark stubble on his chin like she was memorizing the lines of his face. "I love you, Zach. I only wish I had allowed myself to give into these feelings sooner."

"I love you too. And you were worth the wait." His hand slid down her shoulder then back up to her neck and face, gently caressing her. Abbey was beautiful, and Zach felt blessed that she was his.

34

It was already after nine o'clock when Abbey pulled the Jeep into her usual parking spot. Leaving Zach tonight was especially difficult since his kisses and touch sent feelings of desire surging through her body and mind, begging her to stay.

"Hey there," came a voice from the darkened porch. "Was wondering when you might make it home. Must have had a good day at work and a little something afterward." Abbey could barely make out Josie's silhouette in the rocking chair on the porch, but the light of the moon shone on her face.

"What are you doing out here so late?" Abbey asked as she made her way onto the porch and sat down in the other rocker.

"Actually, I was waiting for you. Though I did think you would be here long before now. How did your day go? How did everyone react to the news of you and Zach?"

Abbey shook her head and laughed. "Can you believe they all said it was about time? I guess our attraction to each other was obvious to everyone but me. If it hadn't been for your encouragement, I don't think I would be with him now. Thanks, Josie," Abbey said gratefully.

"I could say the same to you. Michael left just a little while ago. We had dinner but also discussed more about the past. Mostly the mistakes we both made, even though his was a bit more heartbreaking for everyone involved. But it feels so good to let all these pent-up emotions out. All these feelings of hurt and even hatred I have had bottled up for so long. You were the one to convince me to give myself a chance to be happy, and that's what I'm going to do. I can't say I'm not scared, but I'm also feeling happy for the first time in a while. Thank you so much Abbey."

"I don't believe in coincidences. Someone up above must have known that we needed each other to move on to the next step in our lives. There was a reason I chose that apartment upstairs out of all the places I could have picked from when I moved to Key West," Abbey said quietly.

"I need to get upstairs and put the finishing touches on a few little mermaid sculptures that I hope to have ready for Saturday. Probably should have come straight home from work, but Zach's dinner invitation at his place was one I couldn't resist. I hadn't been to his apartment before, and for a single guy, it wasn't too bad. Nothing like my brother's place! If my momma ever saw it, she would have a fit. Anyway, Zach even fixed me dinner. It was nice to just sit and talk, among other things." She grinned at Josie, knowing that she would know the meaning.

"Go get busy, girl. And we will talk more later."

Josie sat on the porch a little while longer, giving more thought to all the changes that had happened since Abbey had arrived in Key West. Her quiet life had suddenly become very busy, and as she thought about it, Josie wouldn't have it any other way. Though the old feelings of abandonment and fear would sometimes creep back into her thoughts, things were getting better each day between her and Michael. Since this was her last week at the resort, only working half days, they had made plans for some afternoon dates to play tourist in Josie's island town. This would give them more time to learn about each other all over again.

To Josie, it actually felt like they were dating for the first time. Michael had been such a gentleman about agreeing to her "rules," as she put it. They did slip up that one night, caught up in the moment, and it had been a night to remember for her. Michael might have been older, but he was still sexy as ever.. The romance that was blossoming between them for a second time was real. Josie could feel it when she let her guard down, which was becoming easier each day.

As for her last week at the resort, Josie's mornings were filled with meetings, helping the new owners make the transition, and going over numbers on the computer. She hated that some of those she had worked with for so long were losing their jobs, but most were able to stay on at the hotel. As she watched all that was taking place with new rules and job descriptions, Josie was glad she had taken the nice severance package, even though the new management was practically begging her to stay on as one of their top employees. In fact, if it wasn't for that nice bonus to stay to make the transition more peaceful,

Josie would have already left. Each day she went to the resort, it was stressful to watch the place she had worked at for so long becoming something entirely different. And there wasn't anything for her to do in the accounting department, since a team in Chicago now took care of the resort's books. Josie was basically there to answer questions till Friday, and then she was unemployed. What helped her get through each morning was knowing that her afternoons would be spent with Michael.

Every day around two o'clock, he would pick her up, and they would head somewhere new on the island. They went to Smather's Beach. The next day they went to Fort Zachary. They spent a good deal of time at the Hemingway House one afternoon, since it was a bit rainy. The next day they just walked Duvall Street, doing a bit of shopping and having dinner at Margaritaville, since Michael had never been to the restaurant. Even though Josie had lived there for twenty-seven years, it was like she was a first-time visitor, seeing Key West through Michael's eyes. She loved his enthusiasm and curiosity about the city that she had initially ran away to but that had become her home.

During their time together, they were always holding hands and stealing a kiss or two wherever they went, not caring who saw them or where they might be. It was official that they were in love for a second time, something Josie honestly thought she would never experience again in her lifetime. Each day she felt more and more like a teenager discovering her first crush. And in essence, Michael was her first love. They had dated their senior year of high school and throughout college. Even though Michael had dropped out, she continued school for her degree in business, and he made his way back to his

.king over the day-to-day work so well that
.een able to retire. They kept their relationship
Josie stayed in school by spending weekends to-
geu.   .e she was only two hours away from him. Their re-
lationsh.p flourished even when Josie went on to complete her
master's degree during the next two years. When she finished
school and was finally back home, within a month Michael
popped the question. It wasn't long before they were planning
the wedding, even though it would be one year away. They
were together, and Josie thought all was right with the world
till that fateful day.

But now, as they spent more time together, those memories from so long ago were fading. Yes, they had happened,
but now it was time to move on in life. And Josie's life was
changing on so many levels. For the first time, she was embracing the changes, even with the excitement and fears that
came floating through her mind.

As Josie and Michael sat in their rockers, talking and laughing,
Abbey and Zach walked through the gate.

"Hey, you guys, come and join us," Michael said, motioning for them to come over.

"We will have to pass again," Abbey said tiredly. "I'm
just about done getting things ready for tomorrow night. If it
hadn't been for Zach's help, I don't think I would have been
able to have a show this week. I might even take next Saturday
off to give me two weeks to prepare. I love that I'm able to do
this, but it is a big commitment. Not like when I was selling my

artwork back in North Carolina. If you guys are out tomorrow, come by the square."

"Don't work too hard," Josie said as Abbey was about to walk away. But then Abbey noticed the four glasses and bottle of wine sitting on the table between the chairs. *Crap! This is Friday, Josie's last day at the resort!* Abbey quickly walked onto the porch, reaching down to give Josie a hug.

"Josie, I'm sorry! I got so wrapped up in everything this week that I forgot that your last day of work was today," she said as Zach quickly walked up behind her.

"Are we celebrating or crying?" Zach asked jokingly, because he already knew the answer.

"We are officially celebrating, and that is why we asked you to join us. But, Abbey, I know how busy you are. Let's say we celebrate tomorrow at the square. We will bring the glasses and the wine."

Abbey leaned down again, hugging Josie tightly. "Thank you," she said before she and Zach quickly went up the steps to her little place.

It didn't take as long to get things together as it had the previous week. And they would have more time the next day. There were two mixed-media art pieces that Abbey wanted to finish in the morning to display after scanning them into her computer to use as art prints in the future. But after the long workday they'd had, they both were tired.

"I really want you to stay for a while, but I know you are tired," Abbey said pulling Zach into an embrace.

"I'm not that tired, but as for you, you look like you could fall asleep standing up," Zach said, giving her a kiss on the forehead before she leaned her head against his chest. "I'll be here early in the morning. As a matter of fact, I'll bring our favorite bagels from the café, along with some cream cheese and coffee."

"You bring the goodies, and I'll provide the coffee."

"It's a date. I'll see you in the morning." Zach pulled her closer to him. Her heart pounded the closer they got, and the kiss that followed all but took her breath away.

When they slowly separated, both were flushed, still touching each other as though they couldn't get enough.

"Till the morning. I love you," Zach said, giving her another small kiss.

"I love you too, Zach. Always."

35

She had just fallen asleep when the phone rang. She could barely make out the caller at the other end of the line, but finally realized it was Lance. As he spoke the words, Abbey felt a complete numbness envelop her body. This had to be a dream — this couldn't be real

"Abbey, are you there?" she heard Lance say.

"Yes."

"Meet us at the hospital. He's going to be fine. Are you OK to drive?"

"Yes. Yes, I'm OK. How did this happen, Lance? When?" Abbey heard herself talking, but she still felt like her whole world had just turned upside down. Everything seemed surreal.

"Let's talk when you get to the hospital. I'll let you know what the police have shared with me," Lance said quietly. "See if Josie can come with you."

"All right. I'll be there in a few minutes," Abbey said emotionlessly, and she clicked the disconnect button on the phone. Even though she still felt paralyzed with fear in her gut, she quickly got up, dressing in the first pair of jeans, T-shirt, and flip-flops she could find. She grabbed her purse and keys then headed out the door.

"Goodness, what has you here so late?" Josie said as she opened her door. Then she saw Abbey's face, tears streaming down her cheeks. "What's happened?"

"It's Zach, Josie. There has been an accident."

Within ten minutes, both women were on the way to the Lower Keys Medical Center. Abbey pulled into the parking lot fast and had barely parked the car before jumping out of her Jeep and running through the ER door, leaving Josie behind her. She saw no one she knew as she looked around at the crowded area. Then Lance came up to her.

"Please tell me he is OK. Lance, please!" The tears began rolling down her face, heavier this time. Josie was finally behind her with her hand on her back for support. Donna was standing behind Lance, eyes red from crying.

"Abbey, they are assessing him now. They won't let anyone see him till they have him stable. Then one person can go back. I thought it might be best to let you, if you are up to it," Lance said softly as he pulled Abbey into a gentle, fatherly hug. Abbey's legs were weak with fear as she began to imagine only the worst.

"What happened?" she asked, terrified to know the details.

"Right now, all the police would say was that he was hit by a woman coming home from work. She was texting and happened to look up just in time to see Zach, but not before hitting him and then running into a tree."

"He was going home from my house," Abbey said numbly.

Just then a doctor approached the small group, talking to Lance.

"Abbey, this is Dr. Simmons. He is the one treating Zach." He then turned to the doctor. "This is Abbey Wallace, Zach's girlfriend."

"Let's go in here where we can talk, since it is a bit crowded in here tonight," Dr. Simmons said, motioning them into a small waiting room.

"What's happening? Is he OK? Can I go see him?" Abbey asked in quick succession. Josie reached for her hand and held it while the doctor gave them the details.

"After talking to the police and examining Zach, it seems that the car that hit him caused him to land on the pavement and sidewalk, the car tire rolling over his left leg and pelvic area, pinning him between his bike and the ground. He has several critical injuries but is in stable condition at the moment. We feel it would be best for him to be flown to Ryder Trauma Center in Miami. As soon as he is able, there is a LifeNet Helicopter ready to take him."

Suddenly Abbey felt faint and started to fall forward. Lance and Josie caught her. "I'm OK, I'm OK," she insisted. But she wasn't. She just wanted to see Zach. To see he was OK. To tell herself this wasn't real. "What are his injuries?"

"His right leg from just above the knee down is badly injured, what we consider a crush injury. He is having a CAT scan done now to make sure he is stable enough to be transported to Miami. We have determined that he has a fractured pelvis, bruised liver, two broken ribs, and a broken left arm right above the wrist. He is extremely lucky that the broken ribs didn't puncture his lung, and it seems he rolled somehow to where he had no severe brain trauma, except a moderate concussion when his head hit the grass instead of the pavement. Thank goodness he was wearing a helmet. Right now, our goal is to get him on the copter to Miami. But someone can go back and see him for a few minutes before he leaves. I just don't know if he will be aware of your presence due to the medication we have given him. We will come and get whoever wants to go back in a few minutes. Right now I can say that even though his injuries are severe, it could have been much worse." As the doctor walked out of the room, they all sat down in silence, trying to comprehend everything they had just heard.

A torrent of tears began to fall from Abbey's eyes. She felt like it was hard to breathe. All the worst possible scenarios crept through her mind. She couldn't lose him. Not now! They had just found each other. If she hadn't been so stubborn, they would have had more time together. But why was she thinking that? Her thoughts were bouncing around in her head so fast, making her dizzy. What was going on in that room? Did Zach know what was happening? Abbey wanted to be in there with him. To hold his hand. To talk him through everything even if he couldn't respond or was just sleeping. All the thoughts that rushed through her head were driving her crazy, and she couldn't take it anymore. "I've got to go outside for a minute," Abbey said as she rushed for the door.

She walked into the parking lot, feeling the light breeze of the night. She stood there looking up into the night sky and closed her eyes. Abbey prayed like she had never prayed before. And as she did, more tears came like a never-ending stream. This wonderful man who had waited so patiently for her to come to her senses was possibly being taken from her. And by someone texting while driving. Her fear was now becoming anger. Anger at the person who had defied all the warnings, putting the love of her life in danger. Then the anger turned quickly to guilt. He wouldn't have been on the bike if he had not come to help her get ready for her show tomorrow night. Zach was always so giving toward others.

Why? Why Zach? Every emotion was flooding her senses like never before. Abbey suddenly wanted her parents. She wanted them to hold her and tell her that everything was going to be OK, just like they did when she was a little girl. She felt very lost. Not knowing what was happening to Zach as he struggled for life had Abbey in a frenzy. But then as quickly as all the emotions had rushed through her physically and mentally, she felt a calmness flow through her. She was still worried and terrified, but all those emotions were finally draining from her, and Abbey was starting to think more clearly. She took a few more deep breaths and headed back into the hospital.

They sat in the quietest part of the waiting room, watching the door that led to the area where Zach was. Within forty-five minutes, a nurse called out, "Family for Zach Isler," and Abbey quickly jumped up.

"Zach has been stabilized for transport, so you will only be able to see him for about ten minutes. He is conscious, but he is on high doses of pain medication, so I'm not sure how much he will talk to you or, if he does, if he will remember that you were here. Just talk to him like you normally would. Also, he has quite a few bandages, cuts, scrapes, and his leg has been stabilized for the flight. It will look a bit strange. If you need anything while you are with him, let us know. Are you or anyone else going to Miami?" the nurse asked.

"Yes," Abbey said, knowing that she would be there as soon as she could, wishing she could fly with him in the helicopter.

Abbey thought that she was prepared to see Zach from the description the nurse had given her, but she barely recognized him. He had a thick bandage wrapped around his head covering a large cut that had required stitches. His broken arm was wrapped, and his leg was stabilized with a big splint to keep it from moving and covered with a bandage, but Abbey could tell that it was not in the proper place. The sight of it sickened her, but she tried to relax and focused on his face. His beautiful face. That was her Zach with just with a few scratches. Even though he was badly hurt, she felt deep in her heart that he was going to be OK. Her inner voice gave her peace about this situation, and she was clinging to it like a flotation device in the middle of the ocean.

She pulled up the chair beside Zach's bed and stroked his hand. Then she pushed some of his hair off the bandage, running her fingers through the rest of hair very lightly. He was going to be OK, Abbey thought as she sat there staring at him. She leaned over and kissed his cheek.

"Hey, Zach. If you didn't want to help me with my show, you could have just told me," Abbey said, trying to smile, though it was so hard as she looked at him. "You're going to be OK. I love you so much. You have to get better for me."

"I've just got a bunch of scratches, that's all," he said in a whisper to her. The joy Abbey felt when he spoke was unbelievable.

"Hey, baby. Kinda messed up our weekend plans, huh?" he said, barely able to speak.

"Shhh, don't try to talk. Just lie there and rest. They are taking good care of you, and I'm right here if you need anything," Abbey said as she clung to every word he uttered. He was awake and aware, which was giving her more hope.

"What happened? All I remember is a car coming up behind me on the street by my house."

"You were hit by a car. You have some broken bones, cuts, and a concussion. They are getting ready to fly you to a hospital in Miami just to be on the safe side. I'm going to follow and be there as soon as I can."

"Can't they just stitch me up and let me go home?" he said in another whisper. But this time Zach fell asleep before Abbey could answer him. The medication they were giving him was so strong that he didn't say anything about pain. As she looked at him battered and bruised, she was grateful that the medicine was doing its job, making him less aware of the situation.

Just as she gave him another kiss on the forehead, the medical team came in to take him to Miami. She watched as he was being wheeled outside, where the helicopter waited. Abbey once again suddenly couldn't control the tears falling down her cheeks.

As soon as the doors shut, Abbey quickly made her way to the waiting room. Lance, Donna, and Josie jumped to their feet, as they could see the look of determination on her face.

"How is he doing?" Josie asked quickly.

"I've got to get home, get a few things, and head to Miami," Abbey said quickly to the three people before her.

"They have already taken him?" Lance asked.

"He's leaving now."

"You're not going by yourself. You're too tired," Lance said quickly.

"We will take her," Josie said. "Michael and I will make sure she's safe."

"Lance, I will call you when I get there and find out more information. Has anyone called his parents?" Abbey asked suddenly.

"I talked to them already, and they can't get a flight till first thing in the morning. I'll call and tell them they are taking him to Miami."

"Lance, I'll bring my laptop and work from there. I won't let our work fall behind, but I need to be in Miami with him." Abbey's nerves were working overtime as she was trying to cover everything that needed to be done, her thought process sped up like she had taken a drug herself. Except the adrenaline that was coursing through her body was coming from her fear.

"Abbey, I'm not worried about that right now. Take care of yourself, and be there for Zach. We will worry about work later. Was Zach able to talk to you?" Lance asked.

"Yes, but he doesn't remember what happened. He asked if they could stitch him up so he could go home." At that, Abbey laughed, even with the tears. That was Zach. The positive one.

"Be careful going to Miami, and call us for anything. I'll let Everly and Roger know what has happened." Lance came over and gave Abbey a hug, as did Donna, but Abbey was ready to leave. Zach was probably already on his way, and she wanted to be on the road too.

Josie took her by the hand and led her outside. "Where are your car keys?" Abbey handed them to her without saying a word. She climbed into the passenger seat to let Josie drive and sat staring ahead, silence enveloping the vehicle.

As they pulled up to their building, both women saw Michael standing on the porch.

"I called to tell him that we might have to take you to Miami," Josie said.

"Give me about ten minutes, and I'll be ready," Abbey said in an almost robotic voice before racing up to her apartment.

"She's still in shock, but I think she will be OK," Josie said to Michael as they watched her sprint up the steps. "Zach is strong. He has some pretty severe injuries, and there is some concern about his leg. We just don't know all the details yet. Let me get my things together," Josie said, walking quickly into her apartment.

As if on automatic pilot, Abbey put together the things she would need to stay with Zach. She stuffed her tote bag with a toothbrush, toothpaste, some clothes, her laptop, and her cell phone. If she needed anything else, she would buy it in Miami. She quickly zipped the case and headed for the Jeep.

"We are going to take Michael's car, Abbey. You can rest in the backseat, so you'll be alert when we get there. Until Zach's parents come, I'm sure the doctors will be looking to you for answers. But we will be right there with you. OK?" Josie said softly, looking over her shoulder at Abbey.

"Thanks." It was all Abbey could say as she grabbed her jacket to lay her head on the side of the interior of the car. Before she knew it, they were on their way, Michael driving just a little faster than the speed limit. But all Abbey could do was look at the clear night sky with its beautiful full moon and wonder why.

She knew she should try to rest during the four-hour trip to Miami, but as hard as she tried, sleep eluded her. All Abbey could see in her mind was Zach—bandaged, scraped, cut, and stitched. And she couldn't forget the sight of his leg. But all she could think about were the whys. Why Zach? Why now? Why had she waited so long to tell him she loved him? This was what haunted her the most. As the fears kept circulating in her mind, she suddenly found herself having a hard time taking a breath. She felt like she was suffocating.

"What's wrong, Abbey?" Josie said alarmingly as she heard Abbey's ragged breath coming from the back seat.

"I feel like I can't breathe."

"Honey, it's just panic. And it's normal for what you have been through tonight. Take some deep breaths, and try to focus on something calming. I know it's difficult right now, but try." Josie's soothing voice was helping her unwind, and Abbey could tell her breathing was beginning to come back to normal.

"Why did this happen, Josie?" Abbey asked her friend.

"I don't know, and I wish I had some answers. Sometimes we just don't know and probably never will. Things happen, but you have to try to stay positive."

"Positive? You've got to be kidding! Josie, I could lose Zach. I just found him, and now I could lose him!"

36

They pulled into the parking lot of the trauma center in Miami within three hours of leaving Key West. In no time at all, Abbey found out that Zach was still being treated in the Trauma Emergency Room and that the doctors would come out soon to talk to them.

The center was busy, but this was Miami on a Friday night. Though Abbey didn't know what to expect, it felt like the walls of the big room were closing in on her. She wanted to know what was happening to the man she felt so connected to like no one else in the world. Whether the news was good or bad, Abbey needed to know.

"Family for Zach Isler?" the woman called out into the busy room.

"Here," Abbey said, grabbing her tote bag and walking fast toward the lady at the door, with Josie and Michael close behind.

"Have a seat in the room here, and the doctor will be with you in a moment," the woman said with a smile on her face and then shut the door. As promised, two doctors came in within minutes.

"Are you Zach's family?" the first doctor said as he looked at Abbey, Josie, and Michael.

"I'm Zach's girlfriend, Abbey Wallace. These are his friends, Josie Collins and Michael Garner. Zach's parents should be here sometime today," Abbey said as she looked at the clock on the wall to see it was 5:30 a.m. "How is Zach?" Abbey asked anxiously.

"As you already know, he has sustained major injuries. We want him to have surgery as soon as possible, and he is being prepped as we speak. His left leg was basically crushed during the accident. He will need extensive surgery to repair the damage to his leg, and if we don't do it as soon as possible, the chances of amputation greatly increase." At those last words, Abbey stomach started to lurch, but she took a deep breath and willed herself to stay calm.

"What about his other injuries?" Josie asked.

"The information they gave you in Key West was correct. But the damage to his leg was more extreme than they thought. That is why surgery is necessary right now."

Both doctors stood up, ready to go out the door. "We will keep you updated on his progress. It could be a while. We won't know what we will find until we are in the operating room. You can go to the waiting room, and we will keep you informed by phone of his condition throughout the surgery. Then we will be back to talk to you after Zach is in recovery."

With that, the doctors disappeared, and they moved back to the bustling room full of people. Abbey didn't even get to see him before surgery. She suddenly felt the wet drops coming from her eyes yet once again. There seem to be no end to the tears.

"He is going to be fine," Josie said as she gave Abbey another hug. "There is nothing we can do right now, so let's get some breakfast, OK?" Though Abbey wasn't hungry, she shook her head dutifully and followed the couple out the door.

Each bite she took had no taste. Abbey only ate because she knew she should. Other than that, food was the last thing she had on her mind. Her nerves were frayed as she imagined what was going on in the operating room. Though Josie and Michael tried to make small talk, Abbey couldn't concentrate on anything. Except Zach. Everything from the horrible phone call till this moment in the cafeteria kept playing in her mind like it was on repeat.

As they headed toward the waiting room, Abbey glanced over and saw the hospital chapel.

"You guys, go ahead. I'll be there in a minute."

"Are you sure?" Michael asked.

"Yes. I just need a minute by myself."

Abbey walked into the chapel, where several other people sat in their own thoughts. It was so quiet and peaceful, almost like the outside world didn't exist. She slowly sat down, closed her eyes, and prayed.

The waiting room was still quite crowded as loved ones waited for patients, like Abbey was waiting anxiously to hear from the doctors about Zach. It had only been a little over two hours, but it seemed time was standing still. It was a blessing that his other injuries wouldn't require surgeries, but they would need a lot of healing time, something she knew Zach wouldn't like. But right now all Abbey could think about was that each minute that ticked by, the surgery was closer to being completed.

"Zach Isler family?" came the familiar voice once again over the crowd of people. Abbey stood up quickly as the woman pointed to the nearby phone. She picked it up tentatively to hear the nurse say that everything was going well so far, but it would be a long procedure. She promised to keep Abbey updated before she hung up the phone.

As Abbey, Josie, and Michael sat, watching the TV or trying to read to keep their minds occupied, Abbey realized that she hadn't called Lance. Zach had now been in surgery for seven hours. Each update she received was positive, but she knew they really wouldn't know what was happening till they talked to the surgeons in person.

"Hi, Lance," Abbey said softly, tired but still running on adrenaline. "He's been in surgery for quite a while. I'm so sorry I haven't called till now. My mind just isn't with it."

"Sweetheart, don't apologize. Just keep us updated. Also, Zach's parents, Sandy and Justin, should be arriving this afternoon. I told them to ask for you. Again, let us know if you need anything," Lance said before she heard the click of the phone.

Abbey looked at the clock on the wall again to see that it was at the ten-hour mark for his surgery. But it wasn't long before Zach's doctor came around the corner, asking them to follow him to the same small room as before.

"Zach is doing well. We were able to stabilize his leg. He had severe damage. Multiple broken bones, damaged muscles, nerves, and blood vessels. The good thing is that no major arteries were cut or severed, which is basically a miracle. But right now we wait and see. I can't say that his leg will be saved—he could still lose it. And if it does heal, we are not sure if he will be able to walk. There are too many unanswered questions that only time will tell. They are getting ready to move him to ICU, and when he is ready, the nurses will come and let one person go back. If you have any questions, let us know."

Abbey sat very still, thinking about the words of the doctor. Lose his leg? Not be able to walk? What about his other injuries? She now had tons of questions, but the doctor had already walked out the door.

But within two hours, Abbey was standing beside Zach's bed, holding his hand, gently stroking it. He probably didn't even know she was there, but the touch of his hand in hers made her feel like everything was going to be OK.

"I was hoping I would see you soon," Zach said in a voice barely above a whisper this time. Though it had been less than twenty-four hours since the accident, he was smiling at her weakly.

"Hi, sweetheart," she said. "Do you need anything?"

"Just you," he said as he barely squeezed her hand. Abbey was doing her best not to cry. She kept thinking about the peace she had felt in the chapel, and that was helping her keep her emotions from betraying her.

"Don't talk. Just rest, and I'll be right here. Your parents will be here soon."

"They didn't need to come. I'm fine," he said as he closed his eyes. He had drifted off back to sleep.

Abbey sat there staring at him, everything still feeling surreal but she knew they would get through this. She laid her head next to Zach's arm and closed her eyes.

"Abbey?" She opened her eyes to see two people she didn't know, but they had called her by her name. "Yes?"

"We are Zach's parents, Sandy and Justin. We just got here. Your friends outside told us about what happened and about the surgery. Thank you for being here for him," Sandy Isler said as she hugged Abbey tightly. Abbey could see that her eyes were red from crying, and Zach's father looked like he hadn't slept in days.

"Mom?" came the voice from the bed.

"Hey, baby. Your dad and I are here. Looks like you decided to pick a fight with a car. How many times did we warn you about that?" His mom's lighthearted joke helped ease the tension surrounding the bed where Zach lay.

"I'm going to go back to the waiting room so you can visit with your parents." Abbey leaned over and gave Zach a very gentle kiss on the cheek before walking out the ICU doors.

She immediately spotted Josie and Michael. Then, looking out the window, all Abbey saw was the beginning of the evening sunset. She had finally run out of adrenaline, and her body let her know it. She felt like she could sleep a week but didn't want to leave the hospital.

"Abbey, let's go to the hotel nearby now that Zach's parents are here. You need to rest," Josie said to her with both hands on Abbey's shoulders.

"I can't leave. I can sleep right over there on that couch. Josie, I can't leave him. What if something happens? And I'm so angry with myself: why did I wait so long to let him know I loved him?" Abbey said, once again, sitting in the chair feeling defeated.

Josie looked at the younger woman in front of her with her glassy eyes and could feel her pain. Josie herself had wondered why she had let so many years go by before giving herself another chance to love. That time wouldn't come back for either of them. The only thing they both could do was move forward.

"I don't know, Abbey. I wish I had some magic answer for you, but I don't. But you do have his love now. Use that to cling to. That will help him also." Josie hugged Abbey tightly and let Abbey cling to her like a child would to its mother.

"Abbey?"

She turned around to see Mr. and Mrs. Isler standing behind her. "We are going to go check in at the hotel close by. We have a room for you too." They motioned to the three people standing before them. "But I think Zach wants to see you one more time before we leave." Abbey shook her head and walked back to Zach's room.

"Hi again," Abbey said as she saw Zach, still half awake, half asleep.

"I love you, Abbey" were the only words Zach told her before his voice trailed off into sleep once more.

"I love you too, more than I can say," Abbey said as she kissed him on the forehead.

37

The next week was a blur of activity. Each day seemed to bring either a triumph or a setback for Zach, with his parents and Abbey waiting patiently, hoping for the day Zach could go home. Every injury he had sustained was healing nicely except his leg. At one point, since Zach could not feel anything from the knee downward, with swelling and infection complicating issues, it seemed like amputation would be the only choice.

Between the pain medication and heavy antibiotics, Zach drifted in and out of consciousness. Abby had either stayed at the hospital or gone to the hotel just long enough for some sleep and a shower. She tried to stay out of the way of Zach's parents as much as possible because he was their son, but she wanted to be with Zach every moment that she could. Even if he was sleeping, she would talk to him, telling him all the things they were going to do when he was healed and back to his normal happy-go-lucky self. To see him injured and in pain at times overwhelmed her.

She got to know Mr. and Mrs. Isler well. They insisted on being called by their first names, and she instantly liked them. She knew immediately why Zach was the type of person he was, because his parents were just like him—warm and genuine.

"You really love him, don't you?" Sandy Isler said one afternoon as they sat across from each other in the cafeteria eating a late lunch while Zach's dad sat with him.

"I do. Mrs. Isler—I mean, Sandy. Zach and I are like best friends. A few weeks back, Zach told me that he was in love with me, and my response was that we could only be friends. I was scared. We worked together, for one thing, and I had just moved to Key West. Then Josie, my friend you met that first day, she talked to me about not waiting. To take opportunities when you can. The next day, I saw Zach in a whole different light. I think I startled him when I told him I felt the same way about him as he did about me. Then this accident. I feel like I wasted so much time." Abbey looked down at her plate, pushing green beans around in a circle like the thoughts that were floating through her mind.

"Zach might not be able to talk to us much right now, but I know he loves you. He already told me. Also said that his dad and I had better be very nice to you," Sandy said, laughing. "I wish we could have met under better circumstances, but I have to say—I'm so glad Zach has you in his life. I can tell you are very special, Abbey. My son is very lucky."

Abbey looked up to see tears forming at the corners of Sandy's eyes. "I'm the one that feels so blessed. Now for him to get well and come home!" Abbey said with enthusiasm that she wasn't feeling.

As they went back to the ICU waiting room, Zach's dad, Justin, met them practically at the door.

"The doctor just left. They are taking Zach into surgery again. It's possible they are going to amputate his lower leg."

The whirlwind that Abbey had felt when this whole ordeal began had subsided, only to be revived with this piece of unexpected news. She sat quickly, feeling weak all over, and looked over to see Sandy crying, being held by her husband.

"Can we go back to see him?" Abbey asked anxiously.

"Yes, I was just coming to find both of you."

They entered the room just as the doctors were talking to Zach about the surgical procedure, but all they heard was a loud voice, struggling to yell.

"You are not taking my leg! Please don't take my leg," he kept repeating over and over. Abbey immediately went to his side, trying to comfort him, telling him everything would be OK while stroking his hair. He finally calmed down, but Abbey looked at Zach as a tear came out of one of his closed eyes.

"We are going to do everything we can. Amputation will only be our last resort, but we have to do surgery early tomorrow morning. We need to reduce the swelling and clean out infected tissue. The longer we wait, the outcome is not as favorable. Do you understand?"

As Zach nodded, Abbey felt like she had when she received the call from Lance the night of Zach's accident. She had known this was a possibility from the moment he was transported here, but he had made such progress this week. To watch Zach go through this was breaking her heart more than she could have ever imagined. *Stay strong for him, Abbey*, she told herself as she took a deep breath, trying to relax.

"If you have any more questions, tell the nurse, and we will talk to you before surgery in the morning."

"Why don't you try to go back to sleep? Get some rest?" Abbey continued to stroke Zach's hair as she watched more tears now falling slowly from his eyes.

"It's OK," Sandy said as she sat on the opposite side of the hospital bed. "They are going to be able to fix you up, and you will be walking in no time." Her voice was gentle and soothing and Abbey could see Zach relaxing ever so slightly at the sound of his mother's voice. But his father stood motionless at the foot of the bed, acting as though he wasn't sure what to say.

"I can't lose my leg. I can't do it." His tears continued to come, but not the crying Abbey had been doing. His face remained emotionless as the drops of water fell down the sides of his face. She knew that there was nothing she could do except be there for him and pray. She reached over and kissed his cheek.

"I love you, Zach. And you are going to get through this just fine. You are a fighter, and you are strong. You always look at the bright side of everything, and you certainly are persistent. Plus, you have so much support. Your parents, me, Lance, and everyone in Key West."

As the nurse came in and administered more medication, Zach fell into a deep sleep once more. He needed rest, and Abbey along with his parents needed time to digest what was happening.

"I'm going outside to make a call to let everyone know the situation. I promised to keep Lance and Josie informed so they could tell everyone else." With that, Abbey slipped out of the room and rushed out of the hospital, needing fresh air on her face and a place to cry or even scream if she needed too.

38

The same waiting room was once again crowded, bringing back memories of Zach's first surgery. It had only been a week ago, but to Abbey it felt like a lifetime. Sitting and waiting, hoping to see the doctor's face come into the room, smiling. She closed her eyes, imagining the scenario over and over. The smile would mean that Zach's leg was OK. She could see every detail of this scene all the way to them being back in Key West, swimming in the waters offshore just like they had not so long ago.

As Abbey opened her eyes, the doctor did indeed come around the corner. He didn't have a smile across his face, but he didn't look grim either. Abbey couldn't interpret his body language.

"Zach is doing well and we didn't have to amputate. Once we were able to look at his leg, remove the infection and some more damaged tissue, we believed that his leg could be saved. It's too early to tell, so we can't gauge the status of the use of his leg at this time. The bones were badly broken, but they were secured with rods and screws to make them stable. They should heal fine, but they will be there permanently. Now it's up to Zach."

As Abbey listened to the doctor, all she could focus on was the fact that they had saved his leg. *Thank you, God*, she said silently, looking toward the ceiling.

"He will still be in ICU for a day or so, but I think he is over that critical stage. We will watch him the next forty-eight hours and then, if possible, move him to a regular room. If all goes well, he can be transferred for follow-up back to the hospital in Key West within a week or so."

Abbey looked over at Sandy and Justin to see smiles and looks of relief wash over their faces. She was sure her face looked the same.

"They didn't have to amputate, so that was good," Abbey said as she talked to Josie. "Hopefully within the next day or two, he will be in a regular room."

"How are you doing?" Josie asked, hearing the weariness in Abbey's voice.

"I'm OK, maybe a bit tired. Zach's parents have been so nice. As soon as they move him to a regular room, I'm coming back to Key West. I'm going to rent a car, because I need to get back to work. I'm so far behind, and now I'll be doing work for me and Zach."

"You need to come home for some 'you time.' This has been a long ordeal, and Zach will need you when he gets home."

"I just hate the thought of leaving him here, but his parents are taking such good care of him," Abbey said, knowing that leaving the love of her life here in Miami and her being in Key West was going to be especially difficult.

"When you are ready to come home, I will come and get you. No need to rent a car—just a waste of money."

"Thanks, Josie. I think I will take you up on that. Would you mind calling Lance to let him know the latest? I'm really tired and don't want to have to explain everything all over again." Abbey was exhausted but didn't tell anyone. She felt like she could sleep for days, but her body was betraying her. It wouldn't let her rest like she wanted to because she had to be—no, needed to be—with Zach.

"That's no problem. I'll give him a call right now."

"Thanks, Josie. I can't thank you enough."

After her call, Abbey had the overwhelming urge to talk to her parents. She knew that they were probably sitting down to dinner, but she had to talk to them. She hadn't called since Zach's accident. As she sat and thought about what had happened, it gave her chills to think how mere seconds could change everything. She quickly dialed her mom's number and was so glad when she picked up. Abbey started crying, barely able to get the words out that Zach had been hurt. At first her mom thought Abbey was injured, but once she got her daughter to calm down, Abbey was able to explain the whole story to her and, by now, also to her dad, since her mom had put her on speaker phone.

"It will be OK, Abbey. We will put him on the prayer list here, and I'll call your brother in Houston, so they will too."

"Thanks, Mom. Everyone keeps telling me he is going to be fine, but no one really knows. I'm so scared, and I've never felt like this before. I can't quit shaking, and I feel like I'm on some kind of wild rollercoaster."

"That's normal, honey. And everyone keeps telling you that because that is what we are hoping for and believing." Her mom's familiar voice helped her breathe more slowly and calm down. By the time they hung up, Abbey was feeling stronger and a bit more steady. Just as she entered the waiting room, Abbey heard her name being called.

"I'm Abbey," she said as she walked toward the nurse.

"Zach has asked to see you." Abbey looked back at his parents, feeling a bit guilty that Zach had asked for her, but both Justin and Sandy shook their heads to motion her toward the recovery room where Zach was.

39

"Hi there," Abbey said softly as she looked at Zach, tubes everywhere and his leg bandaged heavily and elevated. He barely opened his eyes but then smiled at her.

"You are a sight for sore eyes," he said in a low, gravelly voice. He lifted his hand, and she gladly took it, using both her hands like she was protecting him in some way.

"They were able to save your leg," Abbey said, once again speaking very low as though he was sleeping.

"Yeah, I remember the doc saying something about it, but I don't remember any details. I don't care as long as I have my leg." He closed his eyes again, falling back to sleep while holding her hand. Abbey sat there, looking at him as if she was making a mental recording of all his features. She was there with him, and he had made it through surgery once again.

Abbey continued to sit by his side, realizing how lucky they were. Zach was doing well, and for the first time, she felt this ordeal was taking a turn for the better. The doctors sounded encouraging, even though there was still a tough road ahead. But she vowed to Zach as he lay in the bed, this wonderful man who had stolen her heart, that she would be there for him every step of the way.

Abbey looked around at Zach's new room. Though she was happy that he was out of ICU, this meant she would also be leaving soon and she needed to tell Zach's parents.

"The thought of doing this is just harder than I can describe, but I have to go back to Key West tomorrow. I have so much work to catch up on, and until Zach is ready, I'll be working for both of us. The thought of leaving him tears my heart," Abbey said as she was gazing at a sleeping Zach, stroking his hand. Sandy and Justin could see the tears forming in her eyes.

Sandy walked over to her, putting her hands on Abbey's shoulders. "Before you know it, he will be back home recovering. And knowing Zach, he won't let anything get in his way. He has always been that headstrong, and now he has you. So no matter what the future holds for his leg and walking, he won't let it stop him. And the rest of his injuries are healing so nicely. God was watching out for him."

Abbey nodded her head in agreement, afraid to say anything that would cause crying to ensue. But Sandy was right—Zach was a fighter and very persistent. This wouldn't get the best of him.

"Hey there. You are in your own room now," Abbey said as she saw Zach open his eyes. "Maybe we need to decorate this place up with some balloons. Buy you one of those little teddy bears in the gift shop so you have something to sleep with," Abbey said teasingly.

"I won't be here long enough for any of that, and if I have to sleep with something, I would rather it be you," Zach said weakly, not caring that his parents were in the room. Even though he didn't sound like he had much strength, his voice sounded like music to her ears.

"I need to tell you something. I really don't want to do this, but I have to go back to Key West. I told Lance that once you were in a regular room, I would come back to work. But I can't stand the thought of going," she said, not able to finish her sentence as she looked down at her hand intertwined in his. Then he brought it up to his lips, kissing the back of her hand softly.

"It's OK. I don't want you to leave either, but I will be fine. Hopefully I'll be out of this place in a few days," Zach said weakly. Now it was his hand gently wiping the few tears off her cheek as he talked. "My mom and dad are here, so don't worry about me."

"You have wonderful parents, Zach," she said.

"They are. We had our share of rough times when I was growing up, but they have always been there for me, my sister, and my brother. I have to admit—the three of us were a hand-ful. I'm surprised they survived with their sanity intact," he laughed sounding fatigued, but Abbey smiled because this was the Zach she knew.

"I love you, Zach. I loved you before this accident, but this has made me realize even more how precious life is and that when you have something good in front of you, you don't let it go." Abbey stood up and lightly kissed him on the lips. But even in his exhausted state, he wanted more. Their first real kiss since that fateful night.

"Well, hello there." Abbey immediately recognized the voice. It was Josie—her ride back to Key West and away from the man who had stolen her heart. They both parted and looked toward the door to see not only Josie and Michael but Zach's parents too, all smiling.

"Looks like he is in good hands and healing just nicely," Mr. Isler said, laughing.

Abbey knew that her cheeks were probably a nice shade of pink, but she didn't care. She was about to leave Zach, and that kiss would have to hold her through till she saw him again.

"Couldn't let her leave without a proper good-bye kiss," Zach said, his voice sounding a bit stronger.

"If you keep doing as well as you are, hopefully you will be back home in no time," Michael said as they came into the room.

"My goal is by the end of the week."

"What did I tell you, Abbey?" Sandy said.

40

The ride back to Key West was long. Even though Abbey could never get enough of the beautiful scenery of the Florida Keys, this time she felt as though she wasn't looking at anything. Her thoughts were consumed with Zach and the awful feeling she had when she left his room. Panic welled up inside her as they pulled away from the trauma center, only the second time she truly had been away from him since the night she had received the phone call from Lance. But as they were going through Islamorada, she fell asleep from exhaustion.

"Abbey? Honey, we are home." Abbey opened her eyes slowly to see her little apartment before her. Her body felt like lead, letting her know that it craved more sleep, so in her very tired state, she decided she would eat a quick dinner, make sure to have her stuff ready for work tomorrow, and then crawl into bed. Working tomorrow would be a distraction and a reminder that her partner, her best friend, and her love was not with her.

"You go on up and get settled. We left beef stew cooking in the Crock-Pot before we left this morning, and I'll bring some up for you in a bit." Josie smiled and gave her a hug. Then Abbey slowly made her way up the steps.

The shower felt good on her skin, and she stood beneath the warm, falling water, letting her muscles relax and trying to clear her mind. But it was no use. No matter what Abbey did, her thoughts always went back to Zach. The first thing she did after walking in the front door was to make a quick call to Sandy's phone. Zach was sleeping but doing fine. There was still no feeling in the exposed part of his foot, but things still seemed promising. Abbey wanted to hear Zach's voice, and Sandy promised she would have him call if he was feeling up to it. For Abbey, that phone call couldn't come soon enough.

Her apartment was still chaotic with art pieces everywhere. It was supposed to be the next evening that she was to have her second show on Mallory Square, but all that had changed in a blink of an eye. Everything would have to be cleaned up tomorrow after work, she decided, because now she just wanted to crawl into bed, willing her phone to ring to hear Zach's voice on the other end. Then she heard the knock on the door: Josie.

"It smells so good. Thanks for thinking about me and being my ride home. Everything just feels so displaced, like I don't belong here," Abbey said quietly as she put the bowl of stew on her kitchen counter. "I wish I could explain it better."

"Honey, you don't have to tell me. I know how you feel. Just a different set of circumstances for me. All I can say is that it will get better if you let it. Things improved for me. I got used to my 'new normal,' as I called it, but now I can see I could have done even better. But I'm not going to knock myself now. Wouldn't do any good."

Suddenly, Josie found herself enveloped by Abbey's arms, her body trembling as heavy sobs heaved from the girl's chest. Josie had seen Abbey cry since the accident, but nothing like this. It was like every fear, every emotion had been let loose, and Abbey was cleansing it from her body.

"Abbey, he is going to be fine. Look at what progress he's made so far."

"I know. But everything doesn't feel right. Maybe if he was here and not one hundred and fifty miles away, it would be different."

"Eat your dinner and get some sleep. It's still early, but you need it," Josie said as though she were talking to a small child.

"I'm waiting for Zach to call, hopefully. Sandy said he is doing good, and she would have him call if he could."

"Well, you can still crawl in bed while you wait, and if you should fall asleep, I'm positive if that phone as much as beeps, you will wake up. Try to relax. You might not have been in an accident, but you went through a lot of emotional stress. You need to give your body some time to recuperate too. Promise to listen to me? You know I can get cranky if I want to!" Josie said with a slight laugh.

"I'm going to eat and go to bed now."

"That's my girl."

The stew was wonderful after nothing but hospital food for such a long time. Abbey actually ate curled up in her bed, watching

TV for a bit of distraction. But as soon as the phone rang, everything stopped. It was Sandy's number, and she smiled.

"Hello," she said quite excitedly.

"Hi, beautiful," came the groggy voice on the other end of the line. Zach's voice was intoxicating even if he sounded tired, and Abbey drank it all in.

"How are you feeling? I'm having such a hard time not being there with you."

"I wish you were here too, but I understand. Hopefully there isn't a pile of work for you tomorrow," Zach said slowly with a yawn.

"Don't you worry about it. Just get better so you can come home. Being this far away from you feels so wrong. I want you here with me. Get you well so we can do some of those things we talked about." Abbey wanted to keep him talking, but she could hear the fatigue in his voice.

"Go get some sleep. That helps you heal."

"It seems like all I do is sleep," Zach said through another yawn.

"I love you, Zach, so much. Hurry back to me."

"I will. And I love you too," he said softly.

Walking into work the next day felt so odd to Abbey. Like everything else right now, it just felt out of place. She'd had a routine up until the accident, and now it was gone. This was what people called change, and not that she was opposed to it, but a traumatic event unsettled everything. But it would get better, she repeated to herself.

"Abbey, so glad you are back. How is Zach?" It was Everly, giving her a hug and talking to her as she walked to her desk.

"Finally in a room of his own, which was a big step. Today I should find out if and when they might transfer him to the hospital here for rehabilitation. Still has no feeling in his foot that they can tell, so it is just a waiting game."

"Knowing Zach, he will be skiing before you know it," Everly said once again, giving her another hug.

"She is back," Roger yelled from across the room. Abbey looked behind her to see Roger and Lance coming toward her with big smiles on their faces.

"So Zach is doing better?" Lance asked.

Abbey gave them both the same information she had told Everly, and they all agreed that Zach would make it through this.

"He is tough and has such a great attitude. One of the main reasons I hired him. His enthusiasm. And his drive."

Abbey just smiled, wishing she had the same optimistic outlook of her coworkers. She felt good about Zach's recovery but was still haunted by the events of the last two weeks. Her nerves were still on edge, but she hoped diving into the stack of papers on her desk would give her a distraction.

"Don't let the papers overwhelm you. Most of the sites you and Zach were working on are still well within the time frame of completion. Might just have to put in a little extra time to catch up. Everly said she would assist you and cover for Zach when you need any help. Just don't get anxious. We are a little family here, and we are going to help each other." Lance gave her a hug like her own father would and walked back to his office.

Going over the work that needed to be done was a big help for Abbey because it kept her mind occupied, something that she needed, being so far away from Zach. But he was always in the back of her mind. Yes, there was a lot of work after missing so many days, but not anything that couldn't be handled. She spent the morning organizing, waiting for her lunch break, when she could call the hospital.

"Hi, Sandy," Abbey said, feeling happy to hear Zach's mom on the other end of the line. "How is he doing today?"

"Hang on just a minute."

Abbey waited patiently but suddenly had a knot in her stomach. Was something wrong?

"Just wanted to go out in the hall so we could talk."

"What's wrong?"

"The doctor came in this morning. Zach's leg seems to be healing, but he still has no feeling in his foot. They think the nerve damage might have been too great. They are concerned about his ability to walk again," Sandy said with sadness in her voice.

"But he was doing so well. They said that this could happen and that the nerves could regenerate. He just needs more time," Abbey said determinedly.

"They did say today that it would take time. For some people with this type of injury, they heal fast. Others are slower."

"How is Zach doing with this latest news?" Abbey was worried.

"He just sat there, staring at the doctor. I can't really tell what he is thinking. After the doctors left, he just laid the bed down and closed his eyes. He wouldn't even talk to us." Sandy sounded worried.

"Do you think he would talk to me? Maybe tonight once I get home from work? He sounded so good last night except for being tired." Abbey knew she could get through to him.

"Call tonight, and we will see. Hopefully your voice will cheer him up."

After her lunch break, Abbey felt like the afternoon went by so slowly as she anxiously waited for the evening. It had to be a fluke, because the person Sandy had described was not the Zach she knew.

"Hi, Sandy. Can I talk to him?"

"Yes, just a minute. I'll give him the phone, and we are going to step outside to give you two some privacy." Abbey could hear as Sandy passed the phone to Zach. But there was silence.

"Zach, are you there?"

"Hey, Abbey."

"Hi. How are you doing? You sound good, more alert."

"I'm fine. The doctor said that I'm healing good, just waiting to see how my leg is doing. Will be taking the bandages off tomorrow for a better look." The defeat in his voice was clear, and Abbey could tell now why Sandy sounded so concerned.

"That's good. Tomorrow you'll see that it's probably healing fine, just going to take some time."

"Abbey, I'm not stupid. If I can't feel anything, I know the possibility of me walking normal again is probably gone. Listen, I'm really tired. Can we talk more tomorrow?"

She couldn't believe what she was hearing on the other end of the line. The switch in his attitude in just one day was hard to comprehend. "I understand. Get some rest, and I'll call you tomorrow. I love you, Zach."

"I love you too," repeated the monotone voice before they were disconnected.

Abbey suddenly wanted to jump in her Jeep and race back to Miami. She sent Sandy a quick text message saying she could come back if it would help because she could hear the despair in Zach's voice. Sandy wrote back that she would call after the doctors examined his leg in the morning and let her know what was going on.

Work the next day was almost torture. Abbey couldn't wrap her head around the project she was working on, her mind drifting to the hospital room in Miami. What was going on? Had the doctors been in to see Zach? How was his leg? The questions wandering about in her mind left her at times just staring out the window.

"Hey, are you OK?" Everly asked as she walked over and sat beside Abbey.

"Just worried about Zach. He sounded really off last night. He has kept his sense of humor and been as upbeat as possible this whole time, but last night it was like I was talking to a different person. The doctors are removing the bandages to check his leg today for the first time since his last surgery. Just waiting to hear from Zach's mom."

"Looks like you didn't sleep much last night. Are you resting at all?"

"Do I look that bad?" Abbey asked as she looked at her friend.

"You don't look bad, just tired. I know you are under a lot of stress trying to get caught up here and thinking about Zach. Let me help you. You don't have to do it all by yourself. Randy is finishing up the current coding on the website, so I can help you."

Abbey smiled and nodded. Everly grabbed her own laptop and made a place at Zach's desk to work. This was just what Abbey needed. Something else to focus on instead of watching her cell phone for a text message or waiting for it to ring.

"Abbey, that looks perfect! You did it. At least that part is done, thank goodness. I don't think Mr. Watson can complain about that." Everly laughed, and Abbey joined in. And it felt good to smile and laugh. Something she hadn't done in quite a while.

When the phone on Abbey's desk suddenly rang, both girls jumped, startled. It was Sandy.

"Hi, Sandy. How is he doing?" Abbey was almost afraid to ask, but she needed to know.

"Well, there is good news and not so good news. I'm out in the hall so I could talk without Zach hearing me."

"What did the doctors say?"

"All his injuries are healing great except his leg. He still has no feeling from right above the knee down. The nerve damage was greater than they thought, but they keep saying that it could come back. He still can't put any weight on his leg for another five weeks and will have to use a wheelchair to get around till they can take the cast off his arm in about three weeks. Once he can put weight on his leg, they will know more about what they think he will be able to do as far as walking and such. The good news is that he is being transferred back to Key West this Friday as long as he continues to do as well as he is."

He's coming home, Abbey thought, relief spreading through her. She couldn't wait for him to be nearby, closer to her.

"I'm going to stay with him till he is able to move around on his own. But, Abbey, he's not too happy about all this. He won't even talk to us, hardly to the doctors. The nurses are telling me that this is normal, and most patients go through a depression after this type of trauma. I've never seen Zach like this in his entire life. I think it's just going to take time."

"Thanks for letting me know what is going on. Do you think he might talk to me tonight?" Abbey asked, unsure of the answer.

"Call, and we will see. He is having a hard time processing everything," Sandy said. "To be honest, his dad and I are also."

"I understand." *I am too,* Abbey thought.

"Hopefully we can get him home, and he can adjust. I know my son. He doesn't give up. Just need to get him over this hump."

"I'll call tonight. But please tell him that I'm thinking of him every minute, and I will talk to him later, OK?"

"I will. Once again, I can't tell you how glad I am that my son has you in his life. He told us about you during our phone calls over the last few months. He had never talked about a woman like he has you. Zach definitely loves you. He kept telling us he had been dating but just hadn't found the right girl.

But apparently his search is over," Sandy said softly. "Thank you for making him happy."

Tears once again were forming in the corners of Abbey's eyes. "He makes me very happy. I wish I hadn't been so stubborn about admitting we were meant to be together, because he is perfect for me," Abbey said into the phone, the tears now slowly gliding down her cheeks.

"Let's get him home where he can heal. He will have to stay at the hospital in Key West till they feel it is safe for him to be home with a home-health nurse. Then I will stay with him till he is walking," Sandy said in a determined voice.

"That sounds like a wonderful plan to me," Abbey said with a small smile across her face as she drew strength from Sandy's words.

41

Abbey kept watching as each ambulance pulled up to the hospital. Still no Zach. He was being transferred today back to the Lower Keys Medical Center. He had done so well that it was time to come home. Abbey had talked each day to Zach on the phone, but he sounded lost and his depression was obvious. She prayed that once he was back in Key West, among his friends and family, his spirits would lift, and the Zach she fell in love with would be there. Everyone she had talked to told her that what Zach was experiencing was normal, but it hurt her to hear him so down. She had been tempted over the last few days to drive back to Miami, but Zach's parents told her to just wait because they were sure he would be coming home, and now he was.

Abbey watched as another ambulance pulled up to the Emergency Room doors and waited to see who emerged. She couldn't contain her excitement when she saw Zach, on the stretcher, minus the bandage on his head. As she quickly walked over to the door where he was, Sandy and Justin were suddenly beside her. She hugged them both, and they watched as Zach was transferred to his room. He still had not seen Abbey, but she was closely watching him, noticing all the little details. He looked so good, and she couldn't wait till she could touch him, kiss him, and hold him in her arms.

"You can go in now," the nurse said as she exited the room.

"You go first," Justin said to Abbey, motioning toward the door.

"Are you sure?"

"Go."

With a smile on her face, Abbey opened the door.

"Zach?"

He was looking toward the window but slowly turned when he heard Abbey's voice.

"Hi there." He smiled back at her, but it was different. Abbey could tell that he wasn't himself. She walked slowly to the bed and bent over to give his forehead a kiss.

"How was the ride here? And how does it feel to be back home? Well, at least back in Key West?"

"It was fine. I just slept most of the way. But I'm certainly not back home."

"At least you're not so far away. That's progress." Abbey suddenly felt uncomfortable, not sure what to say. They had never had difficulty in conversations since the moment they met, including the little talks they'd had in Miami.

"I guess." He turned his face back toward the window, looking out with glazed eyes.

"Everyone has been asking about you. Be prepared for tons of visitors. But hopefully you won't be here that long. Your mom said that they just had to make sure you were able to be home with a nurse for a while. Then you will start physical therapy once you stand on your leg."

"Did she also tell you that I might not be able to stand on my leg? That I don't have feeling yet? That I might have to learn to walk all over again or that I might need a wheelchair for the rest of my life?" With each sentence Zach spoke, his weak voice was stronger, fueled by anger. Abbey could hear all the hurt and fear in each word that he spoke.

"Yes, she did. But we both agreed that you will walk again because you are persistent—never giving up on the things you want."

"Well, maybe that Zach is gone. He is still lying on the pavement pinned under a bicycle and a car." He still wouldn't look at her, so Abbey went to the other side of the bed.

"You can't give up. You can do this. I know it with every fiber of my being. I love you, Zach and I'm here for you. Anything you need."

"Right now I just want to take a nap." Zach pulled up the blankets and closed his eyes.

"I love you," Abbey said once more as she headed to the door.

"I love you too," came the lifeless voice of the man lying in the bed.

As Abbey made her way home, she felt as though she had been slammed by a wave of sadness as she replayed in her mind the visit with Zach. And even though she talked to Sandy and

Justin about what had happened, she didn't feel any better. Sandy had told her that the doctors had warned them about Depression and Post Traumatic Stress Disorder. They were normal for someone who had been through such a trauma as Zach experienced. She just had to give him time. Abbey was prepared for that, but it was so hard. These last few weeks had been tough. To watch someone you love go through such pain was something she had never dealt with, and the hurt at times was unbearable. Not once did she let it show, but now she felt like she was going to burst. She needed to talk to someone— hopefully Josie would be home.

Abbey knocked on her door, the tears in her eyes yet again threatening to spill forth. She was immediately wrapped in Josie's motherly embrace as they made their way to Josie's couch.

"Is Zach OK?" Josie asked.

Abbey nodded because she was still crying, and no words would come out. Just being here with her friend, Abbey felt safe enough to let out the pent-up feelings that she had felt since she left Zach's bedside.

"Josie, he's different and he barely talked. I know he is depressed and angry. When they got him situated in his room, I was the first to see him, and it was like I was with a stranger. He acts as though he is giving up. He doesn't have feeling in his leg yet, so he thinks he is going to end up in a wheelchair."

"Abbey, you have to accept the fact that he won't be the same. He will be different. Going through an experience like he did changes a person. He is going to be scared, angry, depressed, and the possibility is there that he won't be able to do the things he did before. But he will find a way to make it work because that is the kind of person he is. Don't let this change your feelings for him. You still be yourself. Just know it could be a bumpy ride for a bit, so be prepared. And you need to remember that you are one strong girl. I know you can do it. Look what you did for me!" Josie said, wiping away Abbey's tears.

"I didn't go through a physical trauma all those years ago like Zach has, but mentally, I was devastated. I've told you how I was afterward. I even ran away from home! Then in a brand-new place, I still pushed everyone away for the most part. Stayed at my house. Didn't do much. Really only what I had to. And I was that way till I met you. You gave me the nudge to get out of that miserable comfort zone I had put myself in."

Abbey hadn't thought about how Josie's story was similar to Zach's in some ways, but she was right. Abbey had to give Zach time.

"But, Josie, before I left his room, I told him I loved him. He just murmured it back like he had to, not like he meant it. What if this has changed our relationship? I just found him, and I don't want to lose him." Abbey leaned her head back on the couch and closed her eyes, trying to comprehend everything that was happening.

"I don't think that will happen."

"I'm not sure. I wish I knew what I could do to help him."

"Just be there for him. Zach still has a lot of healing to do. Remember how much time he gave you?"

Abbey looked at her quizzically. "What do you mean?"

"That boy loved you from the minute he laid eyes on you. That is so obvious. He waited, and even after you told him that you only wanted to be friends, he continued to wait. He was patient and persevered. I think it is time that you did the same thing. I won't say that it will be easy, but if you love Zach the way I know you do, it will be worth it."

"I never thought of it that way," Abbey said, wiping another stray tear that fell from her eye. "It's so hard. I want things to be like they were because we were just starting on what felt like a magical journey of sorts."

"You have to remember that things will never be the same as before. But they can be better. Look at me and Michael. Do I yearn for what we had before he left me at the altar? Yes, at times. But now I see that our relationship is much stronger, better than what we had so long ago. We both went through a lot of hell to get where we are today, but it's in those times where you learn and become a better person if you are willing." Josie looked at Abbey, wishing she could take away some of the pain her friend was going through.

Both women stood up, and Abbey hugged her so tight, Josie almost couldn't breathe. "Thank you so much. You know, you are such a good friend, but I feel like you are my second mom. If I had called her, she probably would have told me the same thing about being persistent and patient. But I think you know more of what it feels like, and though I'm sorry you had to go through what you did, maybe your experience is going to help others like me.

"I need to get some food and sleep before work in the morning. I was going to go by the hospital on the way to work, but I think I'll just call to check on him. Give him time to adjust." She hugged Josie one more time and then headed to her upstairs apartment. As soon as she sat down, exhaustion enveloped her, both mentally and physically. She ate, took a shower, got her things ready for work, and went right to bed. She wanted to call and check one more time on Zach but replayed the conversation in her mind she'd had with Josie. *Give him time*, she told herself.

The next week became a strange routine for Abbey. She would work in the morning, visit with Zach at lunch, and then go back to work. In the evenings, she was at the hospital then she went home. Each day repeated itself like a broken record, except for the fact that Zach's anger and depression seemed to deepen during each visit. This raised Abbey's anxiety higher and higher each time they were together.

Physically, Zach was healing fine. Yes, there would be multiple scars, but he was doing great. But he still had no feeling in his leg except some spots that were beginning to tingle, which the doctors confidently told everyone was a positive sign. But they couldn't be sure of anything till Zach could put weight on his leg. That would be the all important test to see if he would be able to walk again.

Each visit, it seemed Abbey did most of the talking. Zach would listen but not offer much input. He would say he loved her, but it was a robotic response, not heartfelt like before. Even his kisses that used to make her weak all over were just routine, like he was acting out of obligation instead of passion. Abbey's heart was breaking as she watched her beloved Zach basically drift away a little each day.

Though each visit was difficult, Abbey put on a smile and acted as though everything was fine. On Friday, the doctors told them that as long as Zach continued to improve, they would let him go home on Monday. Though everyone else was ecstatic, the smile on Zach's face was forced. Abbey could see through the facade. That evening, when his parents went out to get dinner, Abbey finally had to ask.

"Zach, why?"

"What are you talking about?" He looked at her puzzled.

"Aren't you excited about going home? Getting out of here? You are doing so well. Even the doctors are astounded."

"You wouldn't understand."

"Try me," Abbey said, crossing her arms in front of her, standing beside his bed.

"Not now, Abbey," Zach said, dismissing her.

Now what? He wouldn't even talk to her. She didn't want to push too far, but she knew it was time to confront him and his pity party.

"I'll leave you alone. I'm going to be working this weekend, so I will get here when I can. You can always call me though. Anytime. You know that, right?"

"Yeah, I know."

"I love you, Zach."

"Love you too," Zach said as he turned away from her and closed his eyes.

42

"Hey, girl. You are early today. How is Zach?" Everly asked.

"He's doing OK. He got to come home yesterday and is settled in on his couch in front of the TV. His mom is staying with him since he is still in a wheelchair. Hopefully he should have the arm cast off in a few weeks. Then he will be able to use crutches. By the way, thanks for mobilizing his friends and getting that wheelchair ramp built for his house." Abbey quickly hugged Everly so she couldn't see the tears that were forming in her eyes, but suddenly she was crying. It seemed like this was an everyday occurrence for her these days.

"I think you need some time off for you. Maybe a little self-care," Everly said as she directed Abbey to her desk chair. "I remember when I was about eight years old, my dad was in a boating accident. My mom was exhausted between taking care of him and me while working too. We had family around town to help, but it wasn't till one day when my mom fainted that they stepped up and started helping out till my dad was better. I remember being so scared, like I was going to lose my mom and my dad. You need to take care of you. What are you doing after work tonight?" Everly said with a bright smile on her face.

"I'm leaving here to see Zach, then going home. Why?"

"Well, I say we both go see Zach for a few minutes, then it's some girl time. We will sit on the beach with sandwiches from the shop next door. Nothing fancy. Just go, eat, and watch a sunset. Relax a little bit."

"As wonderful as that sounds, I would feel guilty knowing that Zach needs help," Abbey said as she bit her lower lip.

"Zach's mom is helping him. And he knows you need time too. Come on, please?" Everly didn't know that Zach was very depressed and not talking much to Abbey. And she wasn't quite ready to let anyone know what was going on.

"It sounds great, but maybe a rain check for tomorrow? I really want to see Zach tonight."

"Any time would be great with me. Miss 'I Don't Have a Boyfriend' here is available." Everly once again pulled Abbey into a hug. "It will be OK. Promise!"

Abbey sat at her desk, going over the workload. It was enormous. She needed to take this morning just to map out a game plan to get things back on track. All their clients had been more than gracious about the situation, but they needed their websites up and running. Randy and Kim were way ahead of her and Zach as far as the back-end tech issues for the sites they were building. So she took a deep breath, grabbed a pad of paper, and started listing all the ideas, to-dos, and projects to give her some direction and organization. After about three hours, she had a workable albeit heavy schedule that should get them up to speed as soon as possible, barring any major hiccups. At lunch she called to check on Zach, and Sandy told her he was sleeping.

"Tell him that I called and will see him after work." Abbey wanted to see him so badly but had this feeling in the pit of her stomach that the person she really wanted to see wasn't there.

Even though she was apprehensive, Abbey knocked on the door to Zach's little place.

"Hey, come on in. You didn't have to knock," Sandy said with a smile once she saw Abbey.

"He's in the bathroom, and I need to go help him. He is having fits about this, but there is no way around it. I, or should I say 'we,' will be right back." As she left the room, Abbey sat her stuff on the floor next to the door; then she went to sit in the chair next to the spot they had made for Zach in the living room just the day before. Why was she so nervous? Because she wasn't sure what to expect.

"Here he is," Sandy said as the wheelchair came around the corner. Zach said nothing, got up on his one good leg, and was able to make the transfer to the couch. He lay down, propping his arm and leg up, and then looked at Abbey.

"Hi. How's work?"

"Good. Getting caught up, so that's a good sign. How are you feeling? Has to feel better to be home than being in the hospital."

"It does. Harder to get around, but getting used to it." His voice was the same. Emotionless. He even stared at the TV instead of looking at her. So she went and sat on the small coffee table in front of his couch.

"We got another job today. That one Lance has been after for two months, so he was pretty happy about that. And it looks like Josie and Michael are getting a bit cozier. They are going out more, checking out all the tourist traps, and now they have planned a trip to Miami, just the two of them. I think Josie has finally forgiven him and is ready to move on." Abbey tried to think of more topics to talk about, but she was dry. He didn't even look at her when she was speaking.

"Zach, are you even listening to me? If you aren't feeling good, I can leave so you can rest." Abbey wasn't sure what to do or say. She felt like she was walking on eggshells. She wanted to be with him right now, but she could tell if the feeling wasn't mutual.

"Abbey, don't you realize I was hit by a car? I hurt all the time. I can't even go to the bathroom without help. I'm in a wheelchair for I don't know how long. I don't know if I'll be able to walk right again or ski or swim. It hurts to breathe, and all I can do is sit and watch TV all day. It sucks!" Zach's words came out in a rush, filled with defeat and resentment.

"So what are you going to do? Just sit here and feel sorry for yourself? Where is the person I know that would be fighting back, looking for anything that could possibly be good? Where is he?"

"He's gone, Abbey. I'm sorry, but he no longer exits." Zach laid his head back and closed his eyes.

"No, he is not. It is just going to take time."

"You are not the one lying on a couch, having your mom practically help you pee." He looked at her now, anger showing through his eyes. Abbey knew right then that it didn't matter what she said, it wasn't going to be the right thing. She looked at him on the couch, and her heart felt heavy. She loved Zach so much, but it seemed like he was giving up. On life, on himself, and on them.

"If you are feeling up to it, Lance says that we can work here at your house when you are ready. If not, I'm doing OK by myself. Right now, I'm going to go so you can rest. I just wanted to check on you. If you need anything, let me know." With that, Abbey reached over and gave him a kiss on the lips that was weakly returned.

"I still love you, no matter what." When no answer came back, Abbey felt like her heart was going to break into a million pieces.

43

Zach still had his eyes closed, thinking long after Abbey left. What had he done? This woman had been there for him every day since his accident. She had given up so much, and he had acted like a jerk. He felt so helpless. And that he couldn't be the man anymore that Abbey deserved.

"Zach, that was a little harsh. You acted like she was being a pain in the ass when all she is trying to do is be here for you and help. I've never seen you act like that. I know you have been through a lot, but that is no excuse. You might just lose her, you know, and that would be a great loss." His mother's words stung because she was right, but she didn't know his motives.

"I think it would be better if she and I took some time apart except for work. You will be here for my therapy when the time comes, right? I'll see how things go. She doesn't need someone like me keeping her tied down. I'll be nothing more than a nuisance to her."

"Why don't you let Abbey decide that? That girl loves you. And that kind of love is hard to find. I've gotten to know her very well over these last few weeks, through talks we've had when you were sleeping. She is perfect for you, but you are going to screw it up. And you are being completely selfish. Have you thought about her feelings?"

"Mom, just let it go, please." Zach sighed and tried to move, wincing in pain. Though it was getting better, the pain was still there, and the medicine kept it bearable. He did realize his mom was right. He would lose Abbey. But then maybe she would find someone who could give her the life she deserved. Right now he couldn't even work! He also couldn't hold her or kiss her without pain. Going anywhere was out of the question. He didn't know what his future would hold. Zach didn't want Abbey going down that unknown path with him. He wanted her to be happy and free. Not tied down to a crippled man.

The ride home was terrible. Abbey was barely able to see through the wet drops falling from her eyes. How were there any tears left? She had to have expended her allotted amount by now, because she seemed to cry every day. But what she had just experienced hurt her so much, almost as much as the day of Zach's accident when she saw him in the ER for the first time. Why was he doing this? Did he suddenly not love her anymore? Did the accident give him some kind of weird clarity that she was not for him? She tried to cling to Josie's words about giving him space and time. But it was hard, because Abbey just wanted to understand.

She decided that she would start checking on him only once each day by a short trip after work. Then, starting next week, if he had the OK from the doctor, she would insist on working at least half days with him at his house. She would keep everything professional, doing her best not to let any personal feelings show through. This would be hard, but it was the only way she knew how to approach this delicate situation. She wanted "her" Zach back, no matter what the circumstances. She loved him, but the only way she could think of to help him was to treat him like he was treating her. She was going to be nice, though. She hoped that this would heal the rift, not cause it to split further. But at this point, she didn't have anything to lose. Zach was already slipping away and he was the only one that could crawl out of this self-pity and depression hole he had dug for himself. She only hoped their relationship would survive the ride.

The first week was challenging for Abbey, but she followed through on her plan. Zach's attitude had not changed; if anything it was worse. But Abbey still remained cheerful and upbeat. Since she could tell he was getting better, she told him, not asked, that they would begin working on projects at his home every morning starting the next week. Hopefully the work would let him know that he could still be productive. This would also give him something else to occupy his mind and time besides the negative thoughts of his predicament and the TV that stayed on twenty-fours a day.

Abbey also finally broke down and told Lance, Roger, and Everly of what was going on with Zach. The depression. His personality change. The anger. And how she was hoping that time and work would help. Soon physical therapy would be added to the mix, hopefully something else to propel Zach out of this dark place he was in. They all seemed to agree.

But she kept secret how Zach was brushing her off and their relationship. It was too personal and too soon to talk about except with Josie, now her one and only close friend on the island. Was this how Zach had felt when Abbey had told him that she wanted to be "just friends"? If so, it was terrible, but he had continued to be her friend just as she asked. So Abbey would do the same thing for Zach. If it worked out, their relationship would be back on solid ground. If not, they would be only coworkers. Abbey would just have to take one day at a time.

"Here is your laptop, and your mom ordered a table that you will be able to work on. It should be here tomorrow. Today, I'm just going to leave the information on two projects that are due in a few weeks. There are others, but I've got them handled. These seem to be more of your expertise." Abbey was trying to keep it all business, but it was hard keeping her emotions in check.

"I'm not ready for this," Zach said.

"I really need your help. The work is piling up, and Everly has been assisting me, but she has her own work. Can you please try?"

The look Zach gave her was one of indifference as he thumbed through the files, glancing over the papers. Abbey watched him apprehensively, hoping it would spark a conversation like they used to have over work projects. It was like they were brainstorming the next great invention. Happy memories for Abbey and hopefully Zach too.

"I have to go back to work. I'll check on you later, and if you have any questions, just give me a call," she said as she sat his cell phone by the computer.

"You act like I'm completely healed. Like nothing has happened! You don't get it, Abbey! I can't do this. I don't want to do this." Zach was now yelling at her.

"What do you mean?"

Zach was silent as he looked at her. Abbey met his gaze, staying strong and not giving in to the heartache inside. She gently went to his side, gave him a kiss on the cheek, and walked out the front door.

When Abbey pulled up to her little place that evening, she was spent. The morning with Zach had haunted her all day, and she had barely been able to work. Abbey knew what Zach was trying to say to her this morning, but she refused to let it sink in. He didn't want her anymore. But why? What had she done? In her eyes, he was still the Zach she had fallen in love with, just a little battered and bruised. It hadn't changed her love for him, but for some reason, Zach's feelings for Abbey had changed. She just chose not to accept it right now. As she got out of her Jeep, she saw Josie putting a suitcase in the trunk of Michael's rental car. This must be the Miami trip Josie had told her about. Abbey desperately wanted to talk to Josie about what had happened this morning but was not going to ruin the moment, so she kept her thoughts to herself.

"Are you heading to Miami?" Abbey asked, forcing a smile to appear on her face.

"In the morning. We will be gone just for a few days. I hate to leave you right now. Will you be OK?" Josie felt guilty for leaving her, but there wasn't much she could do except be a listening shoulder for her younger friend. And though Abbey was smiling, Josie could tell there was something going on.

"What's wrong?" Josie asked.

"Nothing really. I'm just taking your advice about giving people space. But I will admit it is hard. Also, still trying to get caught up at work, so I'm a bit tired." No way was Abbey going to blurt out the real reason why she looked and felt the way she did. She was not ruining Josie and Michael's trip. They deserved some time away and had done so much for her since Zach's accident. Besides, Abbey wasn't totally alone, because she did have Ella and Garret, both of whom had checked on her and Zach continuously. And she had Everly to talk to at work. It was just different with Josie. She had become Abbey's close friend, something that Abbey had thought was next to impossible those first few days she had arrived in Key West.

"If you need anything, give me a call," Josie said as she hugged Abbey good-bye.

"I hope you two have a wonderful time. Go relax and enjoy. You deserve it."

Abbey walked into her apartment, feeling so alone. As she put everything away and started to fix dinner, her phone rang. The caller ID said it was Hope, and Abbey thought she might start crying all over again.

"Hey you!" Abbey said. "How are my BFF and the munch-kin?" Her best friend in Charleston was now seven months pregnant.

"We are doing excellent, except I am big as a house! More importantly—how are you? And how is Zach doing since he came home?"

Abbey took a deep breath and told Hope details from the beginning till her conversation with Zach this morning.

"You have to admit what he went through was incredible. I work with children, and as resilient as they are, when they go through something major, it takes time for them to heal men-tally as well as physically. I had one little patient that wouldn't even talk after his surgery. It took almost two months of pa-tience and coaxing him along to get him to speak. Nothing was wrong. It was just his way of processing what had hap-pened to him. Don't doubt that Zach still loves you. He just needs more time."

There was that word again—time—Abbey thought as she listened to Hope.

"I pray that you are right, because this feeling is miserable. I get to see him, but he is in his own world where I don't exist. Or if I do, it is only to talk about work. I'm doing my best to keep a positive outlook, but it is so hard. This is the first time I have truly wondered what was I thinking when I moved down here. I've always lived near family, and now I suddenly feel isolated. I have Josie downstairs, but she is finding love all over again with Michael. The people I work with are great, but we only see each other there. And Ella and Garret, the other ten-ants? They are nice, but there is no close connection. Zach was part of my lifeline here, and I feel like he is gone." Though she wasn't crying, her voice was getting softer and more pained with each word she spoke.

"So let's change the subject. You said Josie and Michael are doing good?"

"Yep. As a matter of fact, they are leaving in the morning for a mini vacation in Miami. Just to get away. I tell you, Michael is a charmer, and talk about going after what he wants. He loves Josie a *lot*. He might have screwed up before, but he is making up for lost time."

"Do you think he is sincere?" Hope asked.

"I wasn't sure at first, but the more time I spend with him, getting to know him, I really think he is. It seems like he has really missed Josie something terrible, even if he did get married and have a son."

"What? I didn't know about that! Details, please!" Before Abbey knew it, the two friends had stayed on the phone another hour. And it was the exact medicine Abbey needed to help her feel grounded again and release some pent-up anxiety.

"Hope, you don't know how glad I am that you called. I needed some girl talk. Please pray that this gets better."

"Abbey, it will. I can't say things will be like they were before, but be you. Be persistent. Be patient. Be yourself, just like you were when you moved there. Don't change yourself because Zach has changed. Be who you are, and let him see you just like you were when he met you. He has a lot going on in his head, but he will get through it," Hope coaxed her. "I wish I was there and could give you a great big squeeze, but since I can't, consider yourself hugged."

Abbey had to smile. "I'm so glad that even after we finished college, we remained so close. Give Shawn a hug for me, and take care of munchkin. And I want some side profile pictures of you. I refuse to believe you are as big as you say you are. Love you!"

"Love you too!" Hope said as Abbey heard the disconnect sound on her phone. She wondered what to do next. She had made a list before she left work of what needed to be done tonight, but her phone call with Hope had been more important for her sanity. So now it was time for a shower and to slip into bed. She wondered what Zach was doing as she lay in the darkness of her room. She wanted to talk to him so badly it hurt, but she would hold out for her visit tomorrow.

44

"I hate to leave her right now," Josie said as she and Michael made their way up Highway 1 toward Miami. Even though she was looking forward to this little trip with him, she couldn't help but worry about the situation between Abbey and Zach. Josie and Michael had noticed when they had visited Zach that he wasn't the same person that used to follow Abbey everywhere. He was polite, answering questions and trying to be himself, but the change was noticeable, and after what he had been through, it was understandable. But how long would it last?

"Abbey will be OK. We are only going to be gone for a few days. Maybe when we get back, we can suggest that she take a weekend off and go somewhere. To get away from all the stress she has been under. She needs some time for herself if she will allow it."

"I know Garrett and Ella have been asking me if they could do anything to help, so maybe we can all come up with something for her. But," Josie said, leaning over to kiss Michael on the cheek, "this is our time, and I can't wait to get to Miami. I hope you love it. I've been several times, and to me the city is so exciting. You have to be careful, of course, but there is a vibe you just don't get anywhere else. And I can't believe you booked the Setai! That's one of the most luxurious hotels in Miami—but I'm not complaining." She looked over at Michael to see him with a big grin on his face, which made her smile too. She had never been on a weekend trip with a man. And for it to be Michael made this trip even more special.

He had surprised her two days ago while they were at lunch by handing her an envelope. When she opened it, she saw a beautifully typed confirmation with the Setai Hotel name stamped across the top, and she was intrigued. It was the information on their reservation for a three-day, two-night stay in one of the nicest hotels on South Miami Beach. Michael had even given her a list of choices of what they could do during their getaway, all adventures he had looked into while making plans for their trip. Josie was stunned when she saw all the details he had done to make this trip extra special. She was looking forward to seeing the bright lights and bustle of the city. But what made it the best was sharing it with Michael.

For him, it was the excitement of seeing Josie happy that Michael loved. He knew that he had made the right decision by seeking her out once again. Now he hoped and prayed that she would love the surprise he had waiting on them in the city.

She had been the love of his life, and when he thought back on what he had done so many years ago, he wished he could turn back time. He still remembered it like it was yesterday. A feeling had come over him that consumed him like fire, and he just took off like a bat out of hell. Why, he would never know, and it had cost him the love of this wonderful woman for all these years. But now he had found her again. Josie was just as beautiful inside and out as the young woman he had been going to marry long ago.

The fact that Michael's son had such a huge part in finding her made him proud. Seth wanted his dad to be happy, and he knew that this "Josie" woman was the ticket. His super sleuthing had paid off. Michael still remembered the day when Seth had called to tell him the good news that he had found a woman that matched Josie's description to a T, and Michael had booked a flight to Key West the next day. Then he recalled that evening when he walked up that sidewalk and saw her on the porch. The rush he had felt through his whole body was one he would never forget. All he saw was the beautiful woman from Montana that he so dearly loved. He knew that if he wanted to win this woman's heart all over again, it would take time, and he was grateful that he had a trustworthy manager and his son to take care of business while he was gone on his extended vacation of sorts.

Before they knew it, they pulled up to the Setai. The hotel was beyond breathtaking, Josie thought as she looked around. As they walked through the lobby, Josie couldn't quit smiling, happiness radiating through every part of her. And to look over at Michael to see him as happy made her feel so content. The sexy, older version of Michael brought to life every part of her being.

"My name is Michael Garner, and I have a reservation for this evening for two nights. Is there any chance that the room is ready a bit earlier than your regular check-in time?" he asked, knowing that it would be. He had put much planning into this trip that he hoped it would all go according to plan.

"Hello, Mr. Garner. As a matter of fact, it is. We had an early checkout. Let me just get some necessary information," the clerk said from behind the gorgeous marble counter. Josie had always dreamed of staying in a hotel like this but couldn't believe it was actually happening as she looked at the beautiful decor surrounding her.

Once they had the keys to their room and secured valet service for the luggage and car, they went up to check out the room. It was on the thirty-first floor, overlooking the white, sandy beaches of Miami and the Atlantic Ocean. The room was beautiful in every detail with its Asian-inspired de-cor. The balcony opened to the sound of ocean waves com-ing ashore, and the two reclining chairs graced each side of the open door. Josie could almost imagine falling asleep out there, listening to the waves, watching the stars above with her chair so close to Michael's that it would seemed to be one large chaise lounge.

As she looked around, Michael came up from behind her and wrapped his arms around her waist. "What do you think? Did I pick a good hotel or what?" he said with a huge grin on his face.

"It's stunning, but anywhere with you would have been fine with me," Josie said as she turned in his arms to face him. She gently touched his face and kissed him. What started as a gentle kiss became one that was intense, engulfing both their senses to the point that nothing existed except the two of them. It was at times like this that Josie felt like they were making up for lost time when they were together. She was so in love with him. And she always had been. He was the love of her life, and this time, she wasn't going to let him go. But she felt confident that her fight wouldn't be too hard, because Michael had shown and proved to her so far that this was it. He wanted her and was willing to do whatever it took to win her back. Though she was trying to play hard to get each day, he whittled just a little of her resolve down every time they were together. It had been three months now since she had seen him walk up that street, but she was beginning to feel like they had been together forever.

The sudden knock at the door brought them back to reality. Their bodies separated, and once their clothing didn't looked so rumpled, they opened the door to let the valet in. Apparently they hadn't done a very good job, because the man unloading the bags into the room had a mischievous grin on his face. Josie was sure this wasn't the first time he had caught a couple in the middle of a romantic pose.

"Let's check out the balcony," Michael said as he reached for her hand. "It's beautiful outside—but not as much as you," he said as he gave her another kiss.

They stepped through the glass doors to an incredible sight of beach and ocean. Josie looked out, still smiling at everything that had happened, still feeling like it was all a dream.

"Hey, look. Someone wrote something in the sand with shells. Aww, it says 'Will You Marry Me?' How romantic!" Josie gushed.

"Well?"

"Well, what?"

"Will you marry me?"

"What?" It took a minute for Josie to comprehend what was happening, looking back to the message in the sand and then to Michael again. "You did that? You wrote with seashells in the sand? A proposal?"

"I had some help from the hotel staff. See those people there?" He pointed to the men surrounding the message on the beach. Then he got down on one knee in front of her. "Will you marry me, Josie?" Michael held his breathe, wondering: Was it too soon? Did she really love him? Did she really forgive him for the stupid mistakes of his past?

After the initial shock of what was happening disappeared, Josie wanted so badly to say yes to the man kneeling before her, but the memories of last time suddenly flooded back into her mind like a dam that had burst.

Josie took Michael's hand, pulling him up to stand before her. "How do I know that you won't run like last time? It's only been three months."

"I know this may seem quick, but, Josie, I've known you my entire life. And I have loved you every single second. I want you to be my wife."

"How can you say those words when you were married before? Did you not love her?"

"Yes, but it was different. I loved and cared for her, but it wasn't the relationship I had with you. And it certainly wasn't what we have now. As silly as it may sound coming from a cowboy, you are my soul mate. You were thirty years ago, and you are today." Michael's heart was pounding, hoping he could convince her of his sincerity.

"What about Seth? How would he feel about this?" Josie was asking so many questions when her heart wanted her to blurt out "Yes!" Her mind was blocking her from uttering the word she so desperately wanted to say.

"Seth and I have had long talks about the relationship between his mom and me. Remember, he is the one who found you for me. I had given up on finding love again and decided to live out my life by myself on the ranch, hoping to have some grandkids to play with and keep me company once Seth decided to get married. I was content, or I thought so, till Seth asked about you one day. He told me he could tell that I was still in love by the way I shared the whole story with him. So I think he will be fine, especially if his daddy is really happy." Michael was smiling, hoping and praying inside that this woman in front of him would still say the word he wanted to hear.

"But you didn't answer my first question. How do I know you won't run away?" Josie's heartstrings were being tugged in so many ways, her mind still processing the conversation.

"That one is really simple to answer. Because if you will do me the honor of becoming my wife, we are, if you are willing, going to get married today. Right there on the beach," Michael said, pointing to the spot where the marriage proposal was still written in the sand.

"Today?" Josie said in a squeaky voice.

"Yep, today. First I have to call the minister and tell him your answer. Then it is off to buy rings. After that, there is a wedding planner that will take you to buy a wedding dress while I go and buy my outfit. Then this evening at sunset and in a little circle of shells on the beach, we will get married. All you have to do is say yes."

Josie looked at him, flabbergasted and amazed. She was so happy that she suddenly flung herself into his arms, kissing him quickly on the lips.

"Yes! I will marry you!"

Michael leaned over the railing, giving a thumbs-up to someone, and suddenly they heard clapping from below. She saw that a small group of people had gathered around the shells, clapping and waving.

"Wedding at sunset tonight—same spot," Michael yelled back to the group below, while Josie laughed, hugging him tightly.

45

As Abbey pulled up to Zach's house, she sighed, her heart heavy. The last two days had been so depressing. It seemed as though each time she was with him, his attitude toward her and their work became more distanced, their conversations more sterile. She was coming to the conclusion that she wasn't good at waiting, because she just wanted Zach to be better and return to the man she knew him to be. The world of self-pity he was lost in was so far away from her, and only he could make the journey out.

The knock on the door was answered by Sandy, of course. She smiled and gave Abbey a hug. "He is in the living room," she said then went into the bedroom so she could give them some privacy.

"Hey, Zach," Abbey said as she came around the corner and sat down on the chair opposite the couch. She didn't give him time to answer before she was pulling out the folder of work papers.

"There are a few things that we need to discuss about the Webster site."

"I'm not ready to start working again. I'll try next week." He sat looking at the TV with the remote in his hand. He hadn't even acknowledged her or the papers she had extended to him.

"Zach, we need to talk." He only continued to stare at the TV. This time she couldn't stand it. Abbey got up, yanked the remote out of his hand, and turned the TV off.

"What are you doing?" Zach said angrily.

"I'm trying to have a conversation with my coworker, and I would love to have a talk with my boyfriend. I'm trying to be patient. I know you are still healing, and you are in pain. But why are you shutting me out? What is going on? Why won't you please just talk to me?"

"Next week I'll start working from here. That way you aren't doing everything. But Abbey—we need to take a break. I've got too much going on right now."

Abbey couldn't believe the words she just heard. A break?

"You are breaking up with me?" she said softly, as though the words were the hardest thing to say.

"You deserve better than this," he said, motioning to himself. "I don't even know if I'll be able to walk. Swim. Bike ride. You need someone who can be there for you. I can't."

"You think I fell in love with a bike rider? A swimmer? I fell in love with you, Zach. The guy that is always there for me, said he loved me more than anything, and is so caring. The man that went out of his way to make me happy. The one that loved me even when I said I wanted to be friends. The one that made one of my dreams come true. Are you saying that you aren't that person just because you got hurt?"

"I didn't just get hurt! I got run over by a damn car! I hurt all the time, I'm frustrated, and I don't need all this." Zach turned back to stare at the blank TV screen, not looking at her once.

Now it was Abbey's time to be angry. "Well, it sounds like you are having one big pity party to me. If that is what you want, fine. We can take a break. As for work, I need help now, and you are more than capable. Look at these papers I made for you. Let me know what you think and any ideas you have. When you get a chance, use your laptop to check out the website, and if you need to, notify Randy and Everly of any changes you think are necessary. Each day I will be here at nine o'clock in the morning for a quick meeting to make sure we are up-to-date on our projects. That should give us enough time to decide what we each can do on our own." She put the folder of papers on the coffee table, grabbed the handles of her tote bag, and stood up.

"Hopefully this arrangement will work till you are able to make it back into the office. As for us, since you think I can do better, I'll let you know. But if the Zach I fell in love with happens to reappear and wants to call me, tell him he has my number." With that, she headed out the front door, slamming it hard.

"Abbey!" She heard her name and turned to see that Sandy had followed her quickly toward her Jeep. By this time, Abbey couldn't hide the fact that more tears were flowing down her face.

"Abbey, I'm sorry, but I eavesdropped, and I heard the whole conversation. He has been getting more quiet and withdrawn each day. At his doctor's appointment this morning, we even talk-ed about it, and the doctor suggested some counseling. I thought Zach was going to hit the ceiling. He is so angry. He is depressed and won't admit it. What I'm trying to say is, please don't give up on him. I know that he still loves you. He just feels he isn't good enough for you. I know with all my heart he is going to be able to walk again. The pelvic fracture is healing nicely and so is his arm. Learning to walk again might be a struggle, but I know he can do it. But he is so scared." Now Sandy's eyes were glassy as she talked about her youngest son.

"I'm not giving up on him, but I can't continue to be a punching bag for his feelings. I want to be here more than anything. Everyone I've talked to has told me to be patient, and I am, but I'm going to go ahead and start doing things like going back to my spot on the square to sell my art. Maybe if he sees that life is moving on, he will try to live again. I hate to hear myself say all these words, because it hurts more than I can say. I love your son so much. This accident didn't take that away. If anything, it let me know how truly special that man sitting on the couch in that house is to me. But I'm not going to coddle him anymore. He is the only one that can make the decision to deal with his situation or let it swallow him up in anger. But you don't know how I wish I could do it for him."

Zach's mother hugged Abbey tightly. "Thank you, Abbey. I can see the wisdom of your plan. Most of all, thank you for letting me know you aren't giving up on him. I was so scared he had pushed you away for good when I heard you talking in there."

"Sandy, you can't imagine how hard it was for me to say those words," she said with her voice cracking.

"Now that you have explained it to me, I think I have a pretty good idea how strong you are. Zach picked a wonderful woman in you. Hopefully, he will come to his senses soon." Both women hugged before Abbey got in her Jeep. As she drove home, even though she was upset by the encounter with Zach, she hoped this new approach would help him. If not, then maybe they weren't meant to be together. But Abbey's heart told her otherwise.

46

The drive back home to Key West was one of pure bliss for the newly married couple. She was now Mrs. Michael Garner, the name she was to take so long ago. She found herself smiling as she stared down at the beautiful diamond wedding band on her left ring finger. It felt like a dream come true.

As promised, after the proposal, they found the perfect rings at a jewelry store close by. Michael even paid extra to make sure they were sized that day before the ceremony. Next, they were separated for the rest of the day by two women: the wedding planner named Sara and her assistant, LeAnn. Sara took Josie shopping for a wedding dress, and she picked out a beautiful aqua floral maxi dress with white sandals. LeAnn was with Michael, who picked out a deeper shade of aqua for his shirt after finding out the color of Josie's dress, along with navy pants and a pair of men's sandals. The hotel provided a separate room for the groom to get dressed in so the couple wouldn't see each other until the ceremony. Sara made sure that the beach was decorated with shells and two small pillars that held candles in clear vases to mark the area where the ceremony would take place. And as each was getting dressed, a knock on the door came from the florist delivering a bouquet for Josie and a boutonniere for Michael.

For Josie and Michael, the ceremony couldn't have been more perfect. The minister had met them on the beach at 6:30 p.m., and to the couple's surprise, about one hundred people—beachgoers and those who had helped arrange the marriage proposal in the sand—stayed to watch them officially become husband and wife. If these people had only known how long it had taken for this wedding to become a reality, they would have been amazed at their love story.

The vows Michael had written for her were beautiful, and she was so choked up that when it came time to say hers to him, Josie's voice was barely audible. When the minister pronounced them husband and wife, it seemed like the whole beach was cheering. Michael gave her a sweet, romantic kiss, picking her up off the sandy beach and swinging her around. The photographer and videographer had captured it all on film. She was still amazed at what Sara had been able to do in such a short amount of time. But Michael had planned in advance, finding that she was one of the best wedding planners in all of Miami.

As they were crossing the Seven Mile Bridge, Josie suddenly became curious. "What if I had said no?"

Michael looked at her, perplexed. "What do you mean?"

"What if I had said to no your proposal? You had planned so many things."

"First of all, I had no doubt you would say yes. I could see how much you loved me." He grinned at her, taking her hand and giving it a kiss. "But if you had not accepted, then I would have been out some money. And I would have kept trying till you gave in and realized that we were meant to be together, even if took longer for us to get there."

"I love you, Michael. And thank you for rescuing me," Josie said softly as she put her hand on Michael's cheek.

"I love you too, but I didn't rescue you. You were doing fine on your own. I'm just glad that you accepted me back into your life. You can't imagine how nervous I was on the flight to Key West, and more so as I walked to your apartment. I didn't deserve it, but you found it in your heart to forgive me and to also try again. I feel so blessed that I can now call you my wife. You don't know how long I have wanted to say those words."

As Josie listened to him, her heart swelled, and the happiness she felt inside was immeasurable. It felt almost too good to be true. She had finally let go of the hate and hurt that had been bottled up for so long, and the feeling was so freeing. She only wished she had done it long ago. But the timing was as it should be. They had both become different people over time, wiser and stronger. Now they could build their life together.

"You know, there is one thing we still haven't discussed," Josie said, looking at him with a serious face. "Where we are going to live. I still want to stay here. In the Keys. I'm not ready to go back to Montana. But I also want to be where you are, no matter what."

"Then we will stay here. Josie, I don't have to go back to the ranch, at least not now. My general manager is wonderful. A man I trust implicitly. I will have to visit at least every other month or so, but between the ranch and my investments, we could live here. But I do have one request."

"What?"

"Let's look for our own house, maybe on one of the other Keys. I love Key West, except it can be hot as hell, but it would be nice to have a house, maybe on a canal. We could even have our own boat. Maybe somewhere around Marathon or Islamorada?" Michael looked at her questioningly, since he knew she had always lived in Key West and wasn't sure how she would take his suggestion.

"I think I would like that. Our own house. I've lived in an apartment for so long, I wouldn't know what to do with a big house." The thought of having their own place excited her.

"Just have to make sure to have guest rooms, because I think it won't be long before Seth will be here. As much as he loves the ranching business and Montana, he is a computer geek and wants to see the world. He is always talking about how he wished he could have a—let's see how he put it—a location-independent business. I'm old-school, but Seth says that's possible now with the Internet."

Josie smiled. "He must be good at it, because he was able to find me. And I can't wait to hug him and give him a kiss. Because if it weren't for him, we wouldn't be riding back to Key West with rings on our fingers. Wow—we are really married!" The excitement of the last few days hit her again, and there was no way the smile could be wiped off her face.

Michael looked at his wife, and he felt so lucky and blessed. He had really made a mess of things that day so long ago when he ran away, but, thank goodness, he had found his love again.

They pulled up in front of the apartment house just in time to see Abbey walking toward the gate. They honked the horn to get her attention, and as she looked up, Josie immediately knew something was amiss. Abbey looked like she had aged ten years. Her posture sagged, and the smile she greeted them with was forced. Josie hated to share her happy news while Abbey was going through so much with Zach.

"Michael, don't say anything about the wedding, OK? I can tell something isn't right just by looking at Abbey. She has done so much for me so I want to help her if I can. Hearing about our wedding might make things worse for her."

"I'm fine with that, but, Josie, you are going to have to tell her sometime."

"I know. Just let me figure out when, OK?"

Michael gave his new bride a kiss. "You're the boss!"

"And don't forget that!" Josie kidded him as she opened the door and slid out of the passenger seat.

47

"Hey, how's it going?" Josie said as she approached Abbey.

"Pretty good. I thought you guys would be gone longer. Did you have a good time?" Abbey did her best to sound cheerful, but no matter how hard she tried, the words she spoke were flat.

"Yes, we did, but I can tell that you are lying to me. What is going on, Abbey?" Josie was firm, almost sounding like the woman Abbey had met months ago when she moved to Key West.

"Zach has basically given up on himself and us. As a matter of fact, this morning, he told me we needed to 'take a break.' He is afraid he won't be able to walk, swim, or whatever. He says he's not good enough for me and that I need to move on. He is feeling sorry for himself, and he is taking it out on me. I love him, Josie, but I can't keep putting myself in a situation where I'm continually treated as though I'm a pain in the ass.

I have been giving him time, just like you suggested. Now he can have his own space too."

"Abbey, do you hear yourself? Sounds like you are giving up too!" Josie spat out quickly.

Abbey was angry now. "What do you mean? I've done everything I know to help that man, and no matter what it is, he continues to treat me like someone that gets on his nerves. He doesn't even want me at his house!"

"Who does that sound like, or at least did at one time?" Josie looked at Abbey with her eyebrows raised.

Abbey suddenly made the connection, and her shoulders drooped, as she looked skyward.

"It sounds like you. When I first came here."

"Yes, it does. But you were one persistent young lady, and because of you, I feel like I'm living life again. You have a special gift, Abbey. To see the best in others and help bring that out of them even if they want to stay clammed up in a shell. Zach will have to do the work, but with your encouragement, he will come around. I know him well enough and have seen him with you to know that no matter what has happened, he loves you more than you know."

"You sound like his mom. We had almost this same talk when I left his house this morning. She was scared that his words and the way he was acting were going to chase me away. I told her how much I cared for him but that I had to start living my life. I'm hoping this will show Zach that he can too. So this Saturday I'm setting up on the square again. Do you think you and Michael might be able to help me? I could probably do it on my own, but Zach helped me last time. Once I get the hang of it, I probably won't need the help." Abbey's eyes showed that she hoped they would say yes.

"Of course we will," Michael said has he came walking up with suitcases in each hand. "Didn't mean to overhear your conversation. Helping you this weekend is no problem. As for Zach, it's a man thing, Abbey. We can be stubborn and prideful. Right now he feels less than a man, and that is hard, especially when you want to take care of someone you love. That kept me from looking for Josie all these years. I was embarrassed and felt ashamed, not good enough for her. He is going through something similar. But coming from a man, I agree with Josie. Zach loves you something strong. Hold on to that."

Abbey looked at the couple before her and realized how their journey had turned out. They had found each other again. Maybe it was years in the making, but they were together. So maybe Zach would be hers again. But suddenly, Abbey saw the glistening object on Josie's finger. She reached out, grabbing Josie's hand, bringing it up to her face.

"You got married? Are you married for real?" Abbey couldn't contain her excitement.

Crap, Josie thought. She forgot to take off her ring. "We weren't going to tell you yet with everything you have going on. But yes, you are looking at the now-official Mr. and Mrs. Michael Garner." Josie smiled at Abbey and secretly hoped that this wouldn't hurt her.

Abbey quickly hugged both of them. "I can't believe it! I'm so excited for both of you! But please tell me you aren't moving!"

"Not quite yet. We are staying in Florida, but we are going to look for a house in one of the other Keys. Time to have our own place," Josie said, beaming up at her new husband.

"What about Montana?" Abbey asked quickly.

"I've got people in place to take care of the ranch. I'll—or we—will just have to make visits there. When Josie is ready," he said, looking lovingly at her, "then we will see about going back. But I have to admit—the Keys have grown on me. I think I prefer the sun more than all that snow in the winter." Finally, something good was happening, and Abbey was feeling lighter, something she hadn't experienced in weeks.

"Make sure your new house has room for me, because I will be visiting for sure," Abbey said.

"With Zach." Josie finished her sentence.

"I hope so."

Now Abbey saw Zach only in the mornings, to go over work. Being so close and knowing he did not want her hurt, because she longed to feel his lips on hers, the touch of his hands around her waist. Abbey missed his smile, the way he made her laugh, how he always made her feel so special. In the evenings she kept herself busy by getting ready for her shows at Mallory Square. The first one had been such a hit that she was hoping for a repeat performance.

Every few days she would sneak a call to Sandy to check on Zach and find out how he was healing. Abbey kept up on Zach's physical therapy since he got the green light to put weight on his badly damaged leg. The news wasn't what Abbey had hoped for. The nerve damage was extensive, leaving numbness throughout Zach's leg. He was indeed having to learn to walk again, something, according to Sandy, that Zach wasn't tolerating very well. Abbey also found out that Zach's mood and feelings were the same even when Lance, Randy and Everly stopped by to visit. Zach did show some interest in the outside world when he found out that Abbey was selling her art back on the square, according to Sandy. *That's a good sign*, Abbey thought, but she also knew that she couldn't wait for Zach to stop feeling sorry for himself before she got back to living her life. This man had left an indelible mark on her heart, and letting him go wasn't as easy as turning off a light switch.

Over the next several weeks, Abbey did go about her life, but nothing was the same without Zach. She went to their restaurants. She went back to Bahia Honda Park and went swimming. She had more art showings, and each did so well. She was making a name for herself on the square, and even though time was passing by with minimal contact with Zach now, Abbey found herself still wishing for his presence so she could share the success with him.

Now she only saw him Monday, Wednesday, and Friday, and that was if they needed to discuss something in person. It was too painful to see him, so if work could be discussed through e-mails or over the phone, it was better for her mind and heart. He never asked her about anything personal. She continued to find out about his therapy through his mother, and at times it was even hard to talk to the kind woman who had become a friend to Abbey.

This morning, as she looked out the front window of the office watching the tourists from the cruise ship make their way down Duval Street, a flow of tears came yet once again. When would this ever stop? Abbey asked herself. Sometimes she wished she could jump on one of those docked ships, stow away, and get off on the next island, running away from everything. It was only a fantasy, because she knew running away wouldn't solve the problem. But the thought of it was so enticing.

"How was Zach this morning?" Lance asked, coming up behind Abbey and making her nearly jump, tripping over the desk chair in front of her.

"Didn't mean to scare you."

"I'm sorry. Just a little lost in thought. He was his same self. He is getting around on crutches now, even if it is a bit awkward for him. According to Sandy, physical therapy is not progressing as well because Zach gets so angry at not being able to walk yet. Not a pretty sight, she says."

"At least he is in therapy with two legs instead of one. I wish that boy would think on that instead of fixating on what he can't do." He gave Abbey a hug. Lance was like a dad to her even though he was also her boss. Actually, everyone here was like a little family. She felt so blessed as she looked around the room to see that Randy, Everly, and Donna had been listening to their conversation and were all smiling, thinking the same thoughts that Lance was. This was her Key West family, along with Josie and Michael. She had the best of both worlds. And it wouldn't be long before her parents were coming to visit. She only hoped that the Zach would be there when they arrived.

48

Damn crutches, Zach thought as he caught himself against the wall. Having to keep his leg straight when not in therapy was driving him crazy. But everything was making him feel restless and useless. Things had been so perfect in his life till the stupid driver decided to send a text. How many times had he ridden his bike down that same street, at night? Zach couldn't begin to count, but all it took was one night to change his life forever. Now he felt like he had lost everything, including the only woman he had ever loved. But he wouldn't saddle Abbey with this. He couldn't walk without crutches when they took the removable air cast off his leg each day. Though the therapist said he was making small progress, Zach wanted to tell him to go to hell.

He was hurting not only physically but mentally as well. The TV seemed to be his best friend. His mom was there, thank goodness, but it just wasn't the same as his friends, the people he worked with, and Abbey. He still remembered the way he'd felt the day he told Abbey they needed a break from each other.

When she walked out the door, he felt as though someone had kicked him in the stomach. Zach wanted to yell for her to come back, that he didn't mean it, but he just couldn't utter the words. As badly as it hurt, he knew that she would be better off without him. She had made new friends, was accomplishing much with her art, and was excelling at her job—he didn't want to spoil her new life. But letting her go was harder than he had imagined.

"Are you ready for breakfast before Abbey comes over?" Zach's mom asked when she saw he was awake.

"Thanks. I think I'll text her and tell her not to come today. I still have to work on the website, then that stupid physical therapy. I can do the exercises at home. I really don't need to go."

"Sorry, buster, but as long as I'm here, to therapy you will go. No discussion." Sandy Isler turned her back on her son and began preparing eggs. Even at thirty-one years of age, Zach knew that the conversation had ended, and he wasn't going to start an argument with his mother. She had been his lifesaver, helping at times like he was a newborn, especially those first days back in his own apartment.

And she was right about therapy. Zach had only small spots of feeling in his right leg. It was as though his leg had "fallen asleep." The doctors told him that the small spots of tingling he felt were nerves coming back to life. He only hoped that it would continue to heal. He could stand on his leg, but his mind couldn't register that it was there. Like he had sat in one position too long, losing the feeling of movement. The frustration of making his leg move at therapy made him want to yell at times, though Zach kept his temper in check. Only when he got home did he release the pent-up feelings.

When he heard the knock at the door, Zach quickly looked to see if he was presentable. He had forgotten to text Abbey. Not that it mattered, but he looked forward to seeing her, his bright spot. Though he couldn't tell her, she still brought him a little joy, but then he would get mad and usually screw up any conversation they had. That was when the coldness and anger would come out. Not that he was mean, but he kept things businesslike and impersonal. Though the minute she would walk out the door, Zach would remember holding her in his arms and the way her lips tasted on his. It felt like everything in his life was sheer torture right now, and he was going to crack under the pressure.

"Hey, Zach," Abbey said as she approached the couch to sit in the opposite chair, her normal work space. "I can't stay long this morning. Just wanted to know if you had any questions on the papers from yesterday." Zach noticed that Abbey's voice was cheerful but very indifferent. How could he expect anything else? Especially after the way he had treated her. And he still felt the same way about their relationship. That couldn't change.

"Everything was fine. Still working on a few graphics, but I will e-mail the changes to you."

"How are you feeling?"

"Fine. Still a cripple," Zach said with sarcasm.

"Hopefully physical therapy will help. Just give it time. If you have any questions, let me know. I'll see you in a few days unless I have some other papers from work you might need. Take care." He watched Abbey pick up her things and head toward the door, but not before asking his mom how she was doing and if she needed anything. That was the Abbey he had fallen in love with and missed so much. But he just couldn't see any way to be with her like he wanted to. She deserved so much more than he could give her.

"At least you were civil today," Sandy said to her son as he sat on the couch staring into space.

"Mom, please don't start."

"Just making an observation. Let me know when you need help getting ready for PT," she said before walking outside.

Suddenly Zach threw the papers in his hands across the room, the pieces fluttering to the floor slowly. He just wished he could hit something, yell at someone. Everything seemed so unfair right now. He put both hands on his head, hoping to make all the conflicting emotions just disappear, but no matter what he did or said, the feelings were still there, ready for him to face and deal with. But just as Zach had been doing for these past few months, he pushed them aside, grabbed the remote, and flipped on the TV to find some kind of show he could just get lost in to forget what life had handed him.

"Zach, I hate to say this, but you're hardly trying. You have got to put the weight on your leg and push it forward. Even if it drags. You can do this," Marty said, trying to encourage Zach. Instead it made him angry.

"You don't understand. *It won't move!*" Zach said loudly enough that he drew the attention of the entire room. Once he realized what he had done, he quickly apologized to everyone, especially Marty.

"Hey, man, I know this is tough. I haven't been in your shoes, but I've worked with plenty of people over these last seventeen years. I've seen people with your injury before, and they do walk again. But they bust their ass to make it happen. That is what you are going to have to do if you really want to walk and get your life back."

"What do you mean, 'if I want my life back'?" Zach looked at him with venom in his eyes.

"When you come here for therapy, you act like 'poor me.' I know this isn't professional, but I'm going to tell you like it is. You have to drop the bullshit and start making it happen. You are more than capable of using your leg again. And even if you can't do everything you did before your accident, you are damn lucky to be here—alive. There are plenty of people who never made it through the type of accident you went through."

Zach knew that Marty would have never talked to a patient like that, but they had met each other long before this. And Marty's words at that moment reached a part of Zach that he had closed off to everyone. As he stood there for a few minutes, holding the handrails, he closed his eyes and finally made up his mind that this wasn't going to stop him. Zach had finally hit bottom and had enough. As he made the effort to move his leg with sweat dripping down his forehead, it was as though something had switched inside. He could see what he had been doing to himself and those he loved. Yes, he was mad, but he had taken it out on the people who truly cared for him. Instead, he should have focused that energy into doing everything he could to get better.

"That's it! You are doing it!" Marty exclaimed. When Zach looked down, he saw that he had "walked" about twelve inches. And he smiled, feeling like he had finally made some progress after all this time. Little did Zach know that his mom was watching from across the room with eyes that glistened with happy tears.

As Zach sat back in the wheelchair, he felt complete exhaustion. But it felt good. He had made progress. Progress he could see. For the first time, Zach felt a spark of joy that possibly he could still have the life he had dreamed about.

Once they were in the car to head home, Zach broke the silence and turned to his mom.

"I've been a real jerk. And I am so sorry," he said to his mother. "I felt so lost. I still do in a way, but Marty is right. I'm lucky to be alive, and I've been taking that for granted."

"We knew this wasn't going to be easy, but I have to admit, I never thought I would see you give up like you did. You have always been a fighter your entire life. Always seeing a way out, through or over an obstacle. I was beginning to wonder where my son had disappeared to, but I think he is starting to find his way back." Sandy reached over and gently touched his cheek. This was what she had been praying for since the day Zach came out of intensive care. That was the day she had lost the son she knew, but today, Zach had begun his comeback.

"How about a burger and fries? Then we will go sit by the beach. Have a picnic of sorts," Sandy said to him..

"There is no way to push a wheelchair in the sand!"

"Then we will roll down the windows and sit in the car where we can see and hear the ocean. It's been a while since you have done anything besides stay at home, go to a doctor's appointment, or work. Let this moment be the start of something new."

"Sounds like a plan to me," Zach said, feeling hopeful for the first time. Like he was starting fresh.

49

As Abbey headed to the office, the emotional pain she was feeling overwhelmed her. She thought she was moving forward, but in truth she was stuck. She couldn't help it. Abbey still loved Zach, and every time she had to see him made it even worse. It was like a constant reminder of what her life could have been then realizing that the one person she wanted in her life wanted nothing to do with her. She needed some time alone, and she knew just where to go. Down to the pier.

Abbey loved it there. Watching the tourists and the boats and soaking in the sun with a fresh breeze from the water. These few months had been hard, but she was getting some semblance of order back to her life. She found comfort in her artwork, talking to Josie and Michael in the evenings now that Michael was a permanent resident in the building, and also having an evening out with Garrett.

They had gone to a local bar and grill for some dinner, and as usual, Garret talked mostly about his latest discovery on the reef. Abbey had to admit it was interesting, and it did help keep her mind off where she really wanted to be. Garret had a one-track mind. Abbey wondered if he would ever find that special someone who would take him away from the work he so dearly loved. But now he listened to her as she talked about her life too.

Her art shows at the square continued to be successful, and she was even interviewed for the local paper as part of a street-artist series they were doing. Her excitement over the article was wonderful, but again there seemed to be this dark shadow that hung over her happiness. As time passed she was accepting the fact that her chances of reconnecting with Zach were diminishing. She even dreaded the work hours they had to share together.

This is why coworkers don't date, Abbey thought as she continued to sit on the pier. She knew she should be at work, but she was spent. Her mind and soul needed a break.

"What are you doing here?" The voice came from behind her. It was Garrett.

"Needed some fresh air and a little water time. Are you getting ready to go back out to the reef?" she asked, hoping a little talk with Garrett would help her think about other things.

"No, just working on the boat a bit today since the weather was so nice. I needed a break from the computer and the paper I'm working on." He smiled at her and could tell by the look on her face that something was amiss. "What's wrong with you?" Garrett asked bluntly.

"What do you mean?" she said, trying to put on her best poker face.

"I'm pretty good at knowing when something is up, and with one look at you I can tell you are stressing out big-time."

Abbey sighed and smiled. "I guess you are good at reading someone. It's been a long couple of months, and I've tried my best but gotten nowhere. I feel kinda lost right now." Abbey proceeded to tell Garrett the entire story of Zach and how he had pushed her away for no reason at all.

Garrett sat there taking in the story and not interrupting Abbey. When she finished, they both sat in silence. Abbey looked over to see him staring off into the distance over the expanse of water as though he hadn't heard a word she said.

"Zach doesn't think he is good enough for you now. He is embarrassed. And he feels weak. All of those things are hard on a man, Abbey. We have been brought up that we take care of our mates, that we are the caretakers. To have someone else do for us feels almost wrong. And to know that we might not be able to do the things we once did is a crushing feeling. Don't get me wrong! I'm not saying what he is doing is right, but it's just the way he is handling things. I know you love him very much. He means more to you than just some boyfriend. I can tell by the way you talk about him. And I'm sorry that you have to go through this. But maybe it's time to move on for a bit. I know that sounds harsh, but you can't keep living each day wondering if this is the day he is going to come to his senses. You need to live. Go out and have fun. Do the things you were planning to do once you moved down here. Have you forgotten about those dreams? If so, you need to remember them. That is what brought you down here, not Zach. Start there, and if Zach is meant to be part of your life, he will reappear." Garrett looked at her, smiling, and suddenly leaned over to give her a kiss on the cheek. She then laid her head on his shoulder.

"Thanks, Garrett, for the advice and the insight into the male psyche. You know, you would make an excellent counselor if you weren't into fish so much." Abbey giggled.

"Now that's the girl I remember that first day when she pulled up in her Jeep with a U-Haul full of stuff. She was happy, excited, and smiling. Remember her, Abbey, because that is who you are."

They both stood up, and she reached her arms around him for a big hug. Garrett held her and told her it was going to be OK. And for the first time, Abbey believed it was possible. Garrett, the fish man, as she called him, had just helped her find a little bit of the girl that had such high hopes when she arrived in Key West.

50

As she arrived at Zach's house for another work session, Abbey felt better. A bit of sadness was still there, but it felt different now after her talk with Garrett. He had helped her remember the excitement and giddiness that she had when she arrived in Key West. She remembered her goals, plans, and dreams. They did involve a special someone someday, but Abbey also remembered that she felt free, like she was finally her own woman. She remembered how she had wanted to be an artist at the square, and now she was. Garrett had helped her remember the woman she had been when she moved here. She wanted Zach to be a part of her life, but if it wasn't meant to be, Abbey would remember the brief happiness they had, and she would survive.

As usual, she found Zach on the couch with his leg propped up. But this time he already had paper and pen out, with his laptop now on a tray table next to the couch. Most of the time when she arrived, he was slow to get started. For some reason, he seemed ready to go, but he also had a look of frustration.

"I found some things we need to change on the Webster site. Nothing too intensive. And I've come up with ideas for the research-facility site. I'm sending them to you now."

"Um, hello and good morning. Yes, I'm fine this morning, thank you." She sat there staring at him. "Now I'll check my e-mail." She settled back into the chair and began signing on to her account. Abbey wanted to ask him about his physical therapy, but the way he was acting this morning, she didn't dare. She figured she could ask Sandy later.

"You sure do move fast, don't you?" His words were biting, and she had no idea what he meant.

"Excuse me? What are you talking about?"

"Finding someone new. I guess I should have known better." Zach was red in the face now. Abbey looked at him like he had lost his mind.

"You had better explain that statement and add to it an apology."

"I'm not apologizing for anything. So you are with Garrett now. That didn't take long."

"*What?*" Abbey was shocked. How in the world did this come up? "What gave you that idea? And if it was true, and it isn't, you were the one who wanted a break! Find someone new. I deserved better and all that bullshit." Now she was mad. All the emotion that had been pent up since he pushed her away was coming to the surface, and she was tired of being patient. And she let him know it.

Zach sat in silence, looking at her like she was an alien. But she wasn't giving in and indulging his little fantasy. "I asked you a question. Why do you have this ridiculous idea that I'm with Garrett now?"

"Josh said he saw the two of you at the pier yesterday. That you guys looked pretty close, even kissing."

That was it! "First of all, Josh needs to keep his big mouth shut, especially when he doesn't know the facts. Second, Garrett and I are just friends, and he was giving me some friendly advice about *you!* And even if I decided to date Garrett, it's none of your business. As I said before, *you* were the one who wanted a break. I wanted to be here with you. Help and take care of you. Because I loved you. But you pushed me away, so don't start all this shit and make it sound like it's my fault."

"Why would you talk to Garrett about me?" Zach's voice still sounded irritated but was losing its edge.

"Because I needed some advice from a male's point of view. I was sitting on the pier when Garrett happened to come by and saw me there. We talked. He kissed me on the cheek, and I hugged him for listening and helping me. But why am I explaining myself to you?"

Abbey was so frustrated that she thought she would burst. "You who basically told me to get lost after I stayed with you through your accident, your surgeries. Sitting, worrying in waiting rooms, wondering if I would see you alive that first night. Feeling like my world was coming apart. Remembering how you told me you loved me before they wheeled you into the operating room, my heart feeling like it was being ripped from me to see you in such pain. I did everything I could to be there for you, like most couples that are supposed to be in love would normally do. But you decided to throw the ultimate pity party instead, pushing everyone who cares for you away, especially me! Why? What did I do that was so wrong? I've been patient. Everyone told me that you would come around. Now I don't know anymore. I get it; you're mad. You're angry. But I'm not going to be your punching bag anymore."

She grabbed her laptop and papers. "From now on, we can communicate through e-mails and phone calls. When you are ready to come back to work, fine. Until then, you can do your work here. But I can't come here anymore, Zach. It reminds me too much of what we had at one time, and it hurts. I'm finally ready to let you go, since that is what you want so badly. When you do come back to work, since you were there long before me, I'll seek employment elsewhere." With that last statement, Abbey walked out, slamming the front door.

Zach sat there for a minute before once again throwing papers across the living room, almost adding his laptop to the pile before his mom stopped him.

"I've had enough too. Sorry, I listened in on your conversation, but it was kind of hard not to, as loud as both of you were. I don't like using these words, but you are being a complete asshole." Zach looked at his mother in surprise as she came around and took the seat across from him.

"This has got to stop. I've tried to be patient too. I can't begin to know what you are feeling, because I haven't experienced what you went through. None of us can. But you have got to process this. You were hit by a car, but you survived. You have had surgeries and you are healing fine. Now it's time to start living again. Yes, things will be different, but you can adjust if you try. And if you don't do something, you are going to lose one of the best things that ever happened to you. Abbey is special, and she deserves the best. And that is you, Zach. Let her back into your life. Do you really think that even if you could never walk again, she would run away? That's not the kind of person she is, and you know it. Abbey loves you in a way that most people never get a chance to experience in their lifetime," his mom said, placing her hand on his heart.

Zach sighed, feeling defeated. After therapy yesterday, he'd thought he was starting to conquer this overwhelming despair. But when Josh shared his news about Abbey and Garrett, it all came crashing back down on him.

"Mom, you don't understand. I can't do the things for her or with her like we did before. We went everywhere. On the boat, swimming, to the beach, walking, restaurants. Now if I did something, it would be in a wheelchair or with a walker. I would be placing a burden on her." For the first time since Sandy had come to stay with her son, she saw helplessness in his eyes.

"Have you asked her if it matters? From what I can see, you could have lost your leg, and that girl would have stood by your side, no complaints. Abbey is a true woman, one that is loyal and loving. She cares for others, and, Zach, you might have thought you pushed her away, but you didn't. At least not until today. Your accusations might have been the last straw." Sandy sighed as she looked at Zach. She could tell that the conversation seemed to have gotten through to him. "I'm going to go make us some lunch."

As Zach sat there contemplating everything that had just happened, he knew what his mother and Abbey were saying was the truth. He felt like this whole thing was unfair. Why had it happened to him? And how could he live his life from this point on? Zach felt lost, mainly because he felt like he had no one. He had created this whole mess by isolating himself from everyone. Abbey had been there for him, and he had been so cruel by assuming she wouldn't want him anymore because of a physical handicap. He now felt inferior, but he realized that everyone still saw "Zach," not his leg. He was the one who fixated on what he couldn't do. His friends didn't. The feelings of regret were now surfacing, and he wondered how he could ever fix all the relationships he had seemed to destroy over these last few months.

"Mom I'm really sorry. To use your words, I've been a complete asshole to everyone, even you. That's not me. This whole accident just took me to a place I've never been before, and I didn't know how to handle how it made me feel. Surgeries, pain, physical therapy. This is the kind of thing that happens to someone else, not me. I guess I'm just as vulnerable as the next person." He stared at the food on his plate.

"Zach, it's OK. It will get better, but you better think of ways to live your life. Whether you get full use of your leg or not, don't let this stop you, and don't lose that precious girl. Abbey is the best thing that has happened to you."

He sat eating his lunch in silence and suddenly had an idea. "If you can help me, I think I have a way of saying I'm sorry. I might need Josh's help too."

51

Though Abbey pretty much set up her art booth by herself now, Josie and Michael insisted on coming as much as possible each week to help her. It was always better to have someone with her, even if it was just to talk. Everly had even helped a couple of times, and they had great fun afterward. The thought of Zach was always in the back of her mind. But after the "talk" they'd had this week, she and Zach were finished. Abbey had explained the situation to Lance, and he told Abbey that things would work out somehow. He didn't want her to leave the agency. She was the best at what she did, but she was also like a daughter to him, Lance confessed. Abbey promised to take it one day at a time but said that she would not work with Zach at his home anymore, which Lance agreed was OK. That had given her a reprieve of the stress that each morning would bring when she knew she had to go face the love of her life, though their relationship had dissolved before her eyes.

"I think that about does it," Michael said as the last painting was hung on the background behind her and she placed one more little dolphin sculpture on the table. People were starting to trickle into the plaza to watch the famous Key West sunset, and Abbey was ready for what she hoped would be another busy and profitable night. After the week she'd had with Zach, work, and getting ready for this weekend's show, the stress was taking its toll. Talking with the people who came by her table helped Abbey escape from the reality of her current situation for a little while.

"Abbey, I think you might have a visitor," Josie said as she placed her hand on Abbey's arm to turn her around. Coming across the square was a man pushing another in a wheelchair with a woman beside them, all people Abbey recognized instantly. It was Zach, pushed by Josh, with Sandy by her son's side. In Zach's lap was a huge bouquet of red roses. Abbey stood speechless as the trio finally reached her table.

"Can we talk for a few moments?" Zach asked, looking up at Abbey.

"Why don't the two of you go over to the bench and talk? We will take care of your table," Josie said, motioning to Sandy for her to help.

"I'll help with the wheelchair, then go get something to drink," Josh said nervously, too afraid to look Abbey in the eye.

Abbey followed Josh and Zach to the nearby bench. It wasn't but a second, and Josh nodded his head, walking away from the couple as quickly as possible.

"Not really sure there is much to say," Abbey said coldly.

"I know I don't deserve it, but just hear me out, please?" Zach said in a tone of voice she hadn't heard in so long but sounded like music to her ears.

"It will have to be short, because things look like they are starting to get busy." Abbey wasn't sure how to talk, act, or respond. This was what she had been wanting for weeks, but after the heated argument and accusations earlier in the week, Abbey had finally accepted the fact that they were no longer a couple.

"I really don't know where to begin," Zach said with a shaky voice. "Oh, these are for you." He held out the bouquet of roses, and Abbey sat them on the bench beside her.

"I'll admit I have been the biggest idiot. With everyone, but most of all, you." Zach looked around, like he was afraid to look at her. Or was it embarrassment.

Abbey's shock of seeing him had worn off, but she was still in awe of him coming here. She wanted so badly to reach out, hold him, and give him a kiss despite this week's events. Her body just gravitated toward his, but she held back, still unsure of how she should respond. The rollercoaster he had put her on had finally come to completion with their conversation only days ago.

"I was scared. I know that's not an excuse, but I was scared. I'm not the person I was before the accident. That person you fell in love with is gone, and I just felt you would be better off without me. I'm still a mess, but I'm trying. My physical therapy is coming along slowly. Not even sure about walking again. The doctor thinks I will with time, but I don't know when. And this is so hard to admit, but I'm so damn afraid to do anything. To go out of my house. Get in a car. Be by myself. I know that I'm so lucky to be alive, but I feel like that accident took my life." Zach paused again as though he needed more courage to continue talking.

"What I do know is when Josh came by and told me that he had seen you and Garret at the pier, I was shocked, hurt, mad, and admittedly, jealous. I started having these crazy thoughts, like 'How could she do that to me?'" he said, looking down at his lap.

"Then I realized that I was the reason you turned to Garrett. I had pushed you out. I was so upset that day we talked that my mom finally had enough and gave me a not-so-nice heart-to-heart talk. I guess it doesn't matter what age you are—your parents can still pack a punch when you need some sense knocked into you. She told me that if I didn't change, I would lose the best thing that had ever happened to me—you. Please forgive me. But I hope you understand that I didn't know how to process all this. I'm still having issues. Even coming here in a wheelchair feels humiliating when you're used to being so active and feeling strong. But I want to make things right if that is still possible. You are the only one for me, Abbey."

She was still sitting there, staring at him, taking in all he had said. He had finally hit bottom and was starting to climb back up to live his life. The problem was Abbey was now afraid. These weeks of Zach's refusal to let her be part of his life had stung over and over again, especially every time they were together. He had been so cold and aloof that she was protecting her heart now.

"Zach, I know it took a lot for you to come here. And the roses are beautiful. But words and some flowers can't make up for all the hurt and pain that has been created between the two of us. I know that accident happened to you. But you were a part of me then, and I felt like I had been hit by that car too. To watch you go through surgery, going to the hospital and talking to doctors. I was terrified that I was going to lose you when I had just found you. For you to push me away like you did, like I was a nuisance, hurt in so many ways. I will admit I still love you, but I don't know if things can be repaired. What if something like this were to happen again? What if I was sick? Would you walk away? Maybe our love isn't strong enough to make it over those hurdles. And that's the love I'm looking for. That was the love I thought I had with you." Abbey stood up, roses in hand, wanting so much to tell him everything was fine and finally kiss him like she had dreamed about so much lately.

"I've really got to go, because things are getting busy, but I promise I'll think about everything you have said." She reached over and kissed him on the cheek. "It's good to see you out of the house. I hope physical therapy gets better too."

Zach watched her walk away toward her table, knowing now that he had probably pushed her away for good. He had this grand scenario in his head that he would come here, roses in hand, and win back her love. But the scene played out much differently than he had imagined. He sat there and watched Abbey as she interacted with her customers and the tourists like he had before the accident. She was much more popular, he could tell. Had it been that long ago that he was the one helping her with her table? It seemed like a lifetime, even though it had only been a few months.

"Well, how did it go?" Sandy asked him as she sat where just minutes ago Abbey had graced the spot.

"I think I have lost her, Mom," he said in a downcast voice. "I was so stupid. I let my pride get in the way of the one thing that made me the happiest. But I just want her to be happy now."

"You have taken that all-important first step. Now all you can do is wait. You did put her through hell, Zach. And you are still healing, both physically and mentally. Probably the best thing you could do is throw yourself into working at home and going to physical therapy. Give her some time. Maybe a note here or there. A text message. Just to let her know you are thinking about her. And if it is meant to be, she will become a part of your life once again."

Josh walked around the corner, and then the three of them went back home. Abbey glanced over her shoulder to see if they were still sitting on the bench, only to watch them walking away, pushing Zach's wheelchair over the rough bricks. Every fiber of her being wanted to run to him, tell him that she forgave him and loved him more than anything. But now she was the one guarding her heart. She had finally come to terms with the ending of their relationship, and suddenly he had come to his senses, wanting her love once more. To get her mind off her predicament, she turned and started talking to the score of people surrounding her table.

52

As they folded the backdrop and put it on the cart to take her mobile art display back to the Jeep, Abbey was quiet and lost in thought.

"You want to talk about it?" Josie said when it was just her and Abbey walking a little way behind Michael.

"Yes and no. You know, Josie, I had finally come to the conclusion that mine and Zach's relationship just wasn't meant to be. Even though it hurts like crazy, I accepted that. Then to see him tonight and talk to him, it was like a dream come true. But I'm scared. What if another crisis comes along and he decides to run like he did this time? Or push me away? I don't think I can handle the up and down of a relationship like that. It's too stressful and would be worse than what I'm feeling now. But seeing him, talking to him—it was all I could do not to throw my arms around him and hold on tight. I miss him so much!" Abbey's voice sounded quite pained with each word she spoke.

"When we get home, meet me on the porch. You aren't unloading this tonight, right?"

"No, it's staying in the car. I'll see you at our rocking chairs."

Abbey hadn't sat on the little porch in a long time. Ever since Michael had come back into Josie's life, it seemed that these chairs were their special place to spend time together, especially when Josie finally started talking to Michael once again. And now they were married. To Abbey it was almost like a fairy tale, except for the hurt Josie had experienced all those years ago. As she sat down in the rocker, Abbey could feel the familiar relaxation she remembered of those talks she and Josie used to have after Josie decided to open up.

The two women sat quietly for a few moments, soaking up the relaxing atmosphere of the beautiful evening. Finally, Josie was the one to break the silence.

"Abbey, I know you are anxious about this situation with Zach. Believe me, I completely understand. But please don't do what I did. I got hurt one time, and I completely shut myself off from the world. What Michael did was terrible and humiliating. But had I given it some time and not ran away from what happened, there is no telling how things would be today."

"What do you think would have happened?" Abbey asked quietly.

"I don't know for sure, but I think we would have worked things out over time. Probably gotten married. Who knows? We might've even had children and been grandparents by now. But we reacted in our own way without doing the one thing everyone should do in a relationship: talk. He left me at the altar. I left the town I grew up in so I thought I could start fresh. When I saw Michael for the first time after all these years, all my feelings for him came back to me like a rushing flood. So I know how you feel about seeing Zach tonight. He might have pushed you away, but try to understand why. None of us know how we would react had we been the one on that bike. I'm not giving him a pass for the pain he has caused you, but he is trying to make amends. He still loves you, Abbey. You don't have to miss out like I did by letting the hurt you experienced get in the way of having a wonderful life with him. With you beside him, it will give him the courage to reclaim his life. For you, it will help you heal from his words and actions—to see if he truly means what he told you tonight. And I really think he does. The person we have seen these last few months wasn't the Zach we knew at all. The man you saw tonight is the guy you fell in love with. Please don't throw it all away. Learn from my mistake. If you do, you will make my story mean something. At least I will know that I helped someone, and all that time I spent hurt and angry will not be for nothing."

Abbey looked at Josie, knowing she was right. She didn't want to make a mistake like Josie had by thinking the worst and not giving Zach a chance to prove that he meant what he said. Even though she was scared, she had to talk to Zach and get everything out in the open. She still loved that man. She always had even when he was at his worst. And she wanted to be the one to help him through the rough times. She knew he could do it, and she wanted to be the one to encourage him.

"Josie, thanks for helping me with some clarity. You are right. I love him, and I don't want to let him go. I can't say I'm not hurt by what he did, but it took courage to come to the square tonight in a wheelchair to talk to me. I have to go talk to him."

"It's a little late. Maybe you should wait till the morning? Since it's Sunday, I'm sure he isn't going anywhere."

"He'll be up. I've got to go!" she said quickly as she ran toward her Jeep and headed to Zach's apartment.

Abbey stood at the door to his apartment, shivering, wondering what her reception would be like, especially so late. But she had to see him. She knocked softly on the door. When no one answered, she decided she would come back in the morning. As Abbey turned to go back home, she suddenly heard the door open slightly and turned to see Zach standing there using one crutch to hold himself steady as he leaned against the door.

"Hi," he said, staring at her.

"I'm sorry it's so late. Maybe I should come back tomorrow." Abbey was feeling suddenly exposed, not knowing how things would turn out over the next few minutes.

"It's fine. Mom is asleep, and I was up watching an old movie. Come on in." He opened the door wider, hopping on his good leg and using his crutch to allow her to come in.

As she walked in the front door, the whole place was rather dark, with only the TV glowing, and Abbey suddenly wished she had waited till the morning. Her confidence and resolve were melting away, her heart beating fast in her chest. What exactly was she going to tell him? She couldn't just throw herself at him, though that was what she wanted to do. She was ready to feel his arms around her again and the touch of his lips against hers. She was happy and terrified all wrapped into one.

As she made her way to the chair by the couch, she turned to see him shut the door and begin hopping to the couch using the crutch for support.

"Do you need some help?" Abbey asked.

"No, I'm getting used to this. My left leg and arm are getting into pretty good shape," he laughed. "I'm supposed to be using that walker over there," he said, nodding toward the thing in the corner, "but my arm is still pretty sore when I put too much pressure on it. That is why I have to use a wheelchair most of the time. The bone in the arm has healed, just still hurting. Should get better as time goes by."

They sat in silence as Zach turned the TV off and replaced the light in the room by turning on the lamp beside of the couch.

"Abbey—" Zach began.

"I—" Abbey started, both talking at the same time.

"Please, let me go first," Zach said. "I'm the one who really messed up things. Like I said earlier, this accident left me alive but took away the life I knew. I suddenly felt so vulnerable. I've never been involved in such a situation where in a split second, something can change your entire life. And I honestly didn't know how to handle it. So instead of letting people in and helping, I've seemed to push everyone away who ever cared for me, except my mom, and I think I've even gotten on her nerves a time or two. Probably more! And every time I saw you, every time you came over, it was a reminder of what I felt I couldn't have anymore. My freedom. My carefree lifestyle where I was invincible. I felt weak, and I just couldn't process it.

"I'm so sorry. Sorry for being hateful and mean to you, Abbey, the one person who meant and means more to me than anyone. You are the love of my life. I don't want to lose you, but after these last few months, I could understand why you wouldn't want to be a part of my life. I made things miserable. I know 'sorry' is just a word, but I mean it more than I can say. When Josh told me he saw you with Garrett, I just remember thinking, 'She is mine!' And I suddenly felt like my old self, with a few bumps and bruises and that I had opened a door from a dark place. I was jealous, I'll admit. But in a way I want to thank you. Had that not happened, I don't think I would feel as clearheaded as I am now. Hearing those words from Josh just removed the depression surrounding me and it felt like a voice said, 'Get your ass up and start living.' So if you have moved on, I understand. I still love you, but more importantly, I want you to be happy. But I also want you to know that you saved my life in a way too."

Abbey sat there for a few moments letting everything Zach had said sink in. Then she got up and moved over to sit by him on the couch.

"First of all, I'm not dating anyone. As I said before, what Josh saw down on the pier was one friend encouraging another. As we have talked about before, Garrett is married to his work. You know that." She laughed a bit to gather courage to say what she needed to tell the man before her.

"Like I said earlier tonight, what you did to me hurt so much. I was ready to be there for you through everything. I didn't care if you were permanently in a wheelchair. You were the love I had always looked for. But when you started acting like I was a nuisance to be with, it hurt. It felt like someone had pierced the deepest part of me and that it would never heal. I remember thinking that it was situations like these that kept coworkers from dating, because I knew that I couldn't work with you once you were well. The pain of seeing you everyday would be too much." Abbey paused and looked at the floor, trying to make sure she chose her words carefully. She looked over into Zach's eyes—those that she remembered so well. She was finally looking at the man she had fallen in love with.

"I love you, Zach. I still do, but now I'm anxious. I'm scared that you will walk away again if things get tough. And life is like that. There are hills and valleys, and I need to know that I'll have someone in my life that is ready for anything, as much as one can be."

Zach's head turned, his eyes focusing on the floor. He felt he knew what was coming next, and he didn't want to hear it. She was leaving him for good, and to hear the words coming from her would be devastating, since he knew it was his fault.

"I did talk to someone tonight that gave me some really good advice. This person said not to let mistakes that can be fixed stand in the way of happiness. And this is something that can be fixed. You are my best friend, and I can't imagine spending any more time without you in my life every single day. These last weeks have been so depressing without you. I know you said you are sorry, and I accept your apology. What you went through was horrible, but I never expected you to push everyone away. I'm glad that you had what I call a 'light bulb' moment to help you see that there are so many people who love you and are ready to be here for you no matter what. And I'm first in line." Abbey reached over, lifting his chin so she could see his eyes, and gave him a soft, gentle kiss on the lips, something that she had wanted to do for so many weeks. It was just like she remembered, and her body trembled like it had before so many times when she was with him.

"I'm here for you, but you have to make me a promise. Whether things are great or there is a hurdle to overcome, we will face things together. No hiding our feelings, and we help each other."

"I promise," Zach said, wrapping his arms around her so tightly it felt as though their bodies melted into one. The kiss he received took away all the stress and anxiety from his body. She was back in his life and she loved him just like he was. Zach felt like his whole body was on fire as the memories of holding her, and now having Abbey actually in his arms, consumed him.

"I love you, Abbey, so much. I never thought I could ever feel this way about anyone. You are the love of my life."

"And you are mine," Abbey said.

53

Sandy walked into the living room to check on Zach only to find that there were two people curled up on the couch sleeping. Zach slept in his usual spot, reclined with his leg propped up, and Abbey was next to him in his arms, with her body stretched out on the rest of the couch. Her son was back, she thought, smiling. She wondered how much longer she would really be needed here if these two were finally back together. Not knowing when Abbey had shown up last night or how long they had stayed awake, she got her breakfast quietly and sat at the kitchen table, trying to make as little sound as possible in the small apartment.

When Abbey opened her eyes, at first she was disoriented. Then suddenly she remembered everything from last night. Zach coming to see her at the square with roses. Her talk with Josie. Coming to see him and both of them realizing that they were still in love and that they could get through this. Zach was lightly snoring as she untangled herself from his arms, making sure not to wake him up. The pain meds were doing their job, but Zach had told her last night that they were finally weaning him off the drugs, and he was glad. They made him too "loopy," he said, but they also helped him rest. He promised her that he would give her the full scoop on what his doctors had told him when they got up this morning. She didn't remember falling asleep, but she knew it had to be with a smile on her face, as she lay wrapped in Zach's arms.

Abbey tiptoed to the bathroom, hoping she didn't wake Sandy, when suddenly she saw her sitting at the table. Abbey waved to her and mouthed that she would be back in just a minute.

"I gather you and Zach talked last night?" Sandy said as soon as Abbey sat in the chair across from her.

"Yes, and I'm sorry I was here so late. After you, Josh, and Zach left last night, I had a long talk with Josie, and I came to some conclusions about my relationship with your son. He has gone through so much, and I don't know how that feels. I just wish he hadn't pushed me away. This past week, I had accepted that we were over. But Josie, the wise woman that she is, talked to me last night. I don't know if Zach told you her long story, but her advice was spot-on. If Zach is willing to make this work, so am I. I love him, Sandy, more than I can tell you in words. Any help he needs, like doctor's appointments, physical therapy—anything, I'm here. I need to go home, take a shower, and change clothes, but then I'm going to come back, and we are going to watch movies, especially since it is supposed to be stormy today. Maybe I can even fix dinner, since I know you need a break."

"You just being here with him is enough. And actually, I'm doing fine. It's been nice being here in Key West, except for the reason I had to come. But I'm hoping to go home soon. I miss my husband and my dogs. And I think there are a few grandchildren that are wondering where Grandma is," she laughed.

"Mom, I can do this. You need to go home. You've taken up so much of your time to take care of me. I really can do this now," Zach said as he entered the kitchen, using the walker this time, still not putting a lot of weight on his leg.

"And I'll be here to help him too," Abbey added. "Good morning, sleepyhead," she said as she got up and gave him a kiss.

Sandy couldn't help but watch the way they looked at each other. This must have been a glimpse of how they were before the accident. And Sandy liked what she saw.

"My, now you are ready to get rid of me!" She feigned disappointment with a grin. "Let's see how the next few days go, and we'll go from there."

Abbey looked up at Zach. "I need to go to the apartment, but I'll be back in a little while. I'll stop by the café and get sandwiches for all of us for lunch, if that sounds good."

"All I need is you," he said, kissing her deeply, forgetting his mom was sitting there. But so had Abbey. He was back. Zach was truly back.

Abbey got back to her apartment, took a quick shower, and put together some things she would need, like her journal, her laptop, some snacks, and her Apple TV so they could watch movies. The rain had let up, but the rumble of thunder in the distance let her know that more storms were on the way. As she went to go through the gate, she heard her name called and looked over to see Josie and Michael sitting in the rockers.

"Aren't you guys getting a bit wet?" she said as she headed for the front porch.

"No. Actually, it is staying quite dry under here. I see you didn't come home last night. Is that a good sign?" Josie asked with a big smile on her face. She knew the answer to that question just by seeing the light that practically shone from Abbey's face, but she wanted more details.

"A very good sign! Things are on the mend. And I really have to thank the two of you. Josie, your advice helped me more than I can say. Knowing what the two of you have been through helped me. Zach and I talked for such a long time last night about everything. It is still a work in progress, but I feel like I have him back, and happiness doesn't begin to describe how I feel. I'm sounding a bit mushy, huh?" Abbey stood there rocking back and forth on her feet with the biggest grin on her face.

"I'm happy knowing that the two of you are working things out. Just remember, he still has a ways to go. Patience is the key. And not letting old hurts linger. Let them go so you can enjoy the moment." As Josie said those words, she reached for Michael's hand, and they glanced at each other. They had gotten a second chance, and now Abbey and Zach had too.

"Stay dry today. I'm spending the day at Zach's watching movies. See you later!" She hopped in her Jeep and headed to the café for their takeout lunch.

54

Over the next week, Abbey went to every doctor's appointment and physical therapy session Zach had so she would know what was going on in his treatment. This meant some more time off from work, but Lance gave her the OK, as long as the work that needed to be done was being finished. This gave them permission to work from home. And work they did. They fell back into the same rhythm as before, and some things felt like old times. But after going with Zach to physical therapy and seeing how hard it was for him to use his leg, Abbey knew some things would be different—but that didn't matter.

Zach was learning to use his leg again. She could see the scars from the cuts, scratches, and surgeries. It didn't bother her except for the fact that he had pain and was embarrassed by having to use some type of device to be able to walk. His broken arm was healed, and while he said it was still a little painful, the doctor said that would diminish with time. Even with all this, it was the first time since his accident that Abbey saw determination in his eyes to do everything he could to get better and be in the best possible physical shape. She couldn't help but be in awe of him as he pushed forward.

Marty also noticed the difference at Zach's physical therapy sessions.

"Now I know why you have suddenly started working so hard," Marty said as he looked over at Abbey reading on her iPad.

"She is worth it."

"You are worth it, Zach," Marty said as he encouraged him to move across the floor using the two wooden beams for support.

By the end of the week, Sandy was packed and ready to go back home. She had been there over two months, taking care of her badly injured son. Zach apologized over and over.

"Zach," Sandy said with her hand on his cheek, "there is no other place I wanted to be. You are my son, and this is what mothers do." Zach stood up out of the wheelchair, balancing on one leg to hug his mom for what seemed so long that she might miss her plane.

"Thanks, Mom. I love you, and I couldn't have done this without you." He gave her a kiss on the cheek and sat back in the chair.

Abbey reached out and hugged Mrs. Isler once more, and she heard words being whispered in her ear. "You're a great girl, Abbey. Take good care of him, OK?"

"I promise," she whispered back.

As they watched his mom go through airport security, Abbey glanced down at Zach. "Well, I guess it's just you and me now."

"Looks that way. I have a question for you."

Abbey gave him a quizzical look before turning him around to head out of the airport. "OK—what?"

"Will you move in with me till I don't have to use this chair anymore? Not for any other reason, I promise. You told my mom you would just go back and forth between our apartments, but I have more than enough room and a spare bedroom. Might need a bit of cleaning up, but it would be easier, and then I wouldn't feel so guilty about you having to do so much back-and-forth driving between two places."

"So it's just to take care of you and nothing else?" She smiled and winked at him as they reached the car, and he stood up to get in.

"Well, I could think of other things, but remember, we decided to take this second chance slowly." He smiled back at her, giving her a mischievous grin.

"It sounds like a great idea to me!" Abbey said, and then she kissed him lightly on the lips before he settled down into the car.

55

It was the week after Thanksgiving, and everyone had gone back home. Abbey's parents had visited for the holidays and had threatened to stay since they fell in love with the little city. Everyone also celebrated Thanksgiving dinner at Josie and Michael's new house on Marathon Key—a beautiful two-story home on a deep water canal that led out to the clear waters of the Atlantic Ocean. Abbey remembered looking at the people assembled around the table that day, feeling so blessed to share this holiday with her Key West family and her parents after everything she and Zach had been through these past months.

"Are you up for a little beach time at our park? We haven't been there in quite a while," Abbey asked as Zach was eating his breakfast. "A little walking in the sand might be good therapy for strengthening your leg, and I could go for a swim. Please?" The weather was still warm, and the beach water was just the right temperature. She really wanted to go and wanted it to be just the two of them. It seemed like they had not had any time alone recently and when they did, they both were so tired from work or Zach's PT that they didn't do a lot of things they used to. But at least they were together.

Zach was hesitant about walking in the sand and swimming. He had done some therapy in a swimming pool, but not in the ocean with currents and such. But it would be nice to do something that was familiar and out of his new "normal."

"I'm in. Why don't we get sandwiches on the way and have a picnic too?" He saw the look in her eyes of sheer delight. It felt good to make her happy again. They put everything together they needed, made a quick stop at Abbey's place, and then headed for the park.

The drive was nice, just the two of them. Except for some potential thunderstorms off in the distance, the weather seemed just right. Since the time they had left his house, it seemed like they were in constant contact with each other. His hand on her leg. Her hand on his shoulder. Him giving her a kiss on the cheek as she drove to the park. Another passionate kiss as Abbey helped him out of the car. It almost felt like they had just met for the first time, and she was loving every second of it. Her body seemed to sizzle each time he touched her, like electricity pulsing through every part of her being.

Before they knew it, they were at the park, and there were very few people there. Since it was the Sunday after the holiday, most people were heading home or getting ready for their work week after a long weekend. It almost seemed as though they had the beach all to themselves. They drove down to one of the covered shelters where no one was and decided to take a walk along the beach there before taking a swim.

Abbey could tell Zach was nervous. He was finally walking as some of the nerves came back to life in his leg though he still needed support to take steps. His walk in the sand was slow due to the crutches, but she was there beside him every step of the way. Zach's use of a cane, crutches or a walker was now just part of their life but Zach was still determined that one day he would walk on his own and Abbey believed him. As he stopped to take a break in their stroll along the beach, he leaned over to Abbey, giving her a tender kiss as he looked at this incredible woman and how she cared for him

"Are you ready for a swim?" Zach asked her as he pulled his shirt off. His chest was even more defined than ever since he had started physical therapy and had to rely on his upper body for strength. Abbey called him her "Muscle Man." All she could do was smile as she looked at him and thought, *This is my man.*

"What are you grinning about?" he asked.

"Just admiring you. You are actually quite buff, Zach Isler," she said as she made her way toward him, running her hands across his chest and down to his waist.

"Are you saying I didn't look so good before?" he kidded her.

"You have always looked good, but there is just something about you now." Abbey stood on her tiptoes and kissed him so sensually that he wasn't sure if he wanted to swim or take her back home.

"I think we better go swimming before we decide to do something else instead," he said. He kissed her one more time and then turned to walk toward the ocean. He leaned on her for support as he slowly made his way into the waist deep water.

"You OK?" Abbey asked, concerned.

"Yeah, I just feel a little nervous about using my leg for swimming. I've tried it in the therapy pool but this is different."

"Then let's just float right here," Abbey said as she wrapped her arms around his waist, and they both dunked under the water. The water was perfect and they floated on their backs, holding hands as they gazed up at the sky. Even though the sun was now being hidden behind a dark cloud above, they were so engrossed in each other that they didn't realize a storm was upon them till they heard the thunder.

"I think we better go in. This storm came up pretty quickly," Zach said, looking around at the ominous clouds. But then it started to rain, softly at first and then harder.

"We won't make it back to the car in time," Abbey said, though half her sentence was cut off by another rumble of thunder. Then, they saw a perfect area in the mangrove trees, just big enough for the two of them to huddle down till the storm passed. The trees were so thick that no raindrops could make it past the weave of leaves and multiple branches, leaving the sand mostly dry. So they crawled into the small space and watched as the storm raged on around them.

As they sat huddled together, Zach found Abbey's lips again, kissing softly at first and then hungrily for her. They had come so far in this journey of theirs. Now, between the storm's fury around them and the fire inside each of them, it wasn't long before they were stretched out on the sand, their arms and legs intertwined.

The feel of her skin took Zach's breath away, and Abbey reached up, caressing his chest. Then she gently brought her mouth up to his before he could utter another word. But suddenly they switched places, with her lying on top of him, giving him a wicked smile.

"I think it has quit raining," Abbey said, though she didn't move from her position, having him trapped underneath her. And Zach wasn't fighting her either.

"I do believe you are right. What are we going to do now?" Zach said, raising his eyebrows.

"I can think of a lot of things. There is no one on the beach, and this is a pretty private spot. What do you think?"

He quickly rolled her over so that she was now lying on the sand, and he was propped up beside her, tracing the sand along the skin of her arms and legs. "I think I could stay here all day with you and do things that some couples only dream of. But I'm not that kind of guy unless there is some commitment involved."

"Commitment?" Abbey looked surprised.

"Abbey, I want you to be mine. Totally and completely. Just you and me. I want to spend the rest of my life with you. You bring out the best in me, and each day my love for you grows deeper and deeper. I love you, Abbey Wallace. Forever and always."

"I am yours and always will be. You are the love of my life, Zach Isler. And I love you - always and forever."

ACKNOWLEDGMENTS

First and foremost, I have to thank my most wonderful husband, Jeff. Your love, patience and encouragement help to make this second novel possible. When I felt discouraged, you gave the little push to let me know I could do it. To my mom, Irene – you are simply the best! Thanks for the reading and re-reading, the suggestions, the Zoom time and all that help. Again without you, this novel never would have made it to the publisher!

To all my readers of my first novel: THANK YOU! Your feedback, love and encouragement means more than I can say and helped propel Abbey and Zach's story into a novel. You have also given me the courage to continue writing as more characters from the Florida Keys Romance Novels want and deserve their own stories to be told.

Love and Hugs to all!

Miki

PS – To learn more about the Florida Keys, please visit www.mikibannett.com.

Other Novels by Miki Bennett

"The Florida Keys Novels" Series

The Keys to Love
Run Away to the Keys
Back to the Keys
A Wedding in the Keys

"Camping in High Heels" series

Camping in High Heels
Camping in High Heels: Las Vegas
Camping in High Heels: California

AUTHOR BIOGRAPHY

 Miki Bennett lives in Charleston, South Carolina, with her husband Jeff and her little dog Emma. She wrote this book as part of the Florida Keys Novels Series, which begins with her debut novel *The Keys to Love*. When not working on her latest book, she enjoys creating paintings and experimenting with new arts and crafts projects. She is also known as the family computer geek.

27818435R00207

Made in the USA
Columbia, SC
08 October 2018